BY NIGHT

John **Allison**   Christine **Larsen**   Sarah **Stern**

Volume Two

BOOM! BOX

BOOM! BOX™

Anderson, S.C.
ACL-IVA

BY NIGHT Volume Two, July 2019. Published by BOOM! Box, a division of Boom
Entertainment, Inc. By Night is ™ & © 2019 John Allison & Christine Larsen. Originally
published in single magazine form as BY NIGHT No. 5-8. ™ & © 2018-2019 John Allison &
Christine Larsen. All rights reserved. BOOM! Box™ and the BOOM! Box logo are trademarks
of Boom Entertainment, Inc., registered in various countries and categories. All characters,
events, and institutions depicted herein are fictional. Any similarity between any of the
names, characters, persons, events, and/or institutions in this publication to actual names,
characters, and persons, whether living or dead, events, and/or institutions is unintended
and purely coincidental. BOOM! Box does not read or accept unsolicited submissions of
ideas, stories, or artwork.

BOOM! Studios, 5670 Wilshire Boulevard, Suite 400, Los Angeles, CA 90036-5679.
Printed in China. First Printing.

ISBN: 978-1-68415-399-2, eISBN: 978-1-64144-382-1

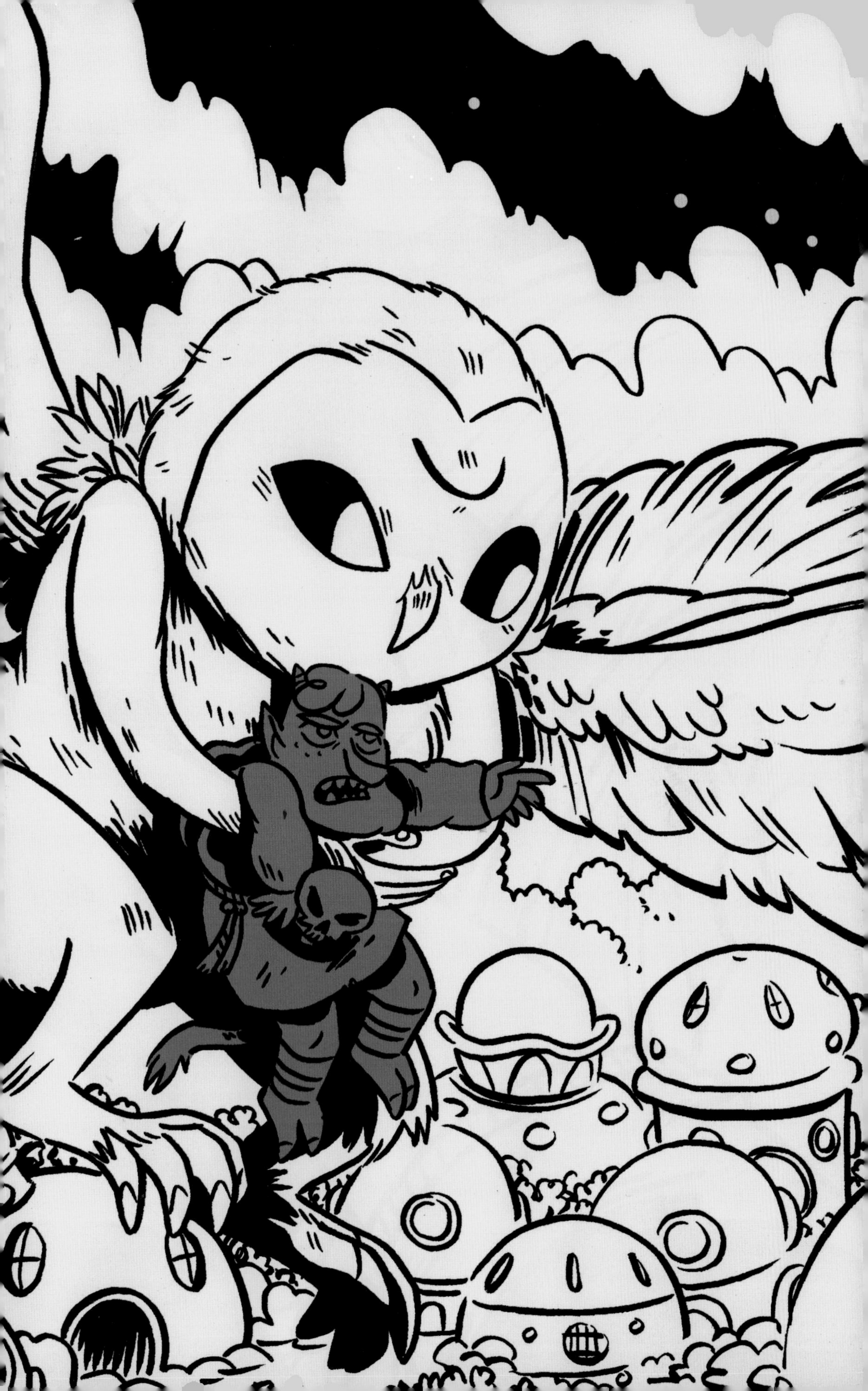

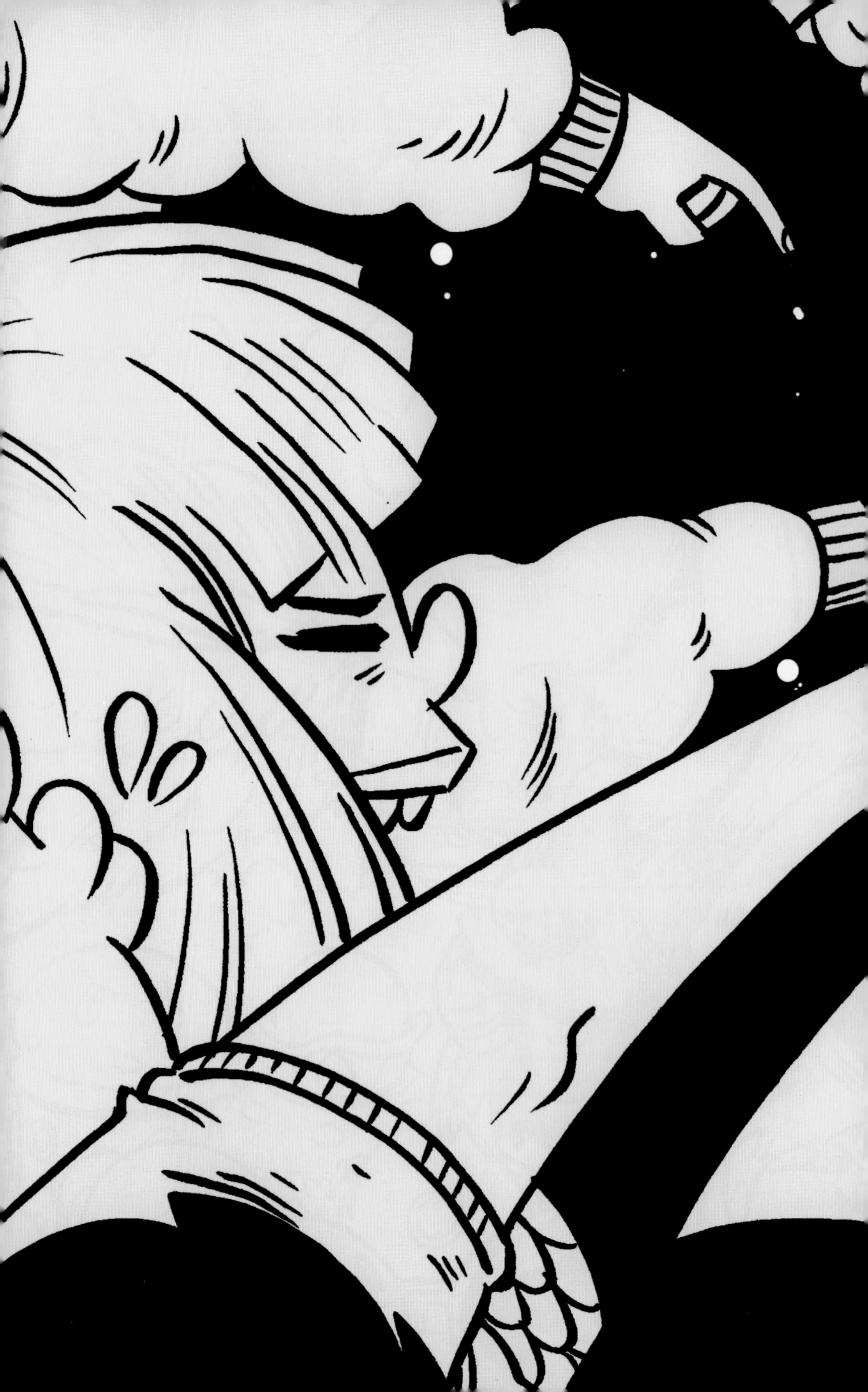

Created & Written by
John Allison

Illustrated by
Christine Larsen

Colored by
Sarah Stern

Lettered by
Jim Campbell

Cover by
Christine Larsen

Series Designer
Michelle Ankley

Collection Designer
Kara Leopard

Associate Editor
Sophie Philips-Roberts

Editor
Shannon Watters

2:00 AM.
JANE--
SLAM
SO...DO YOU EVER THINK ABOUT THE FIRST PERSON WHO TRIED TO RIDE A WILD HORSE?
THE STONES ON THAT GUY. THE ABSOLUTE *STONES.*

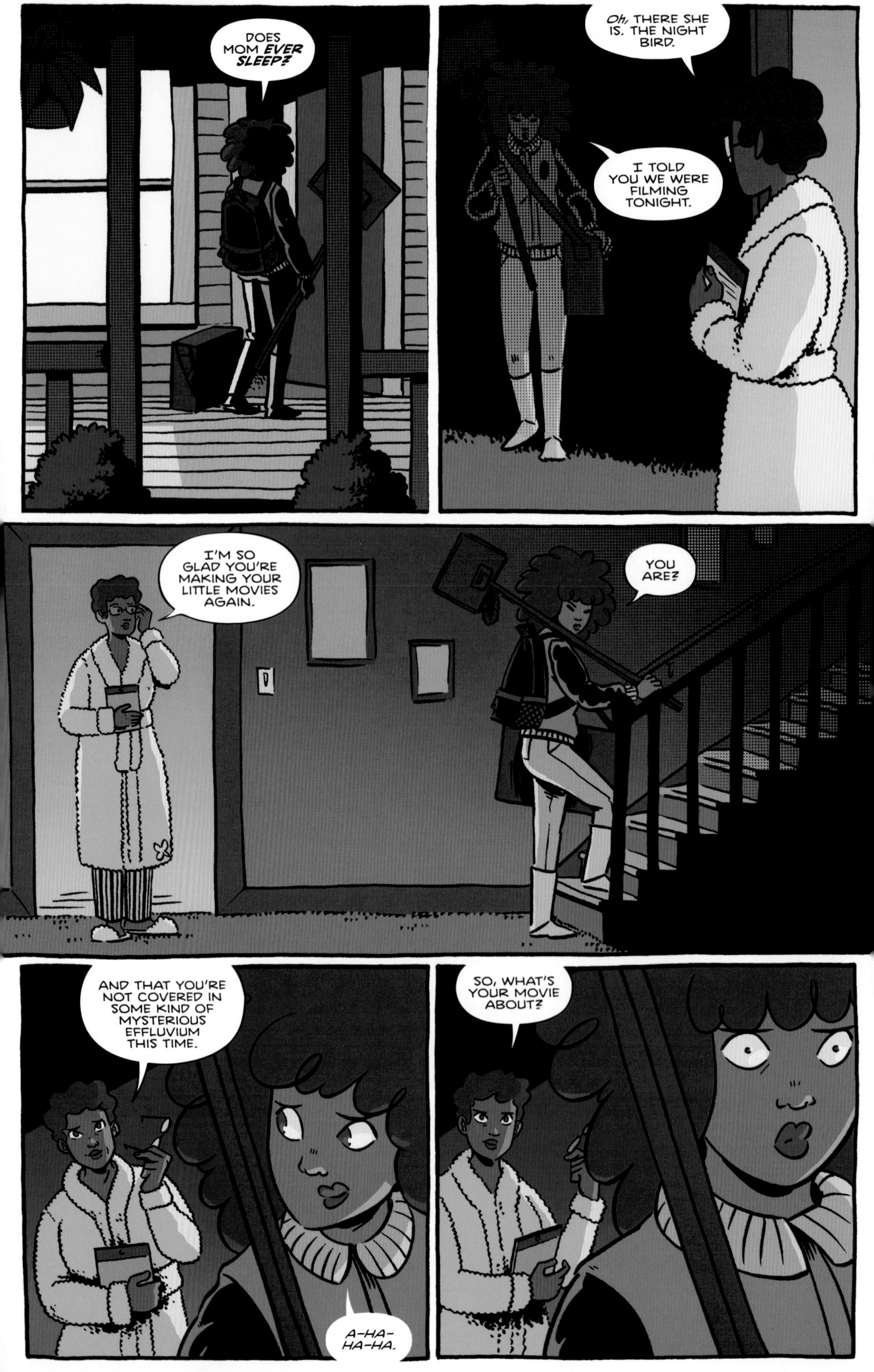
DOES MOM *EVER SLEEP?*
Oh, THERE SHE IS. THE NIGHT BIRD.
I TOLD YOU WE WERE FILMING TONIGHT.
I'M SO GLAD YOU'RE MAKING YOUR LITTLE MOVIES AGAIN.
YOU ARE?
AND THAT YOU'RE NOT COVERED IN SOME KIND OF MYSTERIOUS EFFLUVIUM THIS TIME.
A-HA-HA-HA.
SO, WHAT'S YOUR MOVIE ABOUT?

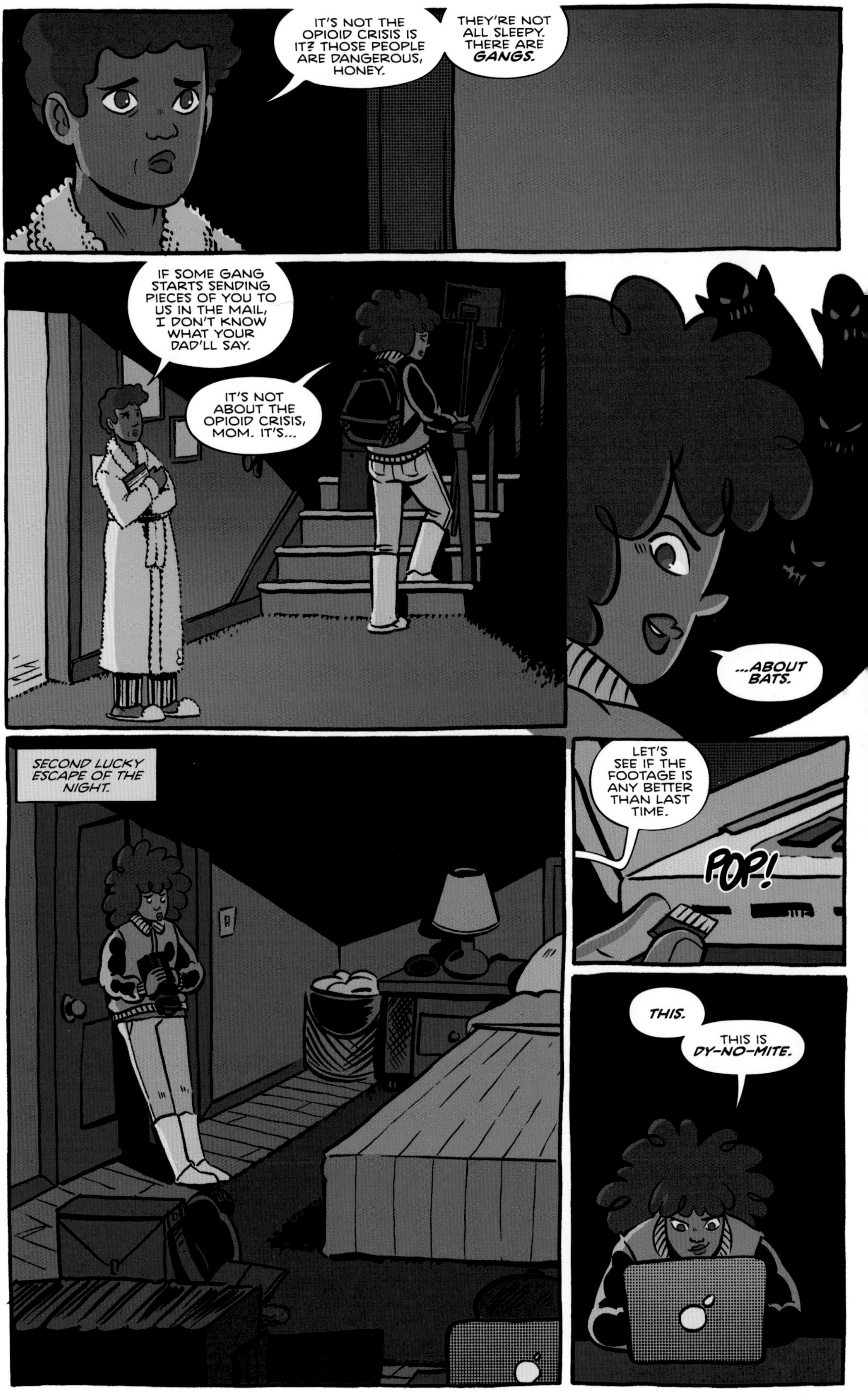
IT'S NOT THE OPIOID CRISIS IS IT? THOSE PEOPLE ARE DANGEROUS, HONEY.
THEY'RE NOT ALL SLEEPY. THERE ARE *GANGS.*
IF SOME GANG STARTS SENDING PIECES OF YOU TO US IN THE MAIL, I DON'T KNOW WHAT YOUR DAD'LL SAY.
IT'S NOT ABOUT THE OPIOID CRISIS, MOM. IT'S...
...ABOUT BATS.
SECOND LUCKY ESCAPE OF THE NIGHT.
LET'S SEE IF THE FOOTAGE IS ANY BETTER THAN LAST TIME.
POP!
THIS.
THIS IS *DY-NO-MITE.*

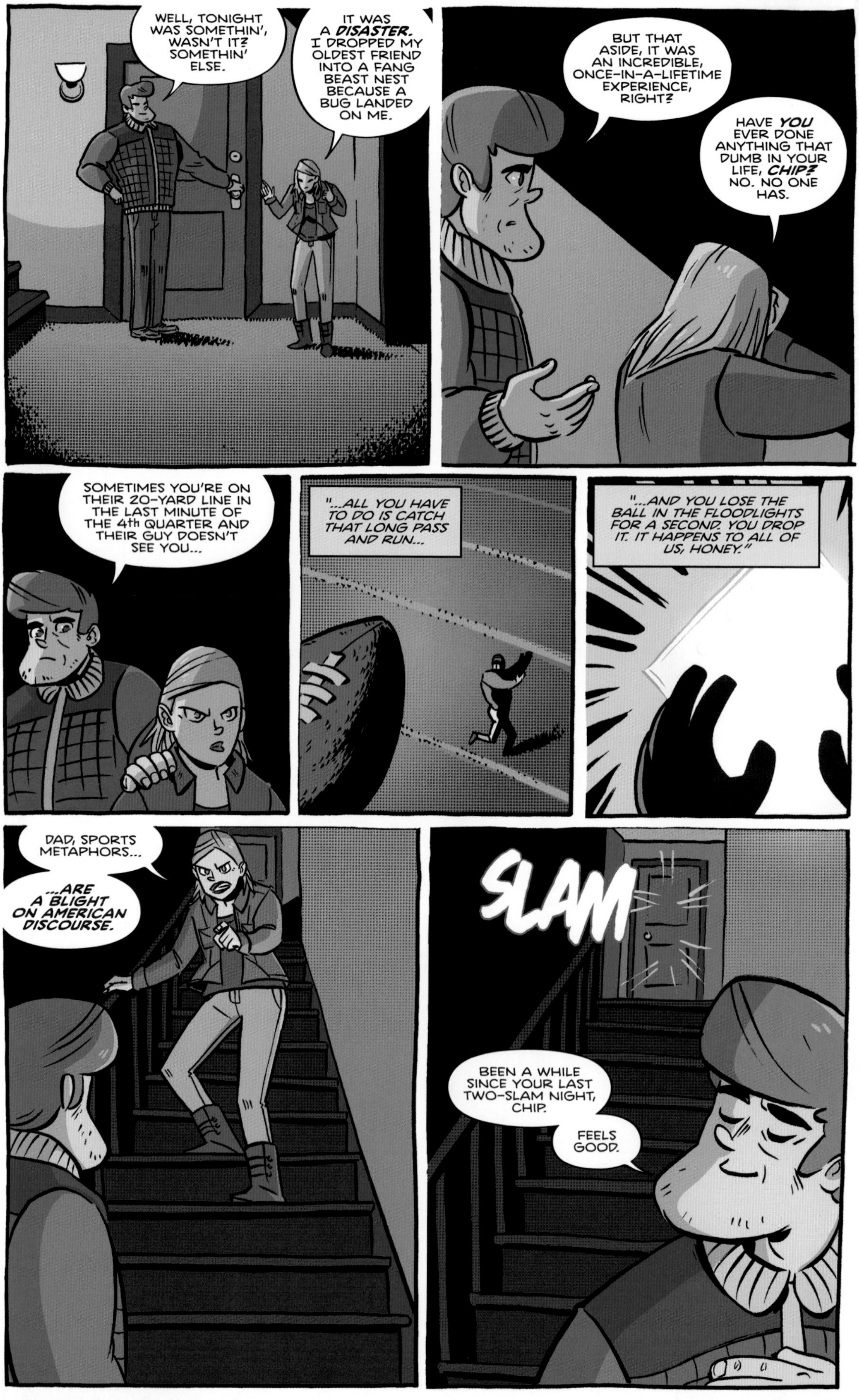

WELL, TONIGHT WAS SOMETHIN', WASN'T IT? SOMETHIN' ELSE.
IT WAS A *DISASTER.* I DROPPED MY OLDEST FRIEND INTO A FANG BEAST NEST BECAUSE A BUG LANDED ON ME.
BUT THAT ASIDE, IT WAS AN INCREDIBLE, ONCE-IN-A-LIFETIME EXPERIENCE, RIGHT?
HAVE *YOU* EVER DONE ANYTHING THAT DUMB IN YOUR LIFE, *CHIP?* NO. NO ONE HAS.
SOMETIMES YOU'RE ON THEIR 20-YARD LINE IN THE LAST MINUTE OF THE 4th QUARTER AND THEIR GUY DOESN'T SEE YOU...
"...ALL YOU HAVE TO DO IS CATCH THAT LONG PASS AND RUN...
"...AND YOU LOSE THE BALL IN THE FLOODLIGHTS FOR A SECOND. YOU DROP IT. IT HAPPENS TO ALL OF US, HONEY."
DAD, SPORTS METAPHORS...
...ARE A BLIGHT ON AMERICAN DISCOURSE.
SLAM
BEEN A WHILE SINCE YOUR LAST TWO-SLAM NIGHT, CHIP.
FEELS GOOD.

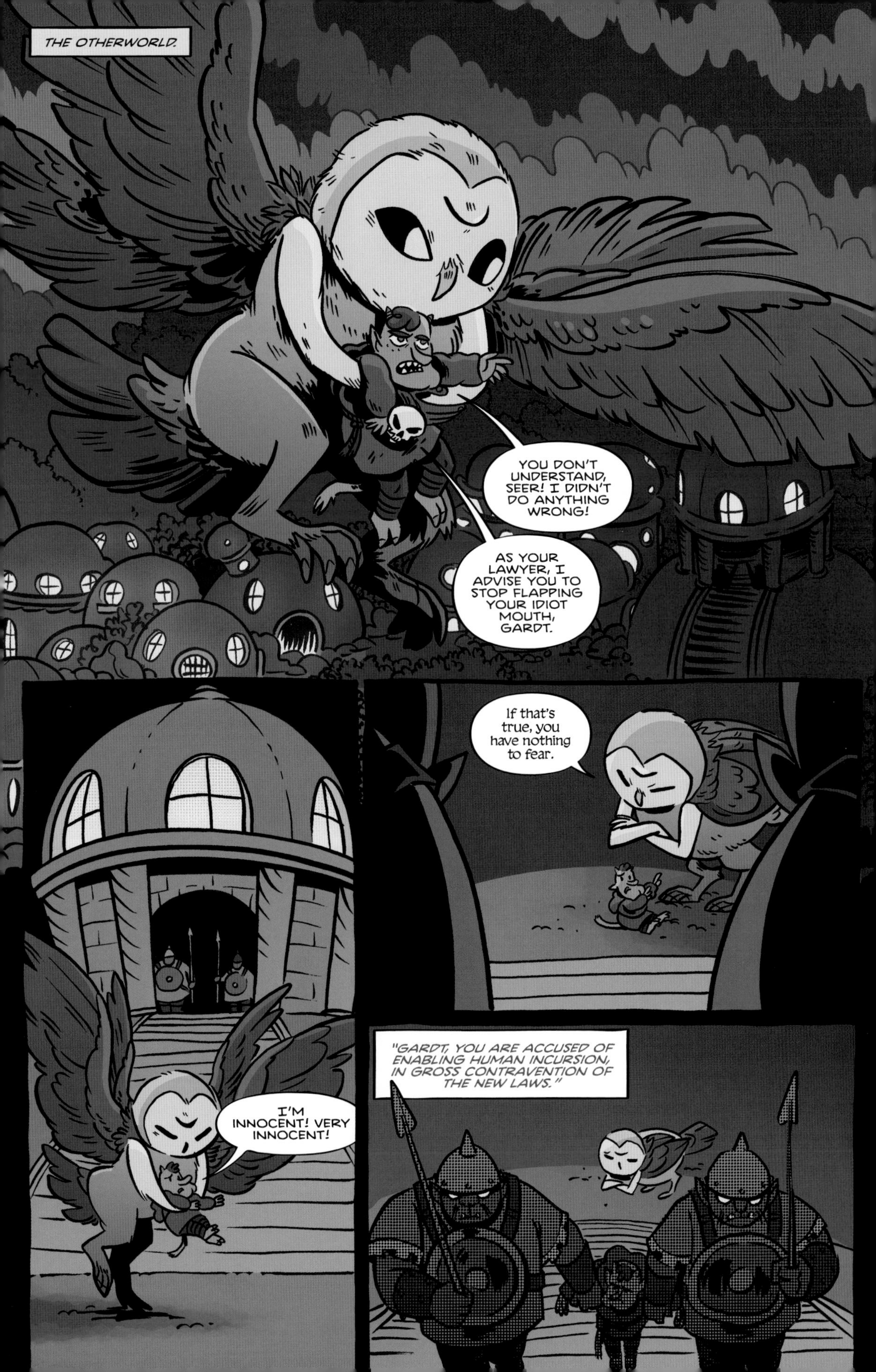
THE OTHERWORLD.
YOU DON'T UNDERSTAND, SEER! I DIDN'T DO ANYTHING WRONG!
AS YOUR LAWYER, I ADVISE YOU TO STOP FLAPPING YOUR IDIOT MOUTH, GARDT.
I'M INNOCENT! VERY INNOCENT!
If that's true, you have nothing to fear.
"GARDT, YOU ARE ACCUSED OF ENABLING HUMAN INCURSION, IN GROSS CONTRAVENTION OF THE NEW LAWS."

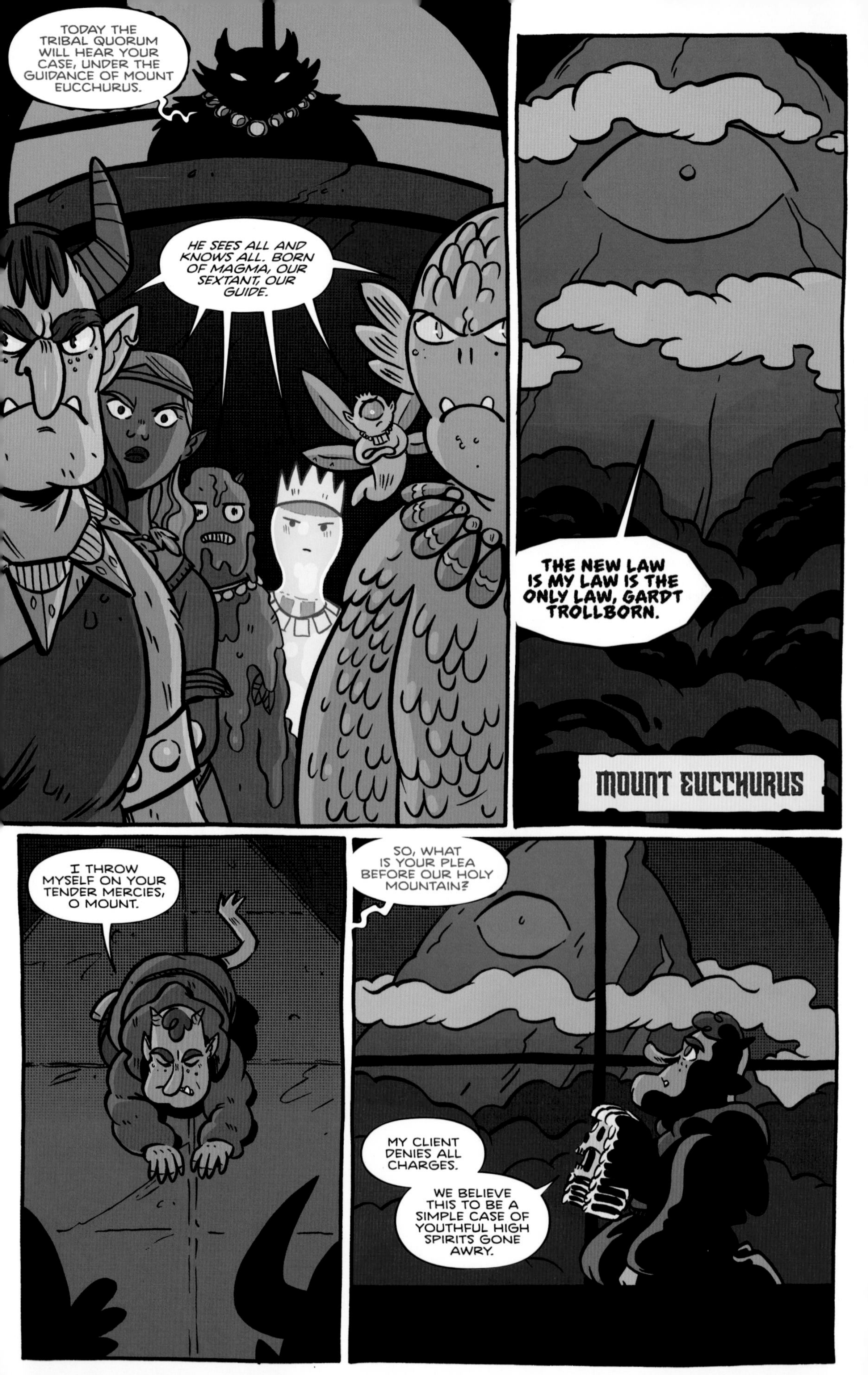
TODAY THE TRIBAL QUORUM WILL HEAR YOUR CASE, UNDER THE GUIDANCE OF MOUNT EUCCHURUS.
HE SEES ALL AND KNOWS ALL. BORN OF MAGMA, OUR SEXTANT, OUR GUIDE.
THE NEW LAW IS MY LAW IS THE ONLY LAW, GARDT TROLLBORN.
MOUNT EUCCHURUS
I THROW MYSELF ON YOUR TENDER MERCIES, O MOUNT.
SO, WHAT IS YOUR PLEA BEFORE OUR HOLY MOUNTAIN?
MY CLIENT DENIES ALL CHARGES.
WE BELIEVE THIS TO BE A SIMPLE CASE OF YOUTHFUL HIGH SPIRITS GONE AWRY.

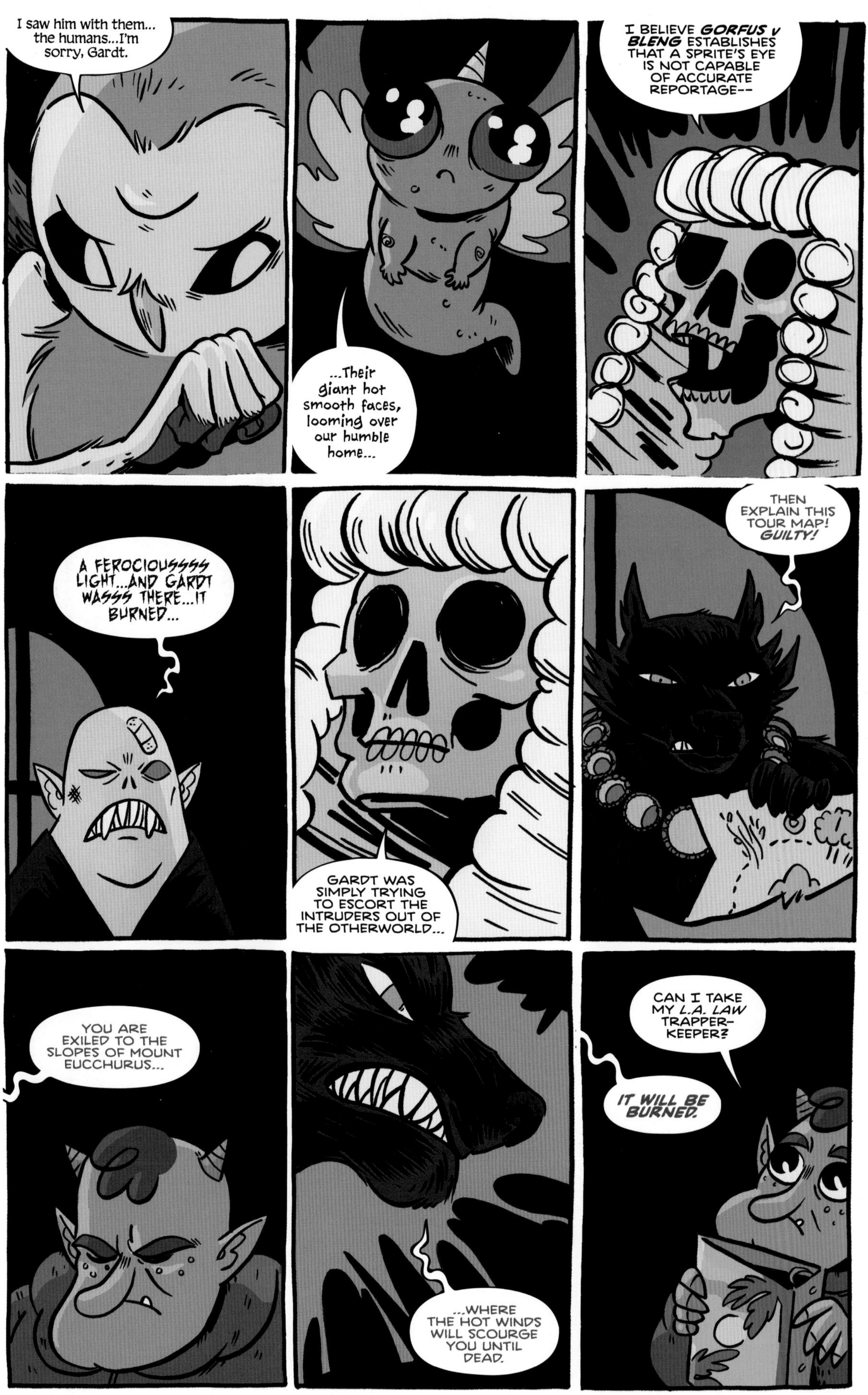

I saw him with them... the humans...I'm sorry, Gardt.
...Their giant hot smooth faces, looming over our humble home...
I BELIEVE GORFUS v BLENG ESTABLISHES THAT A SPRITE'S EYE IS NOT CAPABLE OF ACCURATE REPORTAGE--
A FEROCIOUSSSS LIGHT...AND GARDT WASSS THERE...IT BURNED...
GARDT WAS SIMPLY TRYING TO ESCORT THE INTRUDERS OUT OF THE OTHERWORLD...
THEN EXPLAIN THIS TOUR MAP! GUILTY!
YOU ARE EXILED TO THE SLOPES OF MOUNT EUCCHURUS...
...WHERE THE HOT WINDS WILL SCOURGE YOU UNTIL DEAD.
CAN I TAKE MY L.A. LAW TRAPPER-KEEPER?
IT WILL BE BURNED.

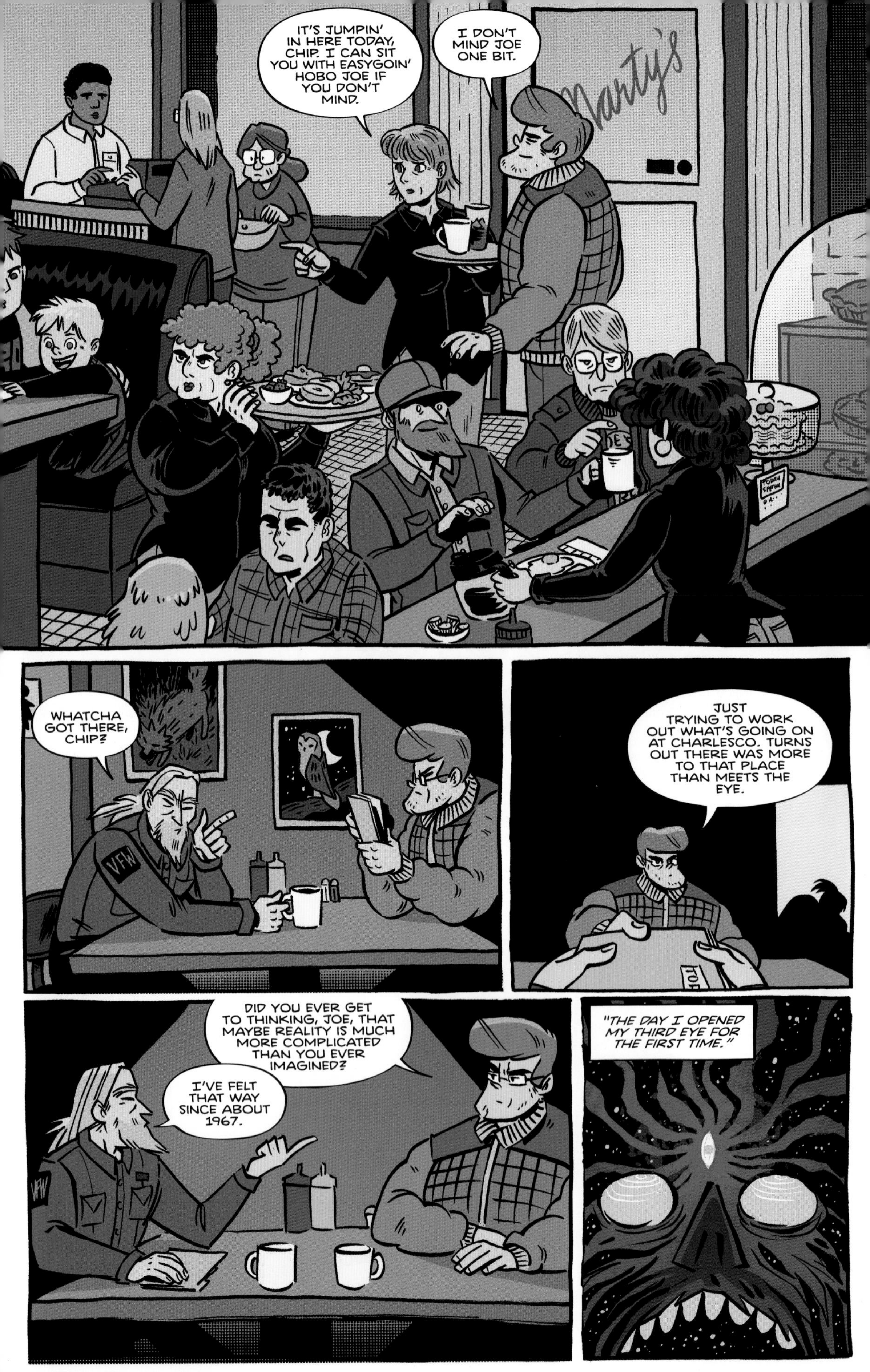
IT'S JUMPIN' IN HERE TODAY, CHIP. I CAN SIT YOU WITH EASYGOIN' HOBO JOE IF YOU DON'T MIND.
I DON'T MIND JOE ONE BIT.
WHATCHA GOT THERE, CHIP?
JUST TRYING TO WORK OUT WHAT'S GOING ON AT CHARLESCO. TURNS OUT THERE WAS MORE TO THAT PLACE THAN MEETS THE EYE.
DID YOU EVER GET TO THINKING, JOE, THAT MAYBE REALITY IS MUCH MORE COMPLICATED THAN YOU EVER IMAGINED?
I'VE FELT THAT WAY SINCE ABOUT 1967.
"THE DAY I OPENED MY THIRD EYE FOR THE FIRST TIME."

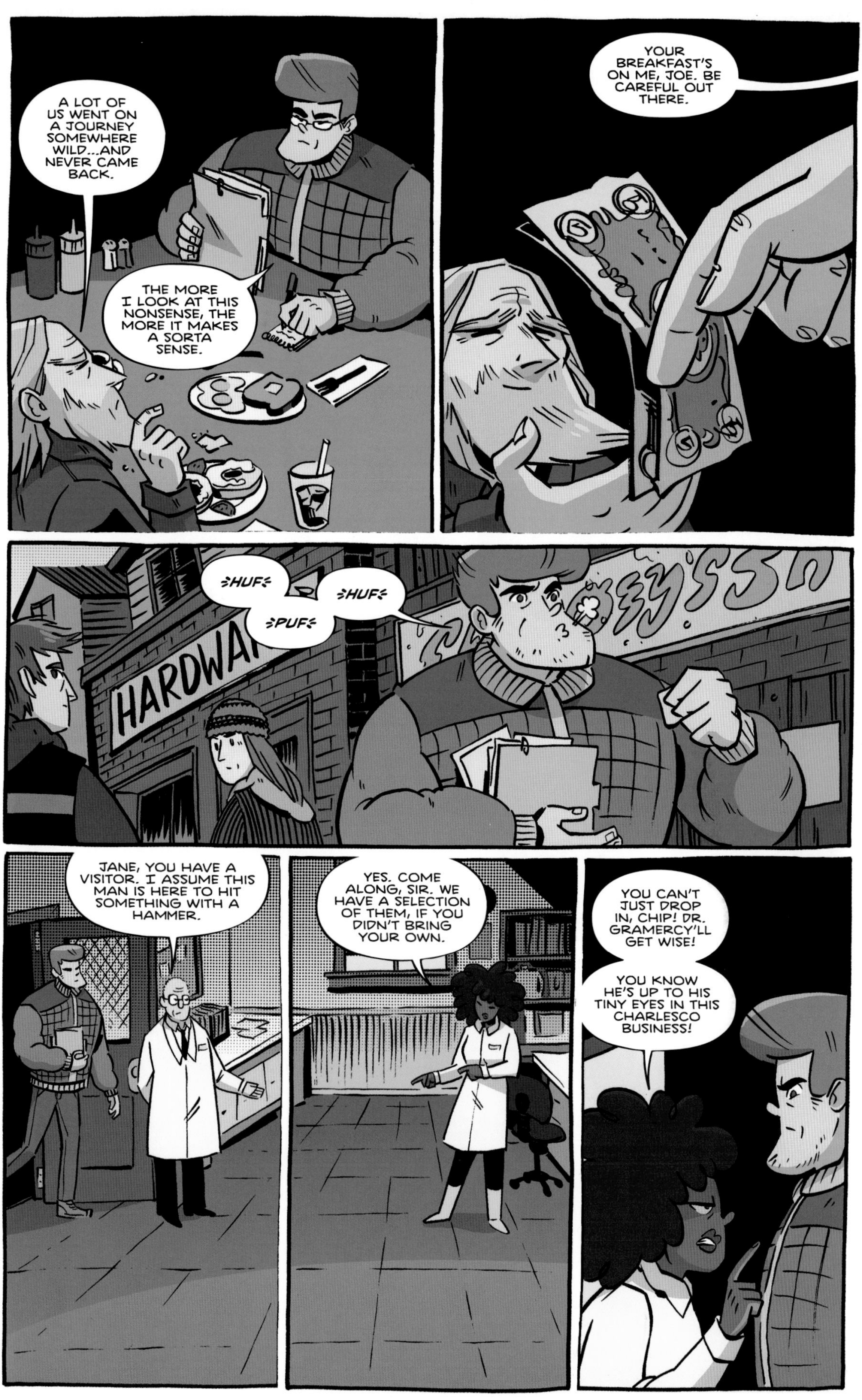
A LOT OF US WENT ON A JOURNEY SOMEWHERE WILD...AND NEVER CAME BACK.
THE MORE I LOOK AT THIS NONSENSE, THE MORE IT MAKES A SORTA SENSE.
YOUR BREAKFAST'S ON ME, JOE. BE CAREFUL OUT THERE.
HUF
PUF
HUF
HARDWA
JANE, YOU HAVE A VISITOR. I ASSUME THIS MAN IS HERE TO HIT SOMETHING WITH A HAMMER.
YES. COME ALONG, SIR. WE HAVE A SELECTION OF THEM, IF YOU DIDN'T BRING YOUR OWN.
YOU CAN'T JUST DROP IN, CHIP! DR. GRAMERCY'LL GET WISE!
YOU KNOW HE'S UP TO HIS TINY EYES IN THIS CHARLESCO BUSINESS!

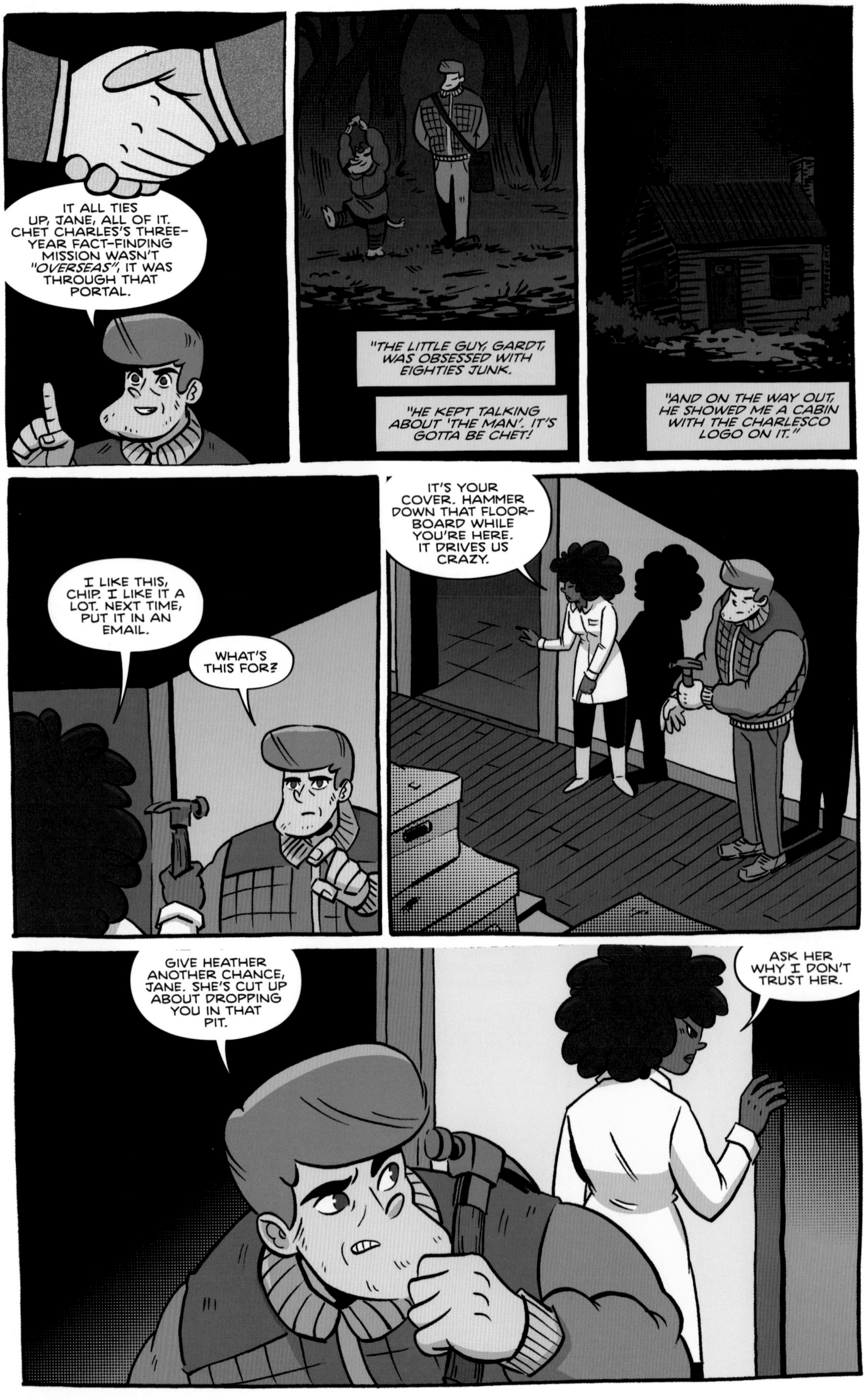
IT ALL TIES UP, JANE, ALL OF IT. CHET CHARLES'S THREE-YEAR FACT-FINDING MISSION WASN'T "OVERSEAS", IT WAS THROUGH THAT PORTAL.
"THE LITTLE GUY, GARDT, WAS OBSESSED WITH EIGHTIES JUNK.
"HE KEPT TALKING ABOUT 'THE MAN'. IT'S GOTTA BE CHET!
"AND ON THE WAY OUT, HE SHOWED ME A CABIN WITH THE CHARLESCO LOGO ON IT."
I LIKE THIS, CHIP. I LIKE IT A LOT. NEXT TIME, PUT IT IN AN EMAIL.
WHAT'S THIS FOR?
IT'S YOUR COVER. HAMMER DOWN THAT FLOORBOARD WHILE YOU'RE HERE. IT DRIVES US CRAZY.
GIVE HEATHER ANOTHER CHANCE, JANE. SHE'S CUT UP ABOUT DROPPING YOU IN THAT PIT.
ASK HER WHY I DON'T TRUST HER.

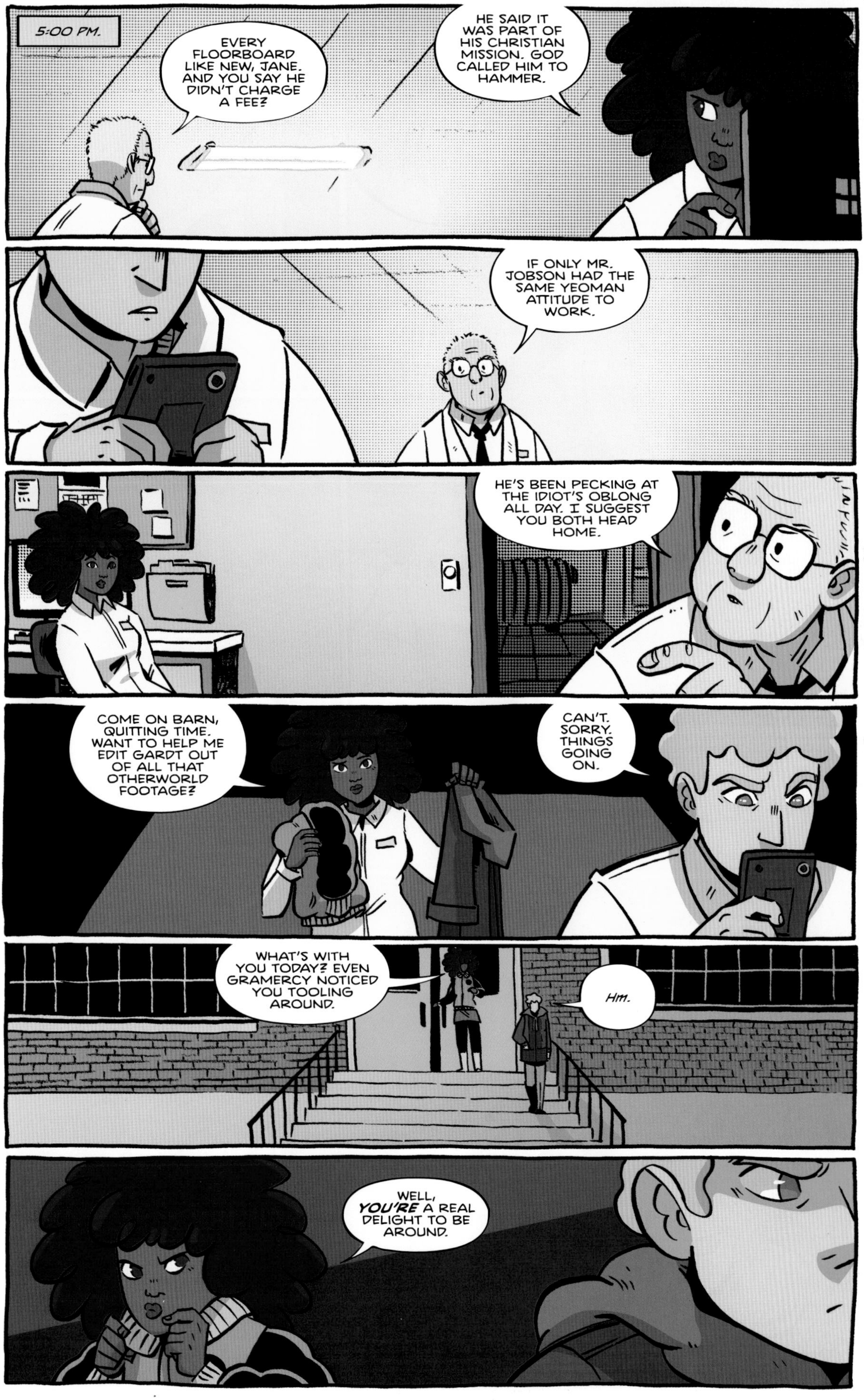
5:00 PM.
EVERY FLOORBOARD LIKE NEW, JANE. AND YOU SAY HE DIDN'T CHARGE A FEE?
HE SAID IT WAS PART OF HIS CHRISTIAN MISSION. GOD CALLED HIM TO HAMMER.
IF ONLY MR. JOBSON HAD THE SAME YEOMAN ATTITUDE TO WORK.
HE'S BEEN PECKING AT THE IDIOT'S OBLONG ALL DAY. I SUGGEST YOU BOTH HEAD HOME.
COME ON BARN, QUITTING TIME. WANT TO HELP ME EDIT GARDT OUT OF ALL THAT OTHERWORLD FOOTAGE?
CAN'T. SORRY. THINGS GOING ON.
WHAT'S WITH YOU TODAY? EVEN GRAMERCY NOTICED YOU TOOLING AROUND.
HM.
WELL, ***YOU'RE*** A REAL DELIGHT TO BE AROUND.

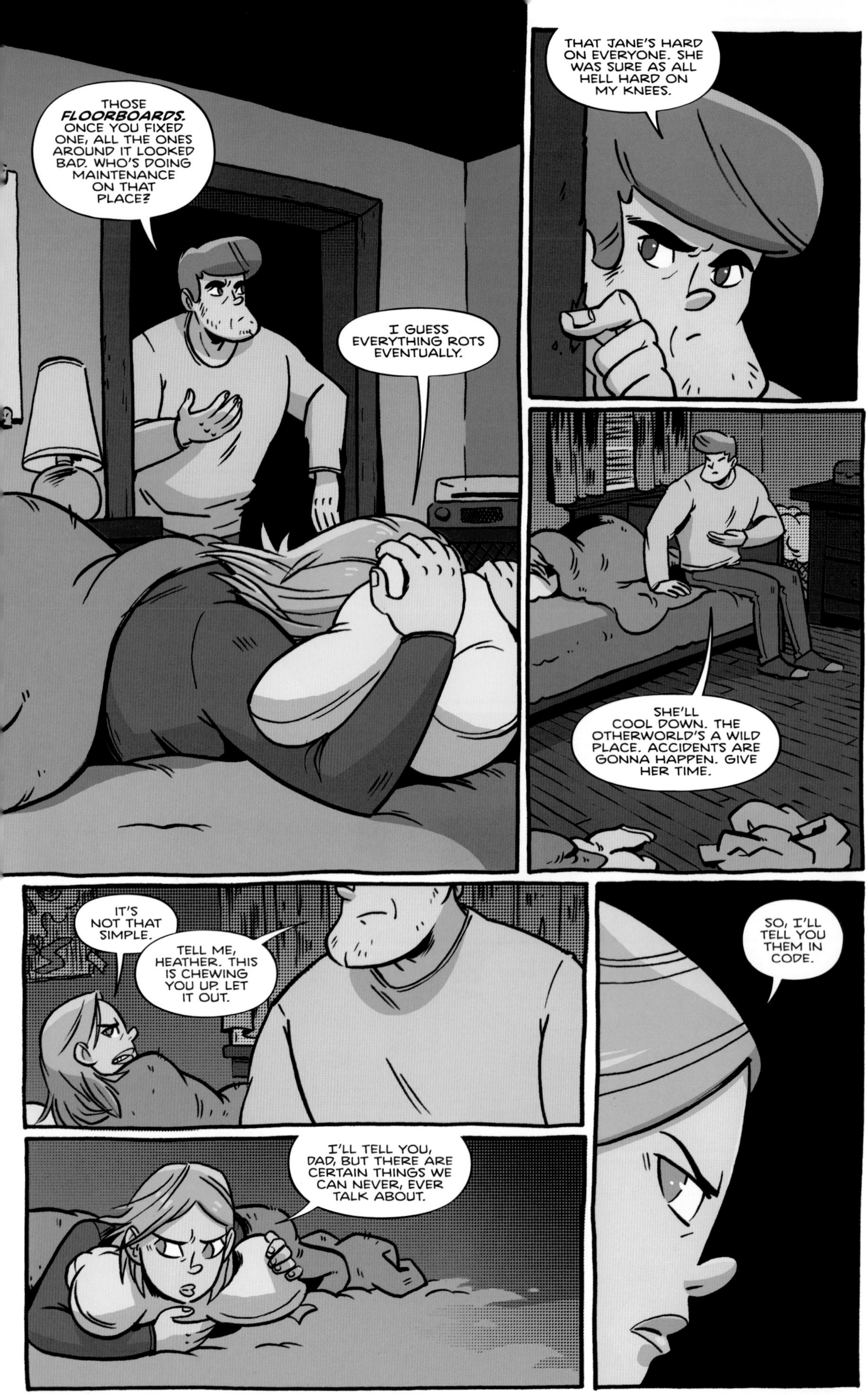
THOSE *FLOORBOARDS.* ONCE YOU FIXED ONE, ALL THE ONES AROUND IT LOOKED BAD. WHO'S DOING MAINTENANCE ON THAT PLACE?
I GUESS EVERYTHING ROTS EVENTUALLY.
THAT JANE'S HARD ON EVERYONE. SHE WAS SURE AS ALL HELL HARD ON MY KNEES.
SHE'LL COOL DOWN. THE OTHERWORLD'S A WILD PLACE. ACCIDENTS ARE GONNA HAPPEN. GIVE HER TIME.
IT'S NOT THAT SIMPLE.
TELL ME, HEATHER. THIS IS CHEWING YOU UP. LET IT OUT.
I'LL TELL YOU, DAD, BUT THERE ARE CERTAIN THINGS WE CAN NEVER, EVER TALK ABOUT.
SO, I'LL TELL YOU THEM IN CODE.

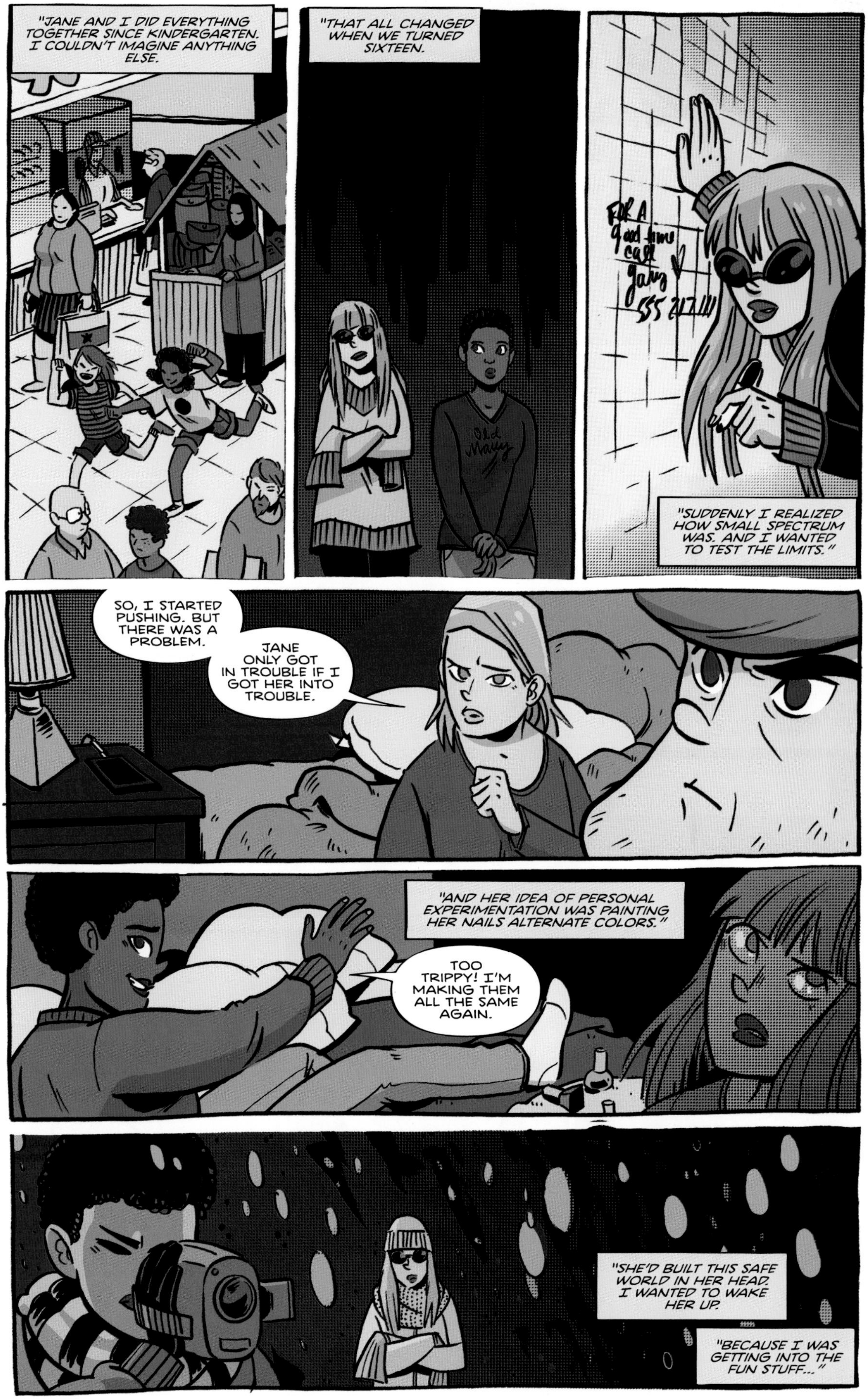
"JANE AND I DID EVERYTHING TOGETHER SINCE KINDERGARTEN. I COULDN'T IMAGINE ANYTHING ELSE.
"THAT ALL CHANGED WHEN WE TURNED SIXTEEN.
Old Navy
FOR A good time call
"SUDDENLY I REALIZED HOW SMALL SPECTRUM WAS. AND I WANTED TO TEST THE LIMITS."
SO, I STARTED PUSHING. BUT THERE WAS A PROBLEM.
JANE ONLY GOT IN TROUBLE IF I GOT HER INTO TROUBLE.
"AND HER IDEA OF PERSONAL EXPERIMENTATION WAS PAINTING HER NAILS ALTERNATE COLORS."
TOO TRIPPY! I'M MAKING THEM ALL THE SAME AGAIN.
"SHE'D BUILT THIS SAFE WORLD IN HER HEAD. I WANTED TO WAKE HER UP.
"BECAUSE I WAS GETTING INTO THE FUN STUFF..."

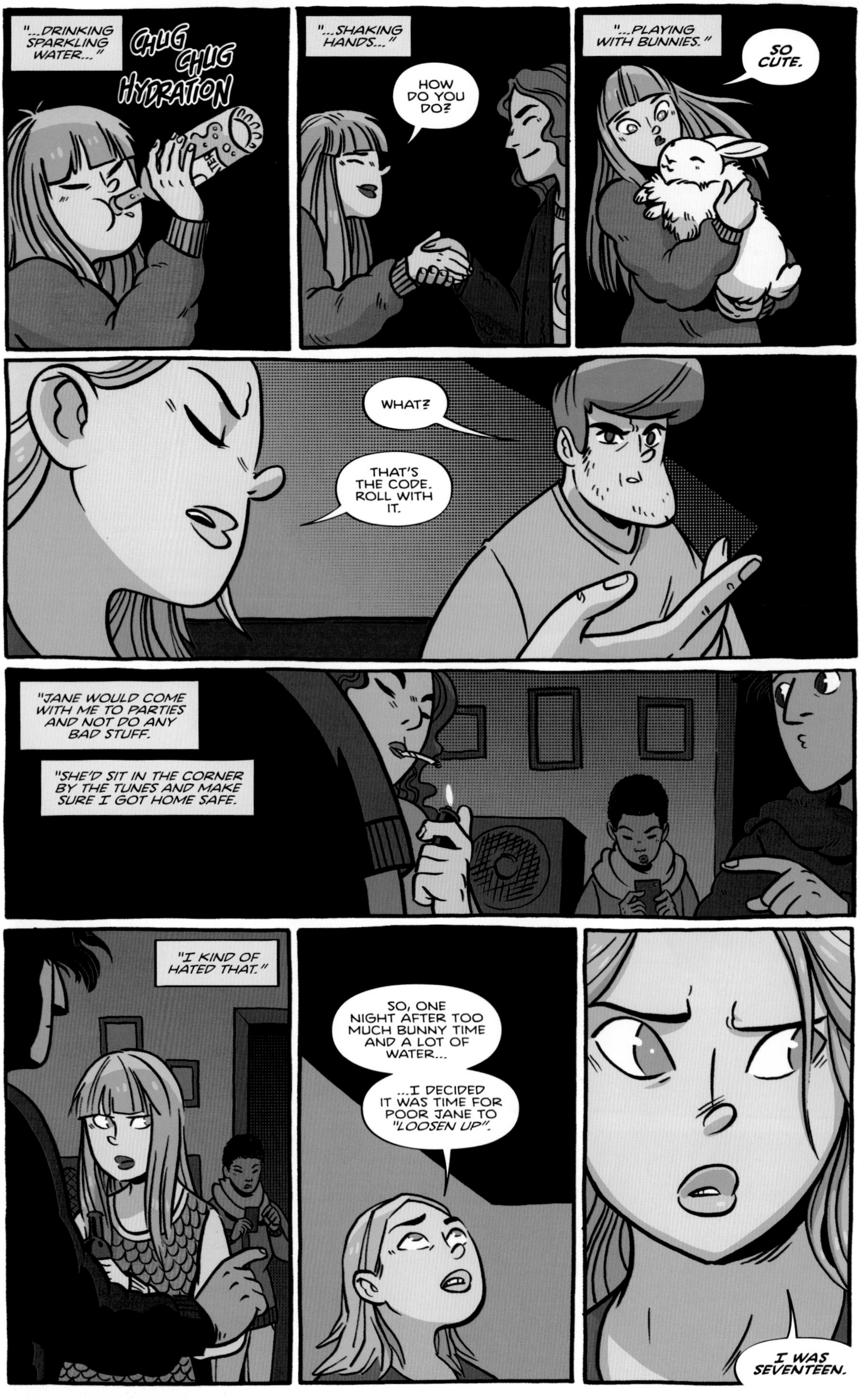
"...DRINKING SPARKLING WATER..."
CHUG CHUG HYDRATION
"...SHAKING HANDS..."
HOW DO YOU DO?
"...PLAYING WITH BUNNIES."
SO CUTE.
WHAT?
THAT'S THE CODE. ROLL WITH IT.
"JANE WOULD COME WITH ME TO PARTIES AND NOT DO ANY BAD STUFF.
"SHE'D SIT IN THE CORNER BY THE TUNES AND MAKE SURE I GOT HOME SAFE.
"I KIND OF HATED THAT."
SO, ONE NIGHT AFTER TOO MUCH BUNNY TIME AND A LOT OF WATER...
...I DECIDED IT WAS TIME FOR POOR JANE TO "LOOSEN UP".
I WAS SEVENTEEN.

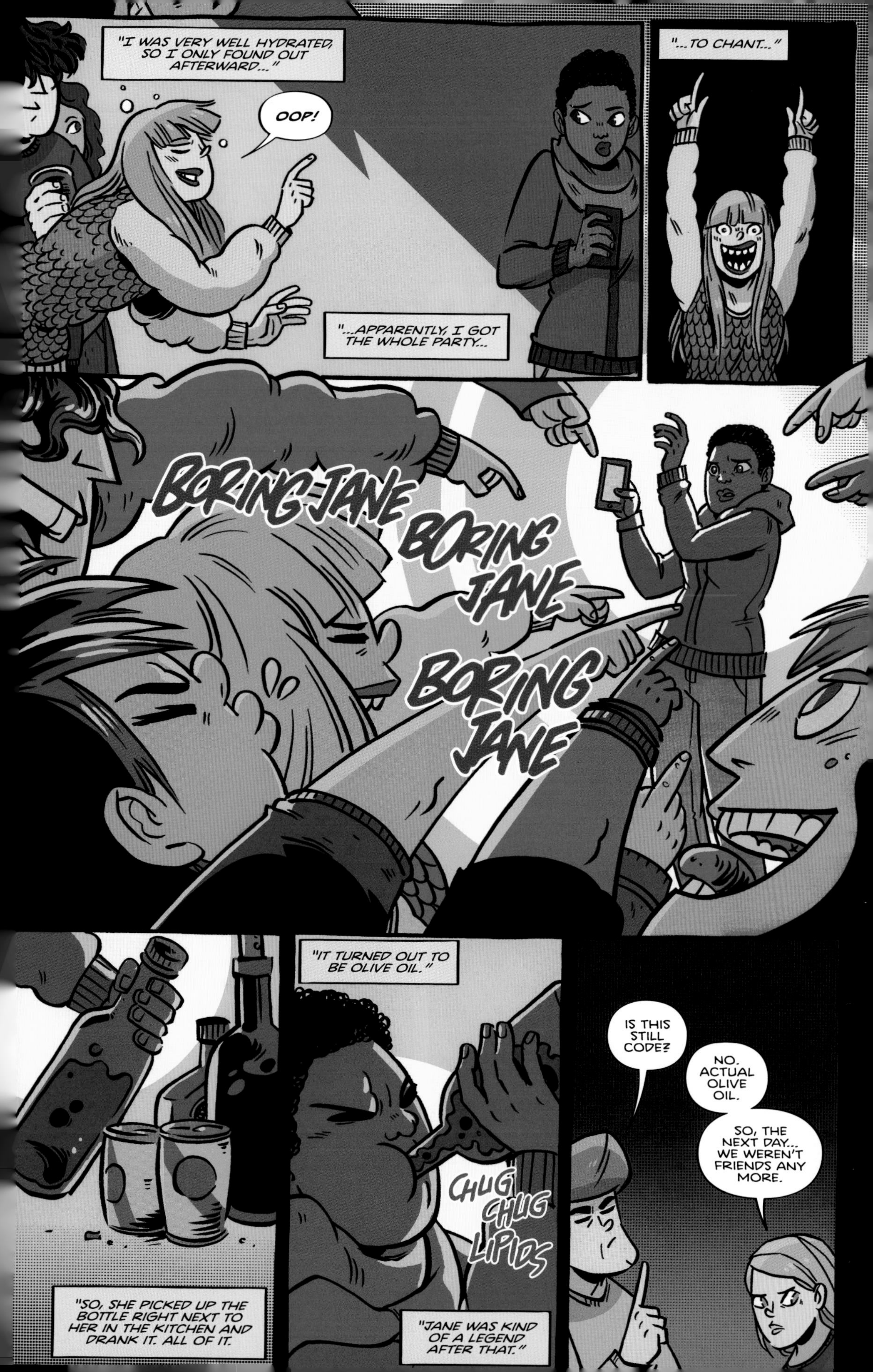
"I WAS VERY WELL HYDRATED, SO I ONLY FOUND OUT AFTERWARD..."
OOP!
"...APPARENTLY, I GOT THE WHOLE PARTY..."
"...TO CHANT..."
BORING JANE
BORING JANE
BORING JANE
"SO, SHE PICKED UP THE BOTTLE RIGHT NEXT TO HER IN THE KITCHEN AND DRANK IT. ALL OF IT."
"IT TURNED OUT TO BE OLIVE OIL."
CHUG CHUG LIPIDS
"JANE WAS KIND OF A LEGEND AFTER THAT."
IS THIS STILL CODE?
NO. ACTUAL OLIVE OIL.
SO, THE NEXT DAY... WE WEREN'T FRIENDS ANY MORE.

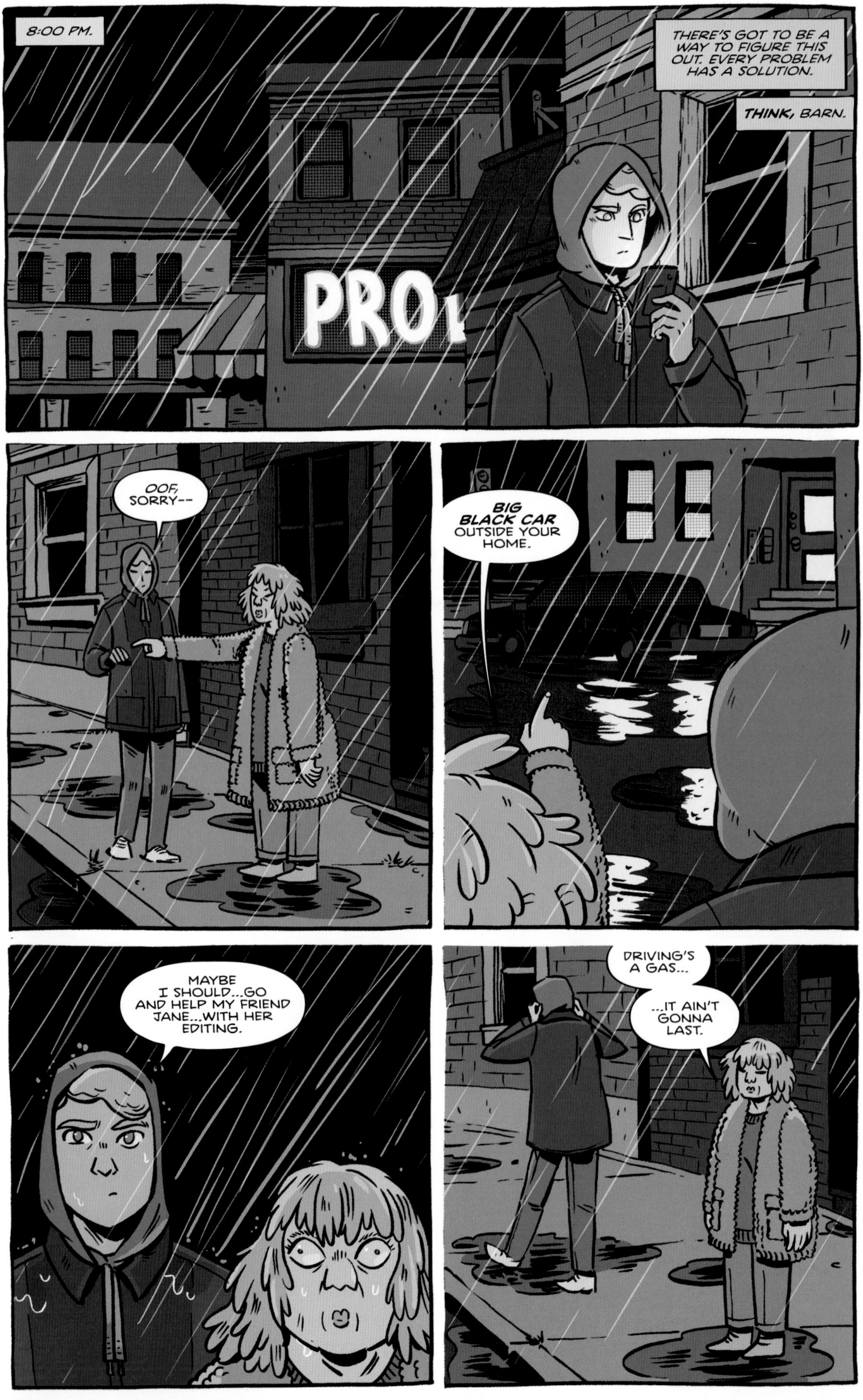
8:00 PM.
THERE'S GOT TO BE A WAY TO FIGURE THIS OUT. EVERY PROBLEM HAS A SOLUTION.
THINK, BARN.
PRO
OOF, SORRY--
BIG BLACK CAR OUTSIDE YOUR HOME.
MAYBE I SHOULD...GO AND HELP MY FRIEND JANE...WITH HER EDITING.
DRIVING'S A GAS...
...IT AIN'T GONNA LAST.

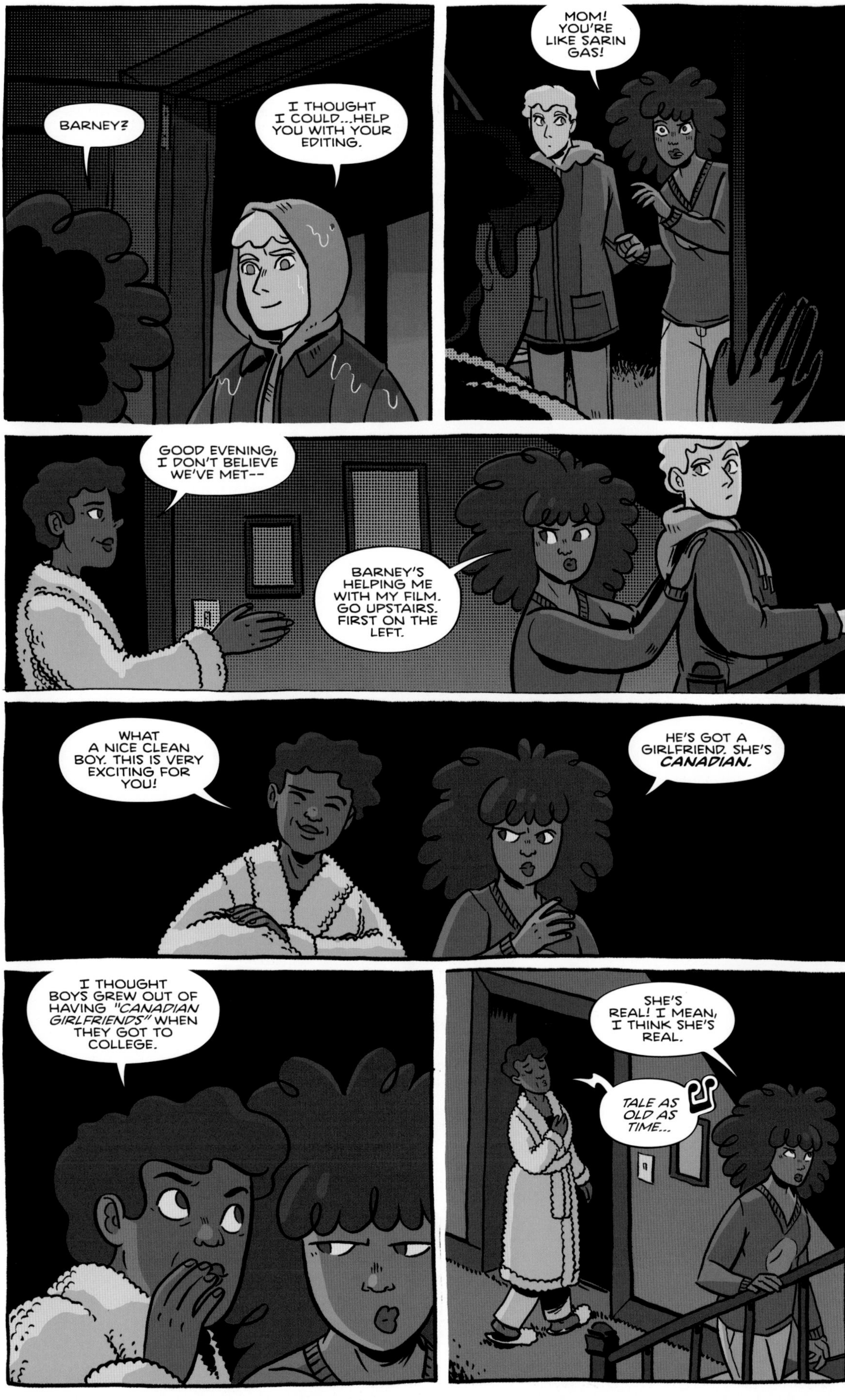
BARNEY?
I THOUGHT I COULD...HELP YOU WITH YOUR EDITING.
MOM! YOU'RE LIKE SARIN GAS!
GOOD EVENING, I DON'T BELIEVE WE'VE MET--
BARNEY'S HELPING ME WITH MY FILM. GO UPSTAIRS. FIRST ON THE LEFT.
WHAT A NICE CLEAN BOY. THIS IS VERY EXCITING FOR YOU!
HE'S GOT A GIRLFRIEND. SHE'S *CANADIAN.*
I THOUGHT BOYS GREW OUT OF HAVING *"CANADIAN GIRLFRIENDS"* WHEN THEY GOT TO COLLEGE.
SHE'S REAL! I MEAN, I THINK SHE'S REAL.
TALE AS OLD AS TIME...

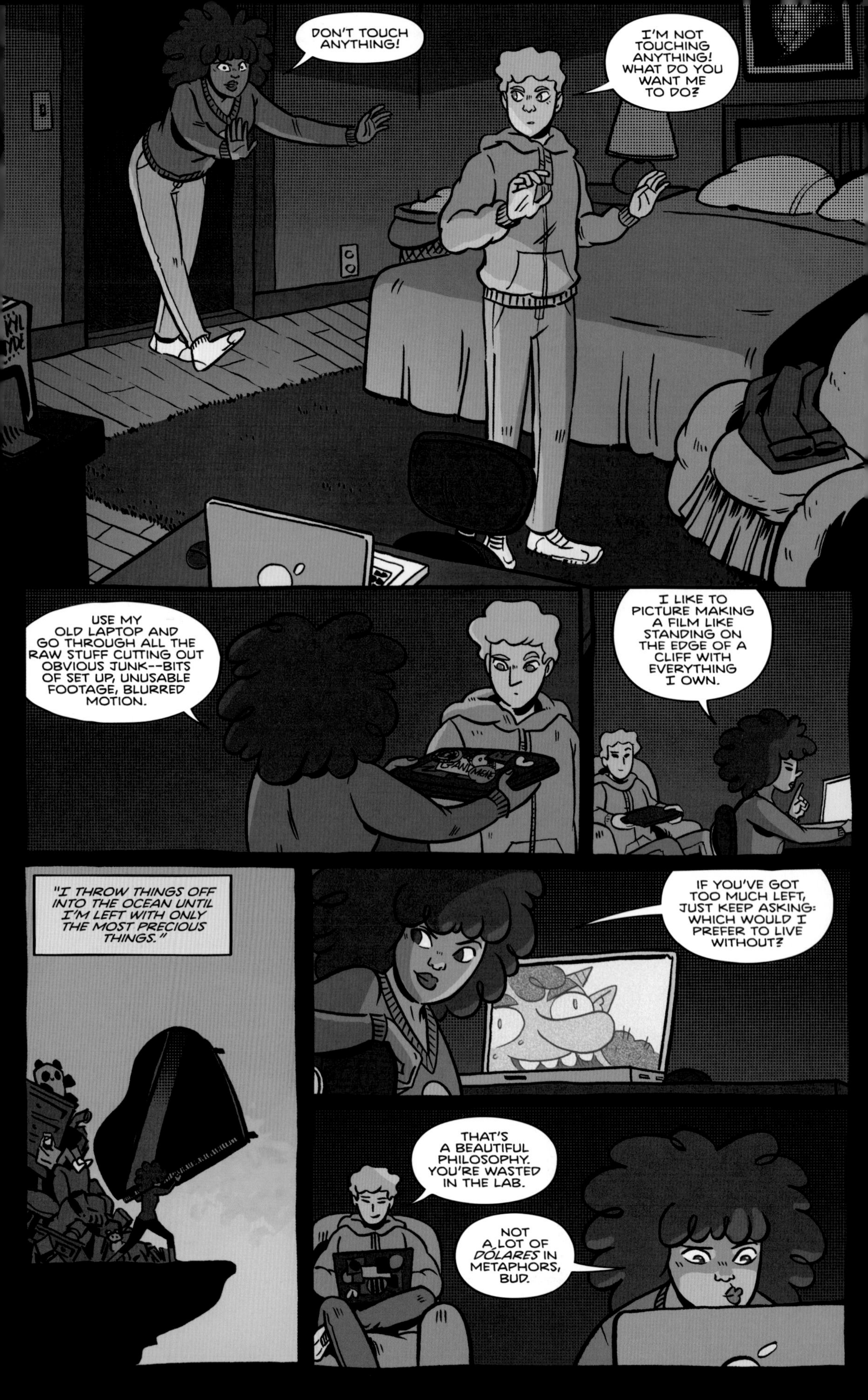
DON'T TOUCH ANYTHING!
I'M NOT TOUCHING ANYTHING! WHAT DO YOU WANT ME TO DO?
USE MY OLD LAPTOP AND GO THROUGH ALL THE RAW STUFF CUTTING OUT OBVIOUS JUNK--BITS OF SET UP, UNUSABLE FOOTAGE, BLURRED MOTION.
I LIKE TO PICTURE MAKING A FILM LIKE STANDING ON THE EDGE OF A CLIFF WITH EVERYTHING I OWN.
"I THROW THINGS OFF INTO THE OCEAN UNTIL I'M LEFT WITH ONLY THE MOST PRECIOUS THINGS."
IF YOU'VE GOT TOO MUCH LEFT, JUST KEEP ASKING: WHICH WOULD I PREFER TO LIVE WITHOUT?
THAT'S A BEAUTIFUL PHILOSOPHY. YOU'RE WASTED IN THE LAB.
NOT A LOT OF *DÓLARES* IN METAPHORS, BUD.

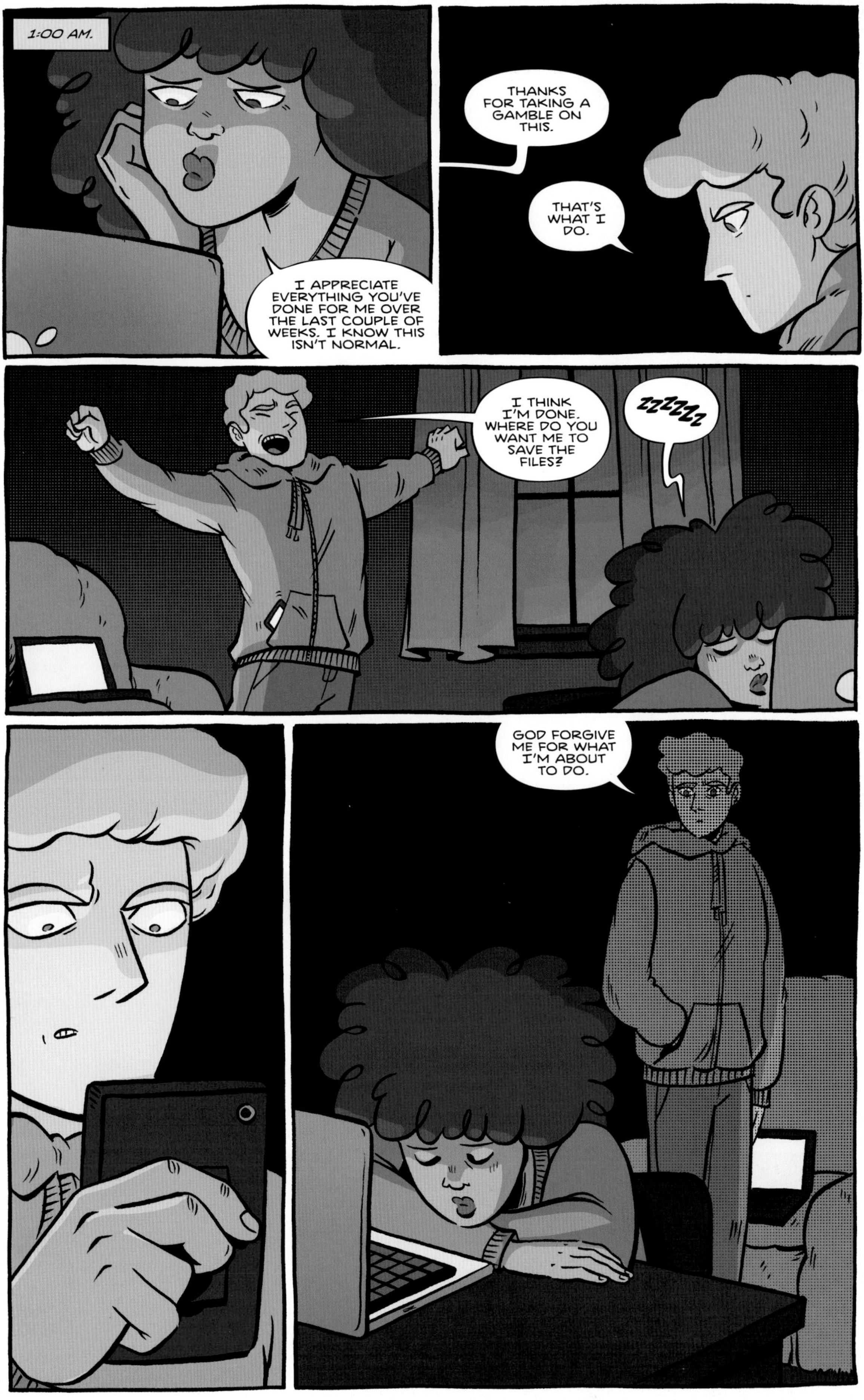
1:00 AM.
THANKS FOR TAKING A GAMBLE ON THIS.
THAT'S WHAT I DO.
I APPRECIATE EVERYTHING YOU'VE DONE FOR ME OVER THE LAST COUPLE OF WEEKS. I KNOW THIS ISN'T NORMAL.
I THINK I'M DONE. WHERE DO YOU WANT ME TO SAVE THE FILES?
ZZZZZZ
GOD FORGIVE ME FOR WHAT I'M ABOUT TO DO.

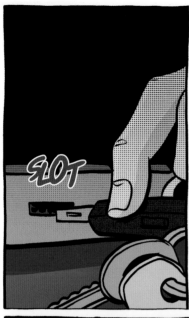

SLOT

WAIT

CRINKLE

CREAK

NEXT TIME YOU COME, YOU MUST TELL ME WHERE'S GOOD TO GO IN CANADA THIS TIME OF YEAR.

CANADA? *Oh* **CANADA.** *Uh,* YEAH, I'LL GIVE YOU SOME TIPS. GOOD NIGHT, MA'AM.

BAD EGG, BRENDA. BAD EGG.

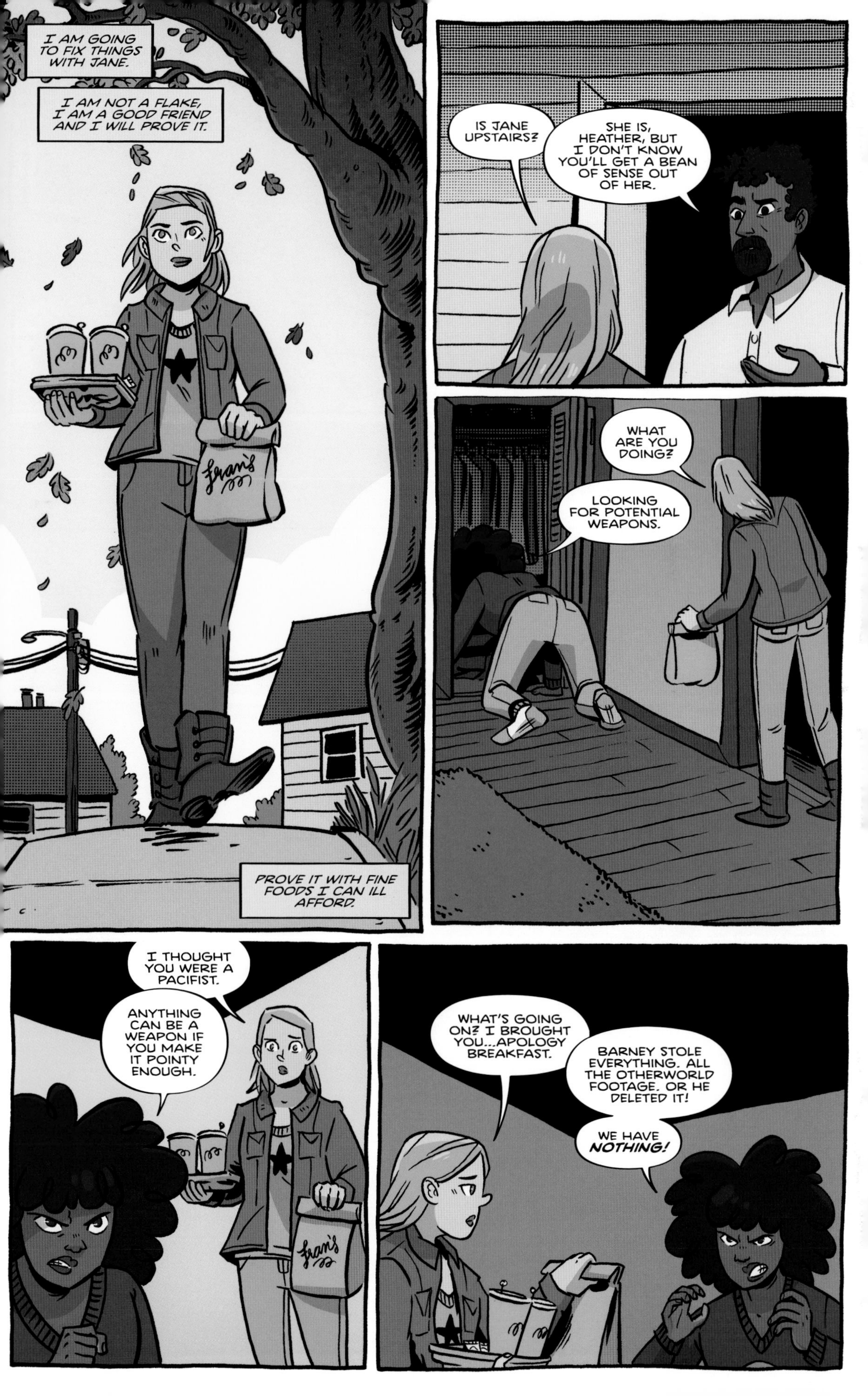
I AM GOING TO FIX THINGS WITH JANE.
I AM NOT A FLAKE, I AM A GOOD FRIEND AND I WILL PROVE IT.
PROVE IT WITH FINE FOODS I CAN ILL AFFORD.
IS JANE UPSTAIRS?
SHE IS, HEATHER, BUT I DON'T KNOW YOU'LL GET A BEAN OF SENSE OUT OF HER.
WHAT ARE YOU DOING?
LOOKING FOR POTENTIAL WEAPONS.
I THOUGHT YOU WERE A PACIFIST.
ANYTHING CAN BE A WEAPON IF YOU MAKE IT POINTY ENOUGH.
WHAT'S GOING ON? I BROUGHT YOU...APOLOGY BREAKFAST.
BARNEY STOLE EVERYTHING. ALL THE OTHERWORLD FOOTAGE. OR HE DELETED IT!
WE HAVE *NOTHING!*

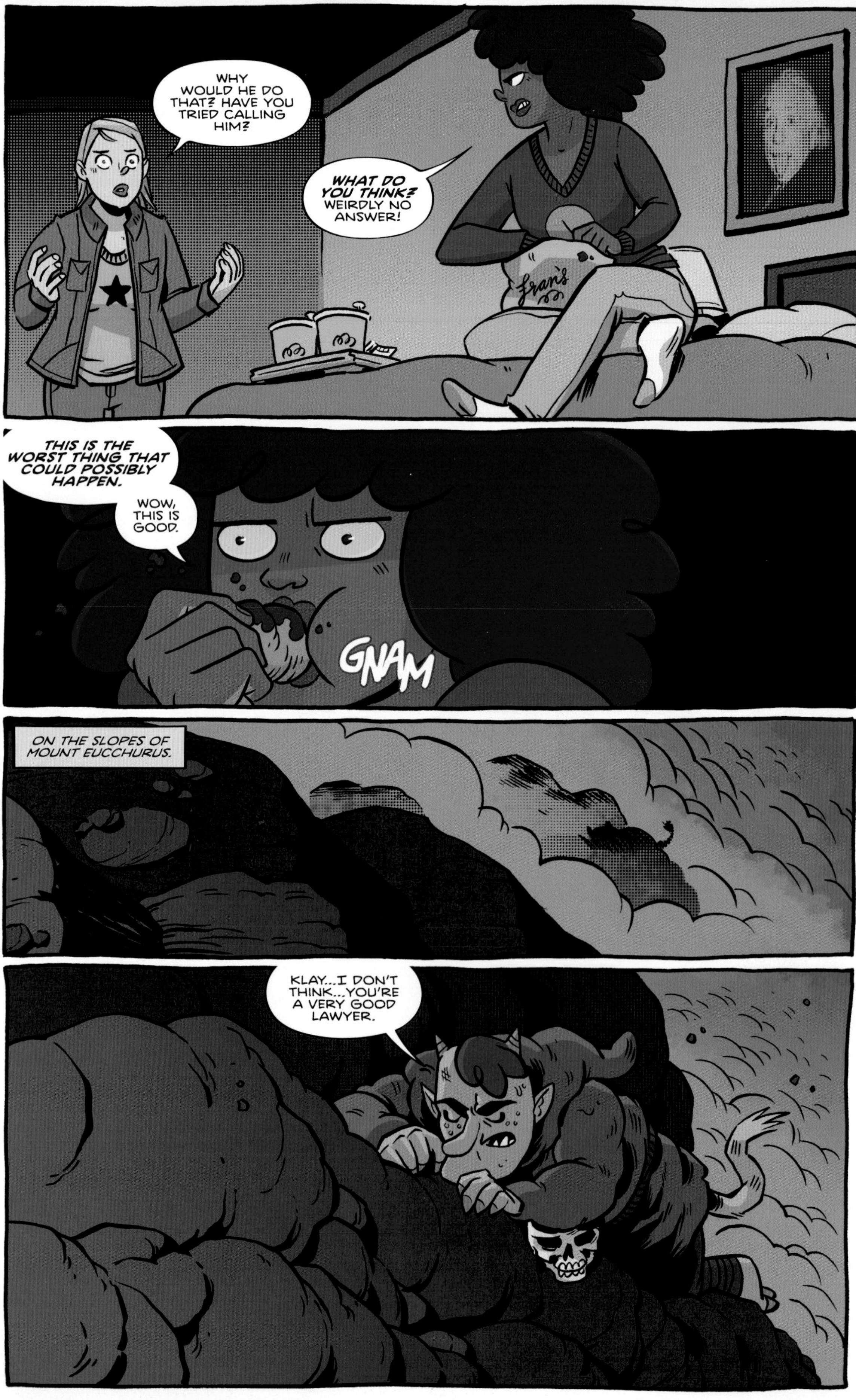
WHY WOULD HE DO THAT? HAVE YOU TRIED CALLING HIM?
WHAT DO YOU THINK? WEIRDLY NO ANSWER!
Fran's
THIS IS THE WORST THING THAT COULD POSSIBLY HAPPEN.
WOW, THIS IS GOOD.
GNAM
ON THE SLOPES OF MOUNT EUCCHURUS.
KLAY... I DON'T THINK... YOU'RE A VERY GOOD LAWYER.

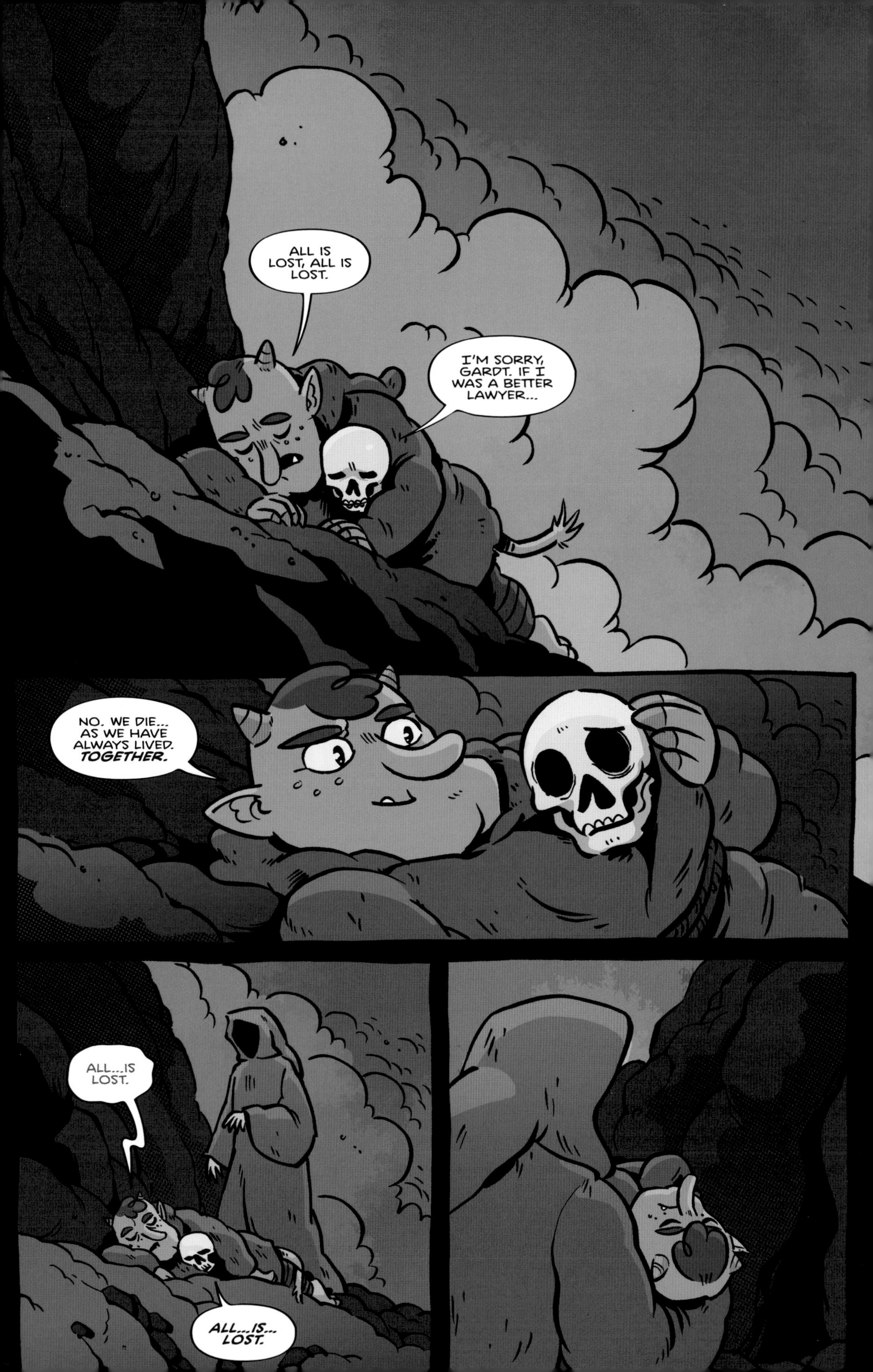
ALL IS LOST, ALL IS LOST.
I'M SORRY, GARDT. IF I WAS A BETTER LAWYER...
NO. WE DIE... AS WE HAVE ALWAYS LIVED. *TOGETHER.*
ALL...IS LOST.
ALL...IS... LOST.

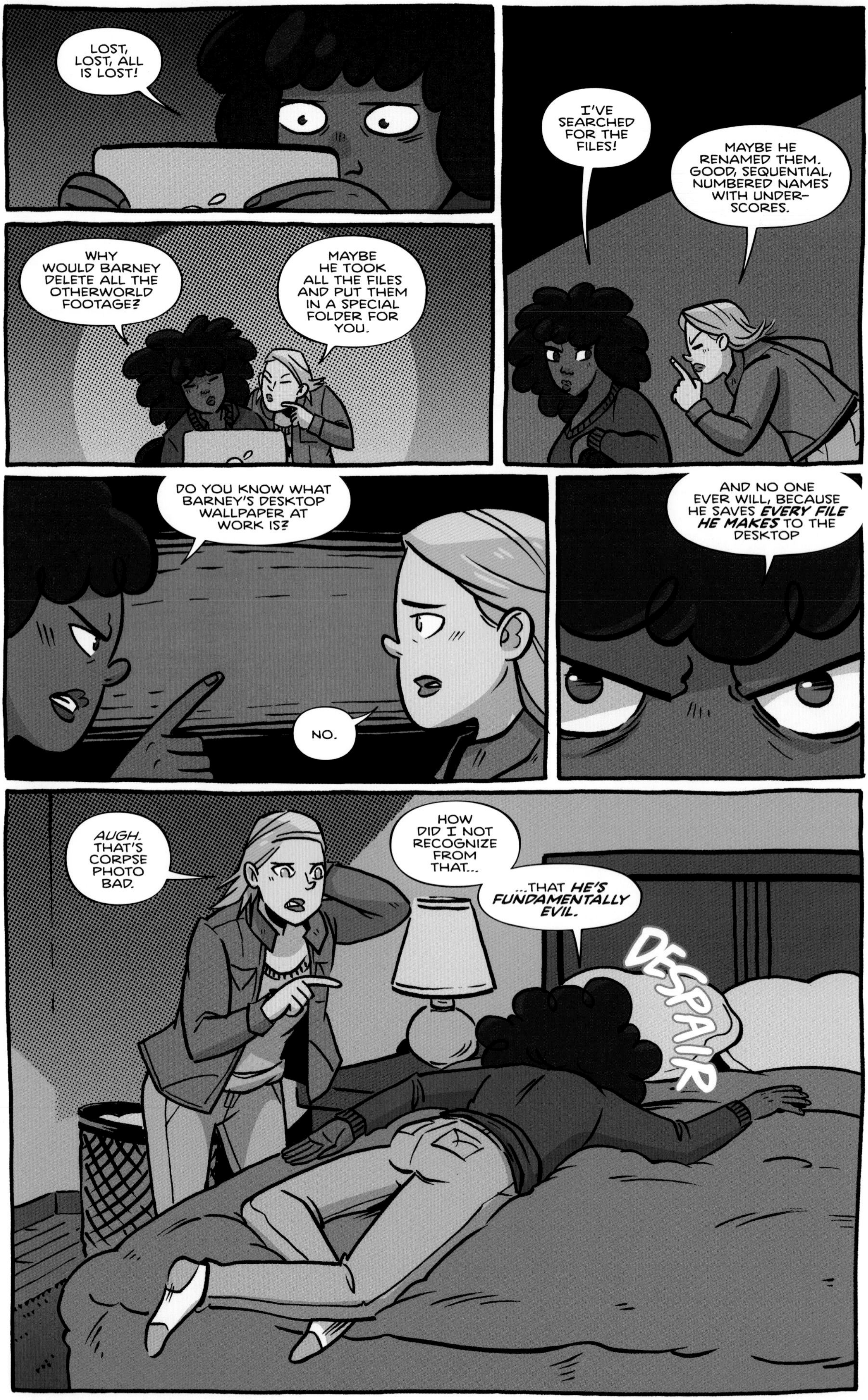
LOST, LOST, ALL IS LOST!
I'VE SEARCHED FOR THE FILES!
MAYBE HE RENAMED THEM. GOOD, SEQUENTIAL, NUMBERED NAMES WITH UNDER-SCORES.
WHY WOULD BARNEY DELETE ALL THE OTHERWORLD FOOTAGE?
MAYBE HE TOOK ALL THE FILES AND PUT THEM IN A SPECIAL FOLDER FOR YOU.
DO YOU KNOW WHAT BARNEY'S DESKTOP WALLPAPER AT WORK IS?
NO.
AND NO ONE EVER WILL, BECAUSE HE SAVES *EVERY FILE HE MAKES* TO THE DESKTOP
AUGH. THAT'S CORPSE PHOTO BAD.
HOW DID I NOT RECOGNIZE FROM THAT...
...THAT *HE'S FUNDAMENTALLY EVIL.*
DESPAIR

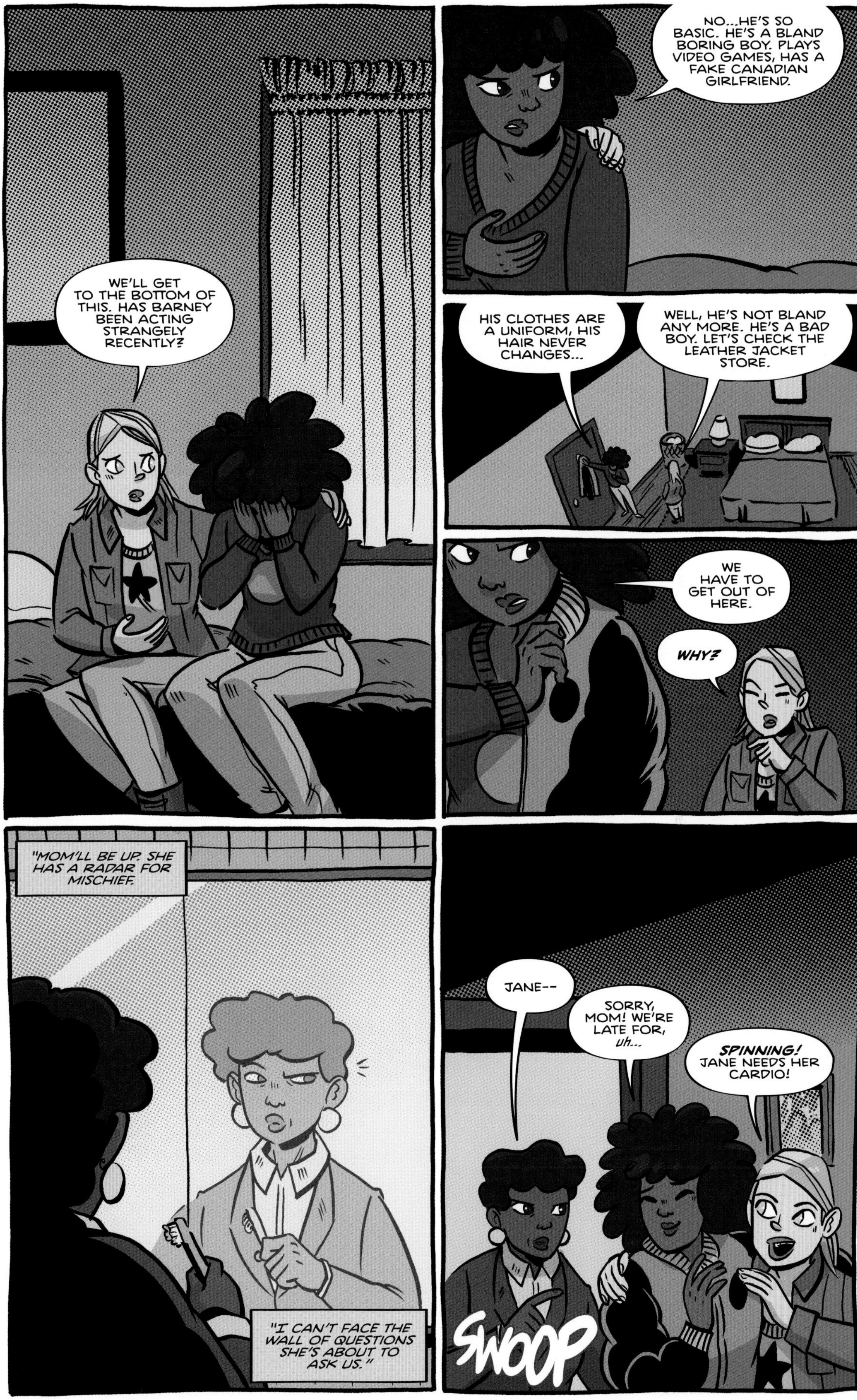
WE'LL GET TO THE BOTTOM OF THIS. HAS BARNEY BEEN ACTING STRANGELY RECENTLY?
NO...HE'S SO BASIC. HE'S A BLAND BORING BOY. PLAYS VIDEO GAMES, HAS A FAKE CANADIAN GIRLFRIEND.
HIS CLOTHES ARE A UNIFORM, HIS HAIR NEVER CHANGES...
WELL, HE'S NOT BLAND ANY MORE. HE'S A BAD BOY. LET'S CHECK THE LEATHER JACKET STORE.
WE HAVE TO GET OUT OF HERE.
WHY?
"MOM'LL BE UP. SHE HAS A RADAR FOR MISCHIEF.
"I CAN'T FACE THE WALL OF QUESTIONS SHE'S ABOUT TO ASK US."
JANE--
SORRY, MOM! WE'RE LATE FOR, uh...
SPINNING! JANE NEEDS HER CARDIO!
SWOOP

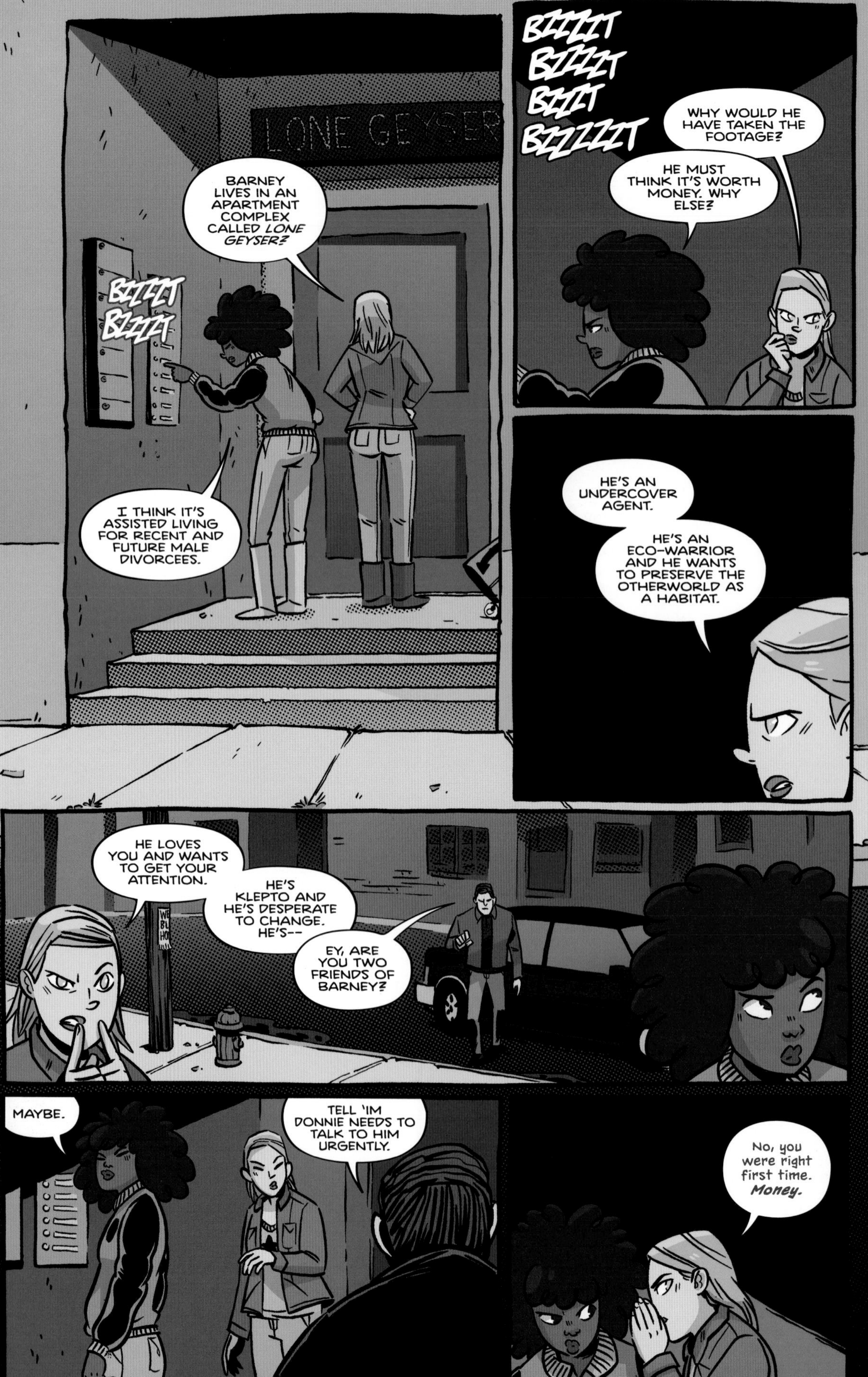
LONE GEYSER
BARNEY LIVES IN AN APARTMENT COMPLEX CALLED *LONE GEYSER*?
BZZZZT BZZZZT
I THINK IT'S ASSISTED LIVING FOR RECENT AND FUTURE MALE DIVORCEES.
BZZZZT BZZZZT BZZZT BZZZZZT
WHY WOULD HE HAVE TAKEN THE FOOTAGE?
HE MUST THINK IT'S WORTH MONEY. WHY ELSE?
HE'S AN UNDERCOVER AGENT.
HE'S AN ECO-WARRIOR AND HE WANTS TO PRESERVE THE OTHERWORLD AS A HABITAT.
HE LOVES YOU AND WANTS TO GET YOUR ATTENTION.
HE'S KLEPTO AND HE'S DESPERATE TO CHANGE. HE'S--
EY, ARE YOU TWO FRIENDS OF BARNEY?
MAYBE.
TELL 'IM DONNIE NEEDS TO TALK TO HIM URGENTLY.
No, you were right first time. *Money*.

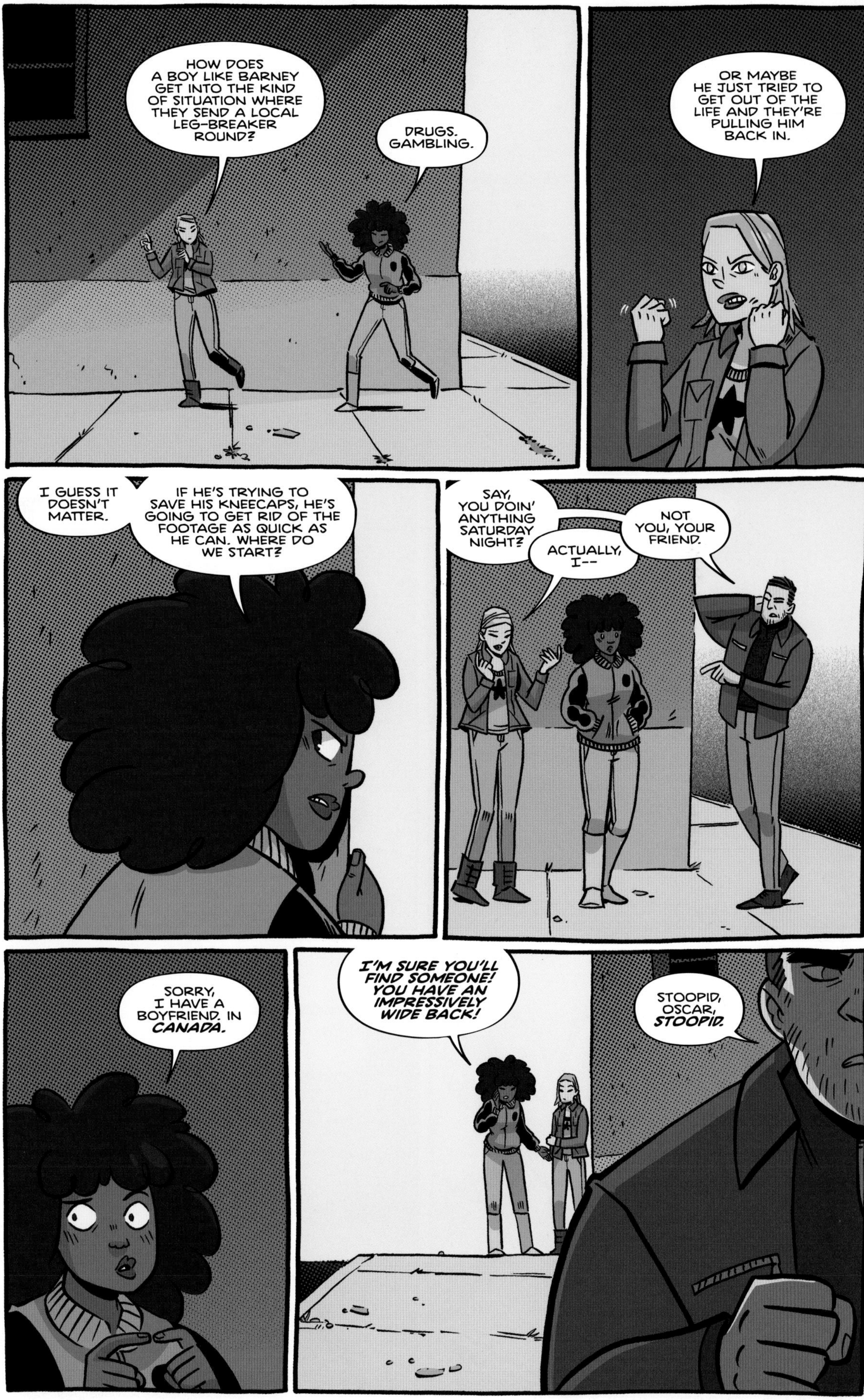
HOW DOES A BOY LIKE BARNEY GET INTO THE KIND OF SITUATION WHERE THEY SEND A LOCAL LEG-BREAKER ROUND?
DRUGS. GAMBLING.
OR MAYBE HE JUST TRIED TO GET OUT OF THE LIFE AND THEY'RE PULLING HIM BACK IN.
I GUESS IT DOESN'T MATTER.
IF HE'S TRYING TO SAVE HIS KNEECAPS, HE'S GOING TO GET RID OF THE FOOTAGE AS QUICK AS HE CAN. WHERE DO WE START?
SAY, YOU DOIN' ANYTHING SATURDAY NIGHT?
ACTUALLY, I--
NOT YOU, YOUR FRIEND.
SORRY, I HAVE A BOYFRIEND. IN *CANADA.*
I'M SURE YOU'LL FIND SOMEONE! YOU HAVE AN IMPRESSIVELY WIDE BACK!
STOOPID, OSCAR, ***STOOPID.***

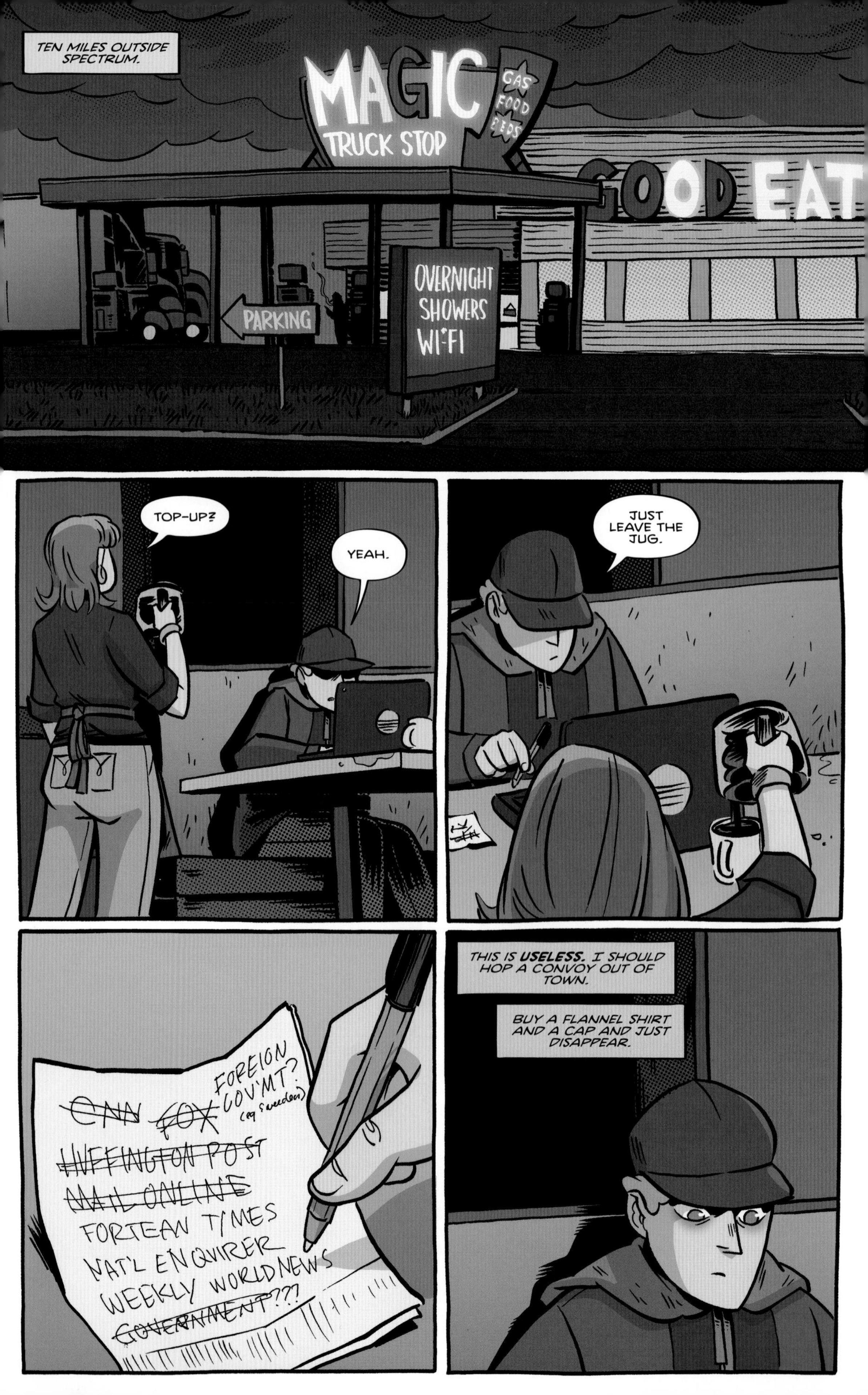

TEN MILES OUTSIDE SPECTRUM.
MAGIC
TRUCK STOP
GAS FOOD BEDS
GOOD EAT
PARKING
OVERNIGHT SHOWERS WI-FI
TOP-UP?
YEAH.
JUST LEAVE THE JUG.
CNN FOX
FOREIGN GOV'MT?
(eg Sweden)
HUFFINGTON POST
MAIL ONLINE
FORTEAN TIMES
NAT'L ENQUIRER
WEEKLY WORLD NEWS
GOVERNMENT???
THIS IS USELESS. I SHOULD HOP A CONVOY OUT OF TOWN.
BUY A FLANNEL SHIRT AND A CAP AND JUST DISAPPEAR.

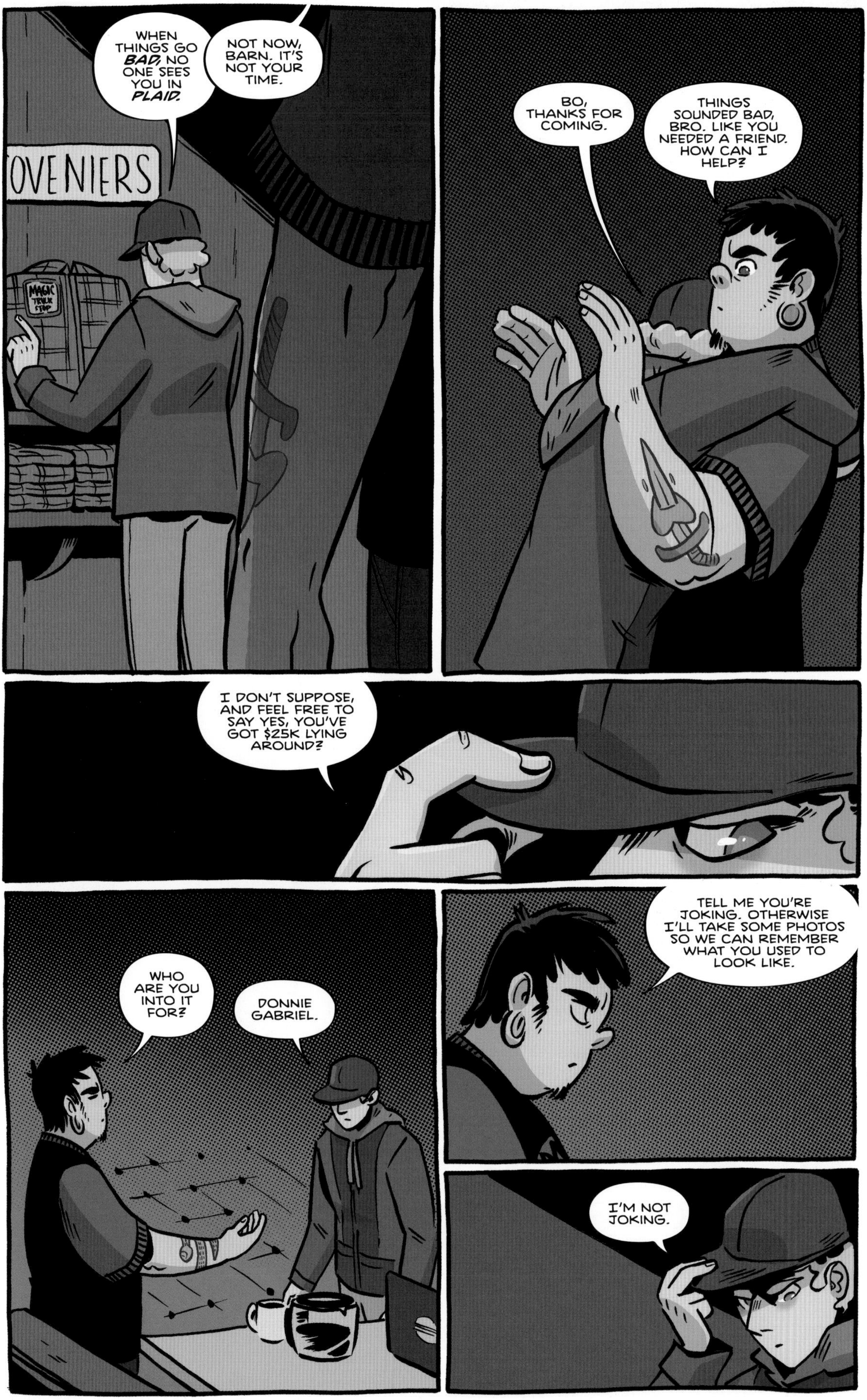

WHEN THINGS GO BAD, NO ONE SEES YOU IN PLAID.
NOT NOW, BARN. IT'S NOT YOUR TIME.
OVENIERS
MAGIC TRUCK STOP
BO, THANKS FOR COMING.
THINGS SOUNDED BAD, BRO. LIKE YOU NEEDED A FRIEND. HOW CAN I HELP?
I DON'T SUPPOSE, AND FEEL FREE TO SAY YES, YOU'VE GOT $25K LYING AROUND?
WHO ARE YOU INTO IT FOR?
DONNIE GABRIEL.
TELL ME YOU'RE JOKING. OTHERWISE I'LL TAKE SOME PHOTOS SO WE CAN REMEMBER WHAT YOU USED TO LOOK LIKE.
I'M NOT JOKING.

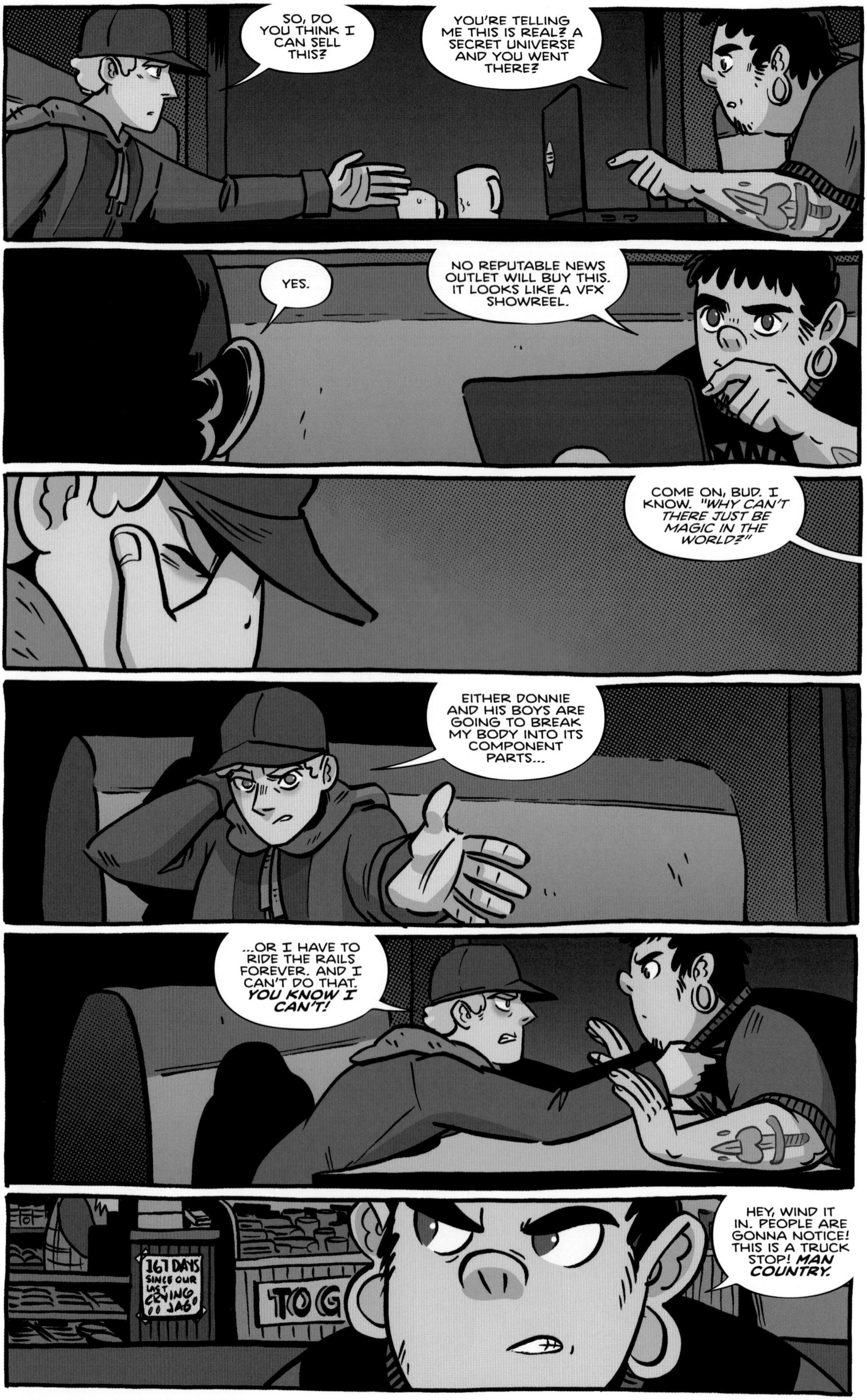
SO, DO YOU THINK I CAN SELL THIS?
YOU'RE TELLING ME THIS IS REAL? A SECRET UNIVERSE AND YOU WENT THERE?
YES.
NO REPUTABLE NEWS OUTLET WILL BUY THIS. IT LOOKS LIKE A VFX SHOWREEL.
COME ON, BUD. I KNOW. *"WHY CAN'T THERE JUST BE MAGIC IN THE WORLD?"*
EITHER DONNIE AND HIS BOYS ARE GOING TO BREAK MY BODY INTO ITS COMPONENT PARTS...
...OR I HAVE TO RIDE THE RAILS FOREVER. AND I CAN'T DO THAT. ***YOU KNOW I CAN'T!***
HEY, WIND IT IN. PEOPLE ARE GONNA NOTICE! THIS IS A TRUCK STOP! ***MAN COUNTRY.***
167 DAYS SINCE OUR LAST CRYING JAG
TOG

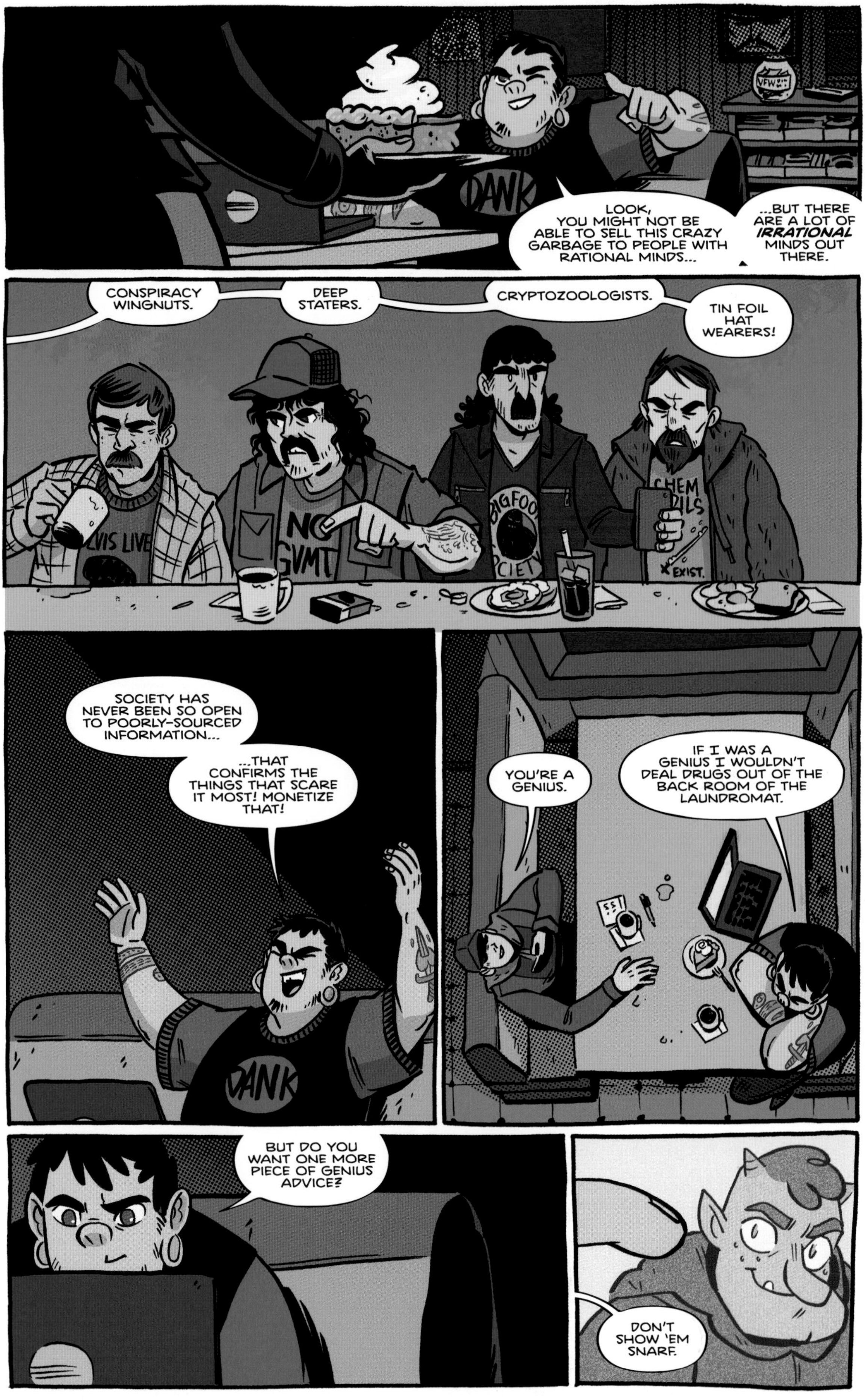
VFW
DANK
LOOK, YOU MIGHT NOT BE ABLE TO SELL THIS CRAZY GARBAGE TO PEOPLE WITH RATIONAL MINDS...
...BUT THERE ARE A LOT OF IRRATIONAL MINDS OUT THERE.
CONSPIRACY WINGNUTS.
DEEP STATERS.
CRYPTOZOOLOGISTS.
TIN FOIL HAT WEARERS!
ELVIS LIVE
NO GVMT
BIGFOOT SOCIETY
CHEM TRAILS
EXIST.
SOCIETY HAS NEVER BEEN SO OPEN TO POORLY-SOURCED INFORMATION...
...THAT CONFIRMS THE THINGS THAT SCARE IT MOST! MONETIZE THAT!
DANK
YOU'RE A GENIUS.
IF I WAS A GENIUS I WOULDN'T DEAL DRUGS OUT OF THE BACK ROOM OF THE LAUNDROMAT.
BUT DO YOU WANT ONE MORE PIECE OF GENIUS ADVICE?
DON'T SHOW 'EM SNARF.

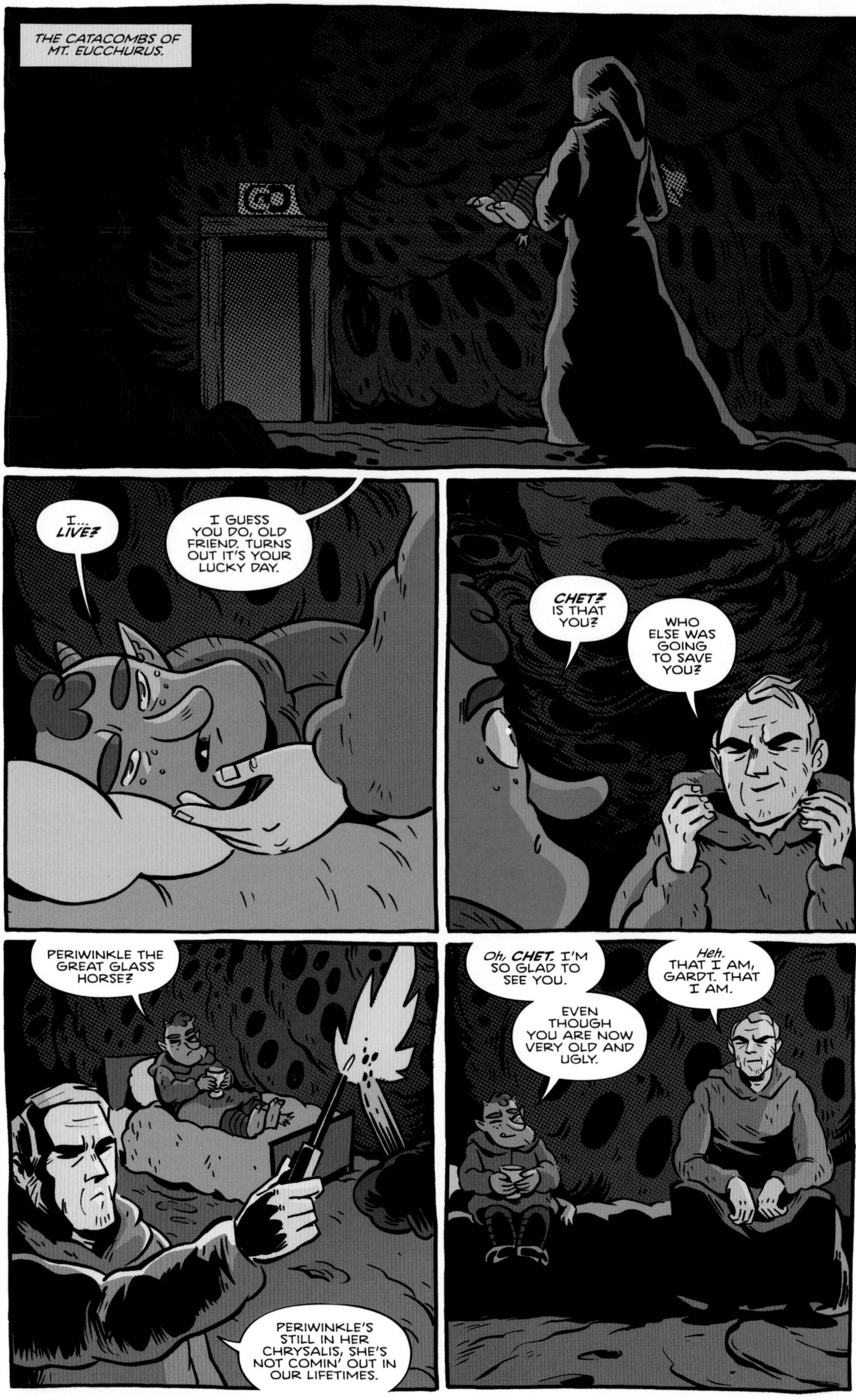
THE CATACOMBS OF MT. EUCCHURUS.
I... LIVE?
I GUESS YOU DO, OLD FRIEND. TURNS OUT IT'S YOUR LUCKY DAY.
CHET? IS THAT YOU?
WHO ELSE WAS GOING TO SAVE YOU?
PERIWINKLE THE GREAT GLASS HORSE?
PERIWINKLE'S STILL IN HER CHRYSALIS, SHE'S NOT COMIN' OUT IN OUR LIFETIMES.
Oh, CHET. I'M SO GLAD TO SEE YOU.
EVEN THOUGH YOU ARE NOW VERY OLD AND UGLY.
Heh. THAT I AM, GARDT. THAT I AM.

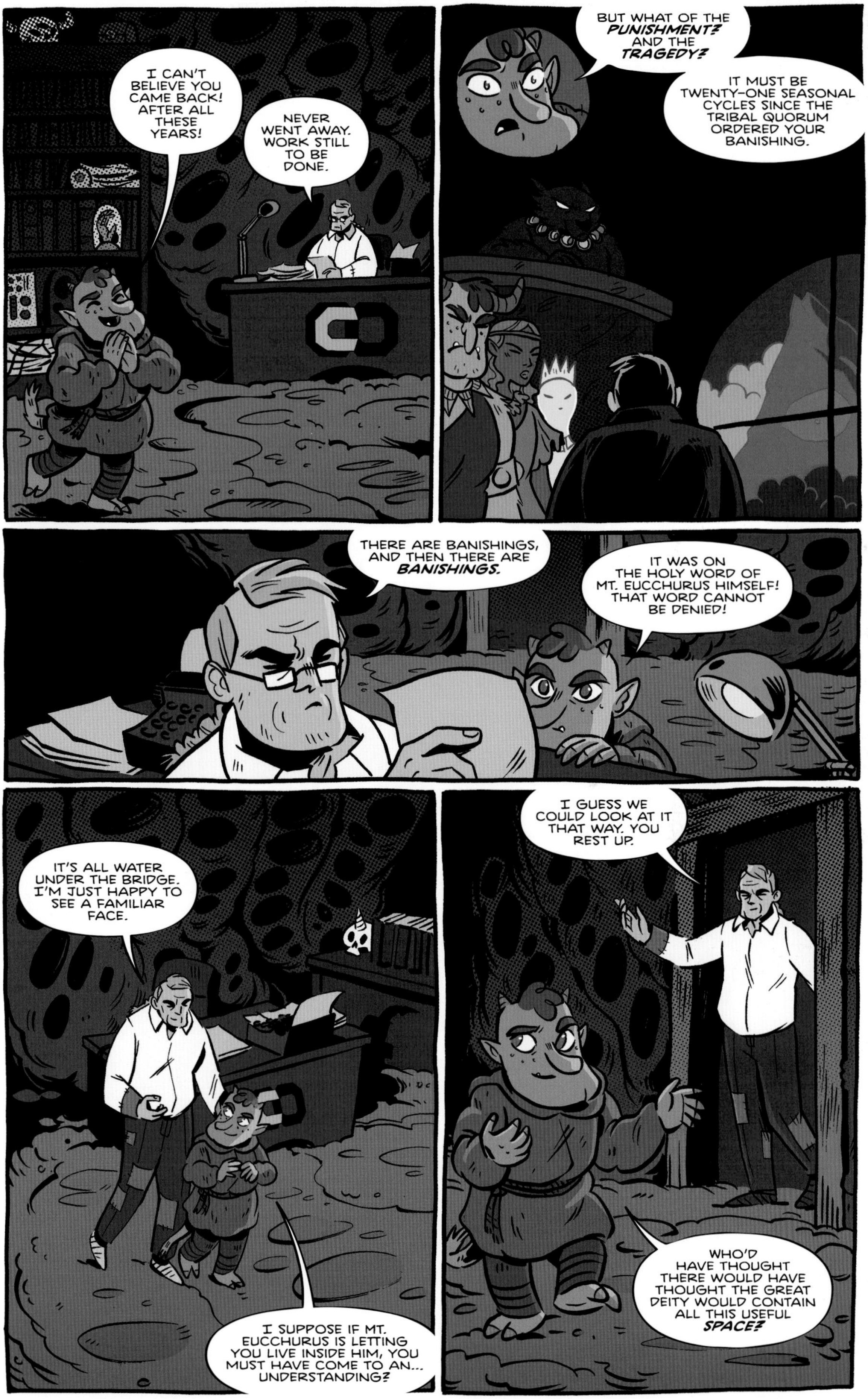
I CAN'T BELIEVE YOU CAME BACK! AFTER ALL THESE YEARS!
NEVER WENT AWAY. WORK STILL TO BE DONE.
BUT WHAT OF THE *PUNISHMENT?* AND THE *TRAGEDY?*
IT MUST BE TWENTY-ONE SEASONAL CYCLES SINCE THE TRIBAL QUORUM ORDERED YOUR BANISHING.
THERE ARE BANISHINGS, AND THEN THERE ARE *BANISHINGS.*
IT WAS ON THE HOLY WORD OF MT. EUCCHURUS HIMSELF! THAT WORD CANNOT BE DENIED!
IT'S ALL WATER UNDER THE BRIDGE. I'M JUST HAPPY TO SEE A FAMILIAR FACE.
I SUPPOSE IF MT. EUCCHURUS IS LETTING YOU LIVE INSIDE HIM, YOU MUST HAVE COME TO AN... UNDERSTANDING?
I GUESS WE COULD LOOK AT IT THAT WAY. YOU REST UP.
WHO'D HAVE THOUGHT THERE WOULD HAVE THOUGHT THE GREAT DEITY WOULD CONTAIN ALL THIS USEFUL *SPACE?*

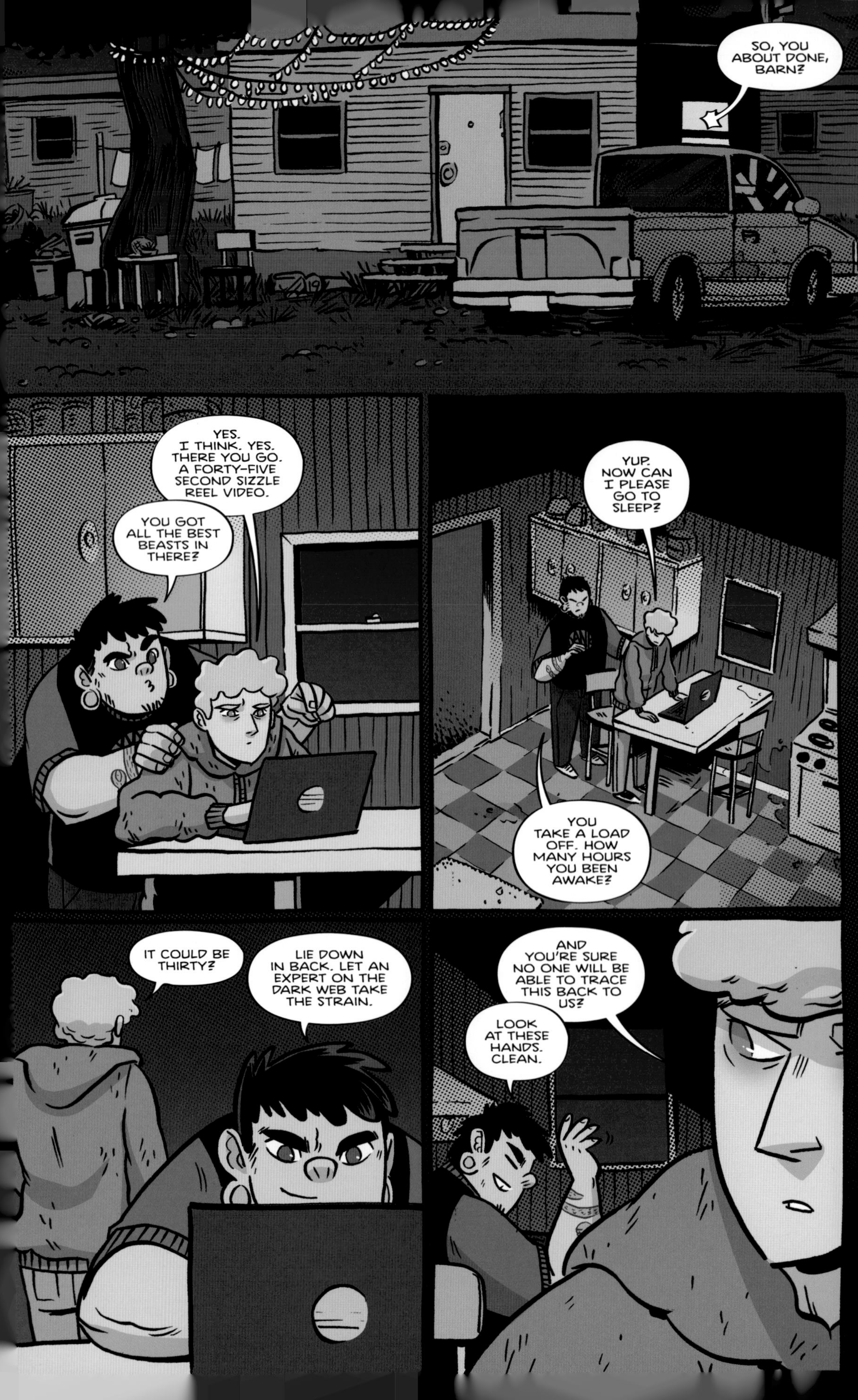
SO, YOU ABOUT DONE, BARN?
YES. I THINK. YES. THERE YOU GO. A FORTY-FIVE SECOND SIZZLE REEL VIDEO.
YOU GOT ALL THE BEST BEASTS IN THERE?
YUP. NOW CAN I PLEASE GO TO SLEEP?
YOU TAKE A LOAD OFF. HOW MANY HOURS YOU BEEN AWAKE?
IT COULD BE THIRTY?
LIE DOWN IN BACK. LET AN EXPERT ON THE DARK WEB TAKE THE STRAIN.
AND YOU'RE SURE NO ONE WILL BE ABLE TO TRACE THIS BACK TO US?
LOOK AT THESE HANDS. CLEAN.

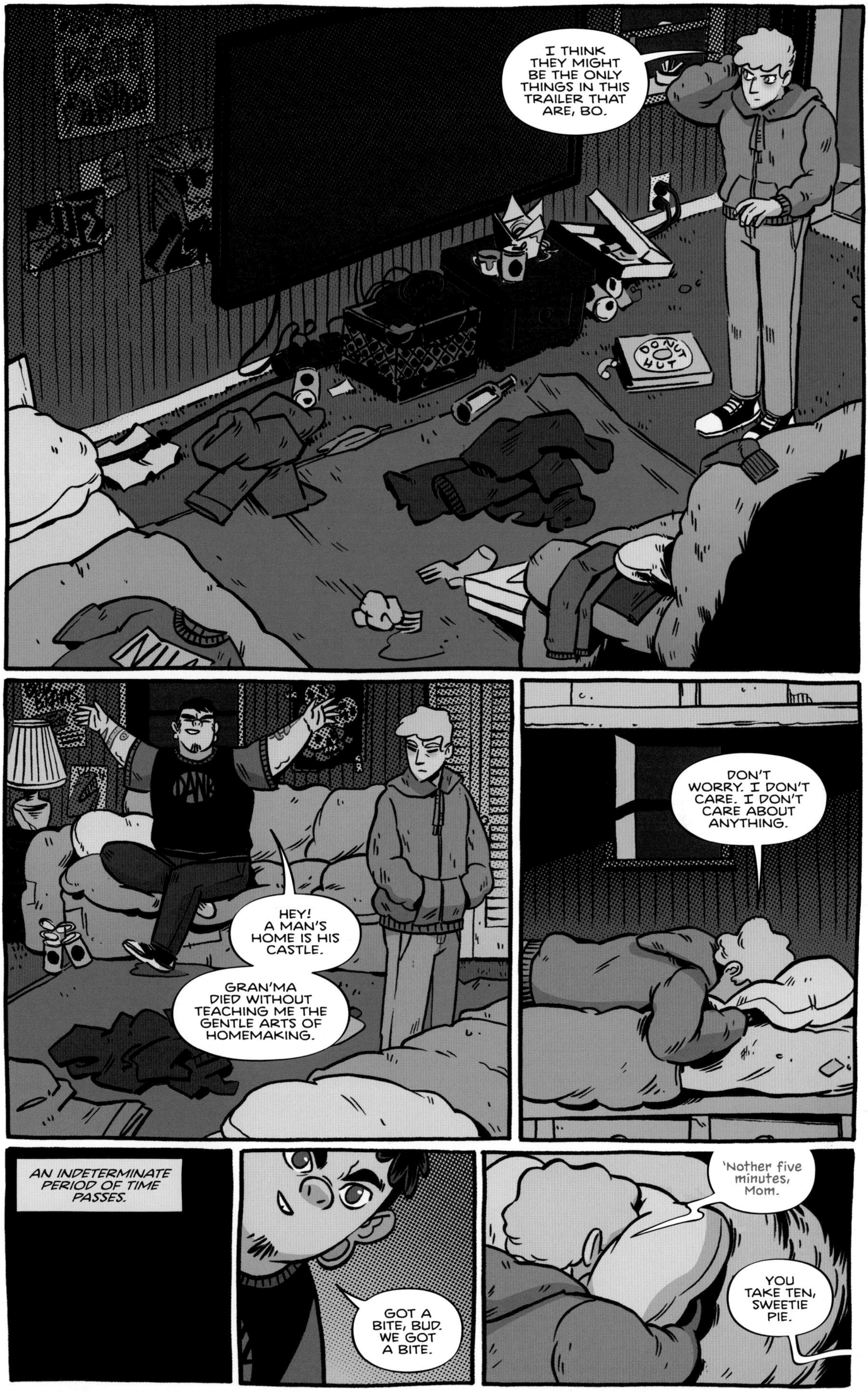
I THINK THEY MIGHT BE THE ONLY THINGS IN THIS TRAILER THAT ARE, BO.
DONUT HUT
HEY! A MAN'S HOME IS HIS CASTLE.
GRAN'MA DIED WITHOUT TEACHING ME THE GENTLE ARTS OF HOMEMAKING.
DON'T WORRY. I DON'T CARE. I DON'T CARE ABOUT ANYTHING.
AN INDETERMINATE PERIOD OF TIME PASSES.
GOT A BITE, BUD. WE GOT A BITE.
'Nother five minutes, Mom.
YOU TAKE TEN, SWEETIE PIE.

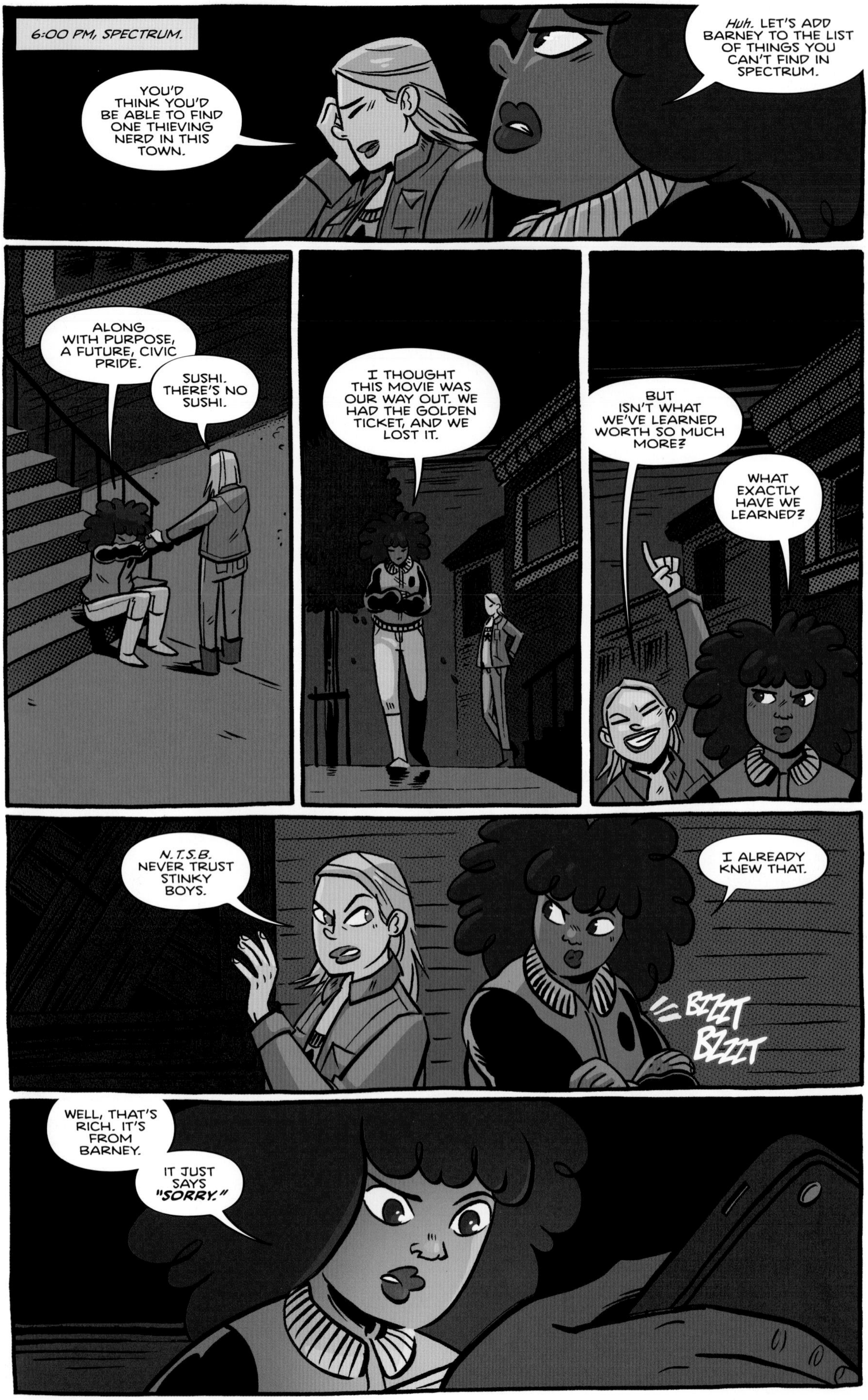
6:00 PM, SPECTRUM.
YOU'D THINK YOU'D BE ABLE TO FIND ONE THIEVING NERD IN THIS TOWN.
Huh. LET'S ADD BARNEY TO THE LIST OF THINGS YOU CAN'T FIND IN SPECTRUM.
ALONG WITH PURPOSE, A FUTURE, CIVIC PRIDE.
SUSHI. THERE'S NO SUSHI.
I THOUGHT THIS MOVIE WAS OUR WAY OUT. WE HAD THE GOLDEN TICKET, AND WE LOST IT.
BUT ISN'T WHAT WE'VE LEARNED WORTH SO MUCH MORE?
WHAT EXACTLY HAVE WE LEARNED?
N.T.S.B. NEVER TRUST STINKY BOYS.
I ALREADY KNEW THAT.
BZZZT BZZZT
WELL, THAT'S RICH. IT'S FROM BARNEY.
IT JUST SAYS "SORRY."

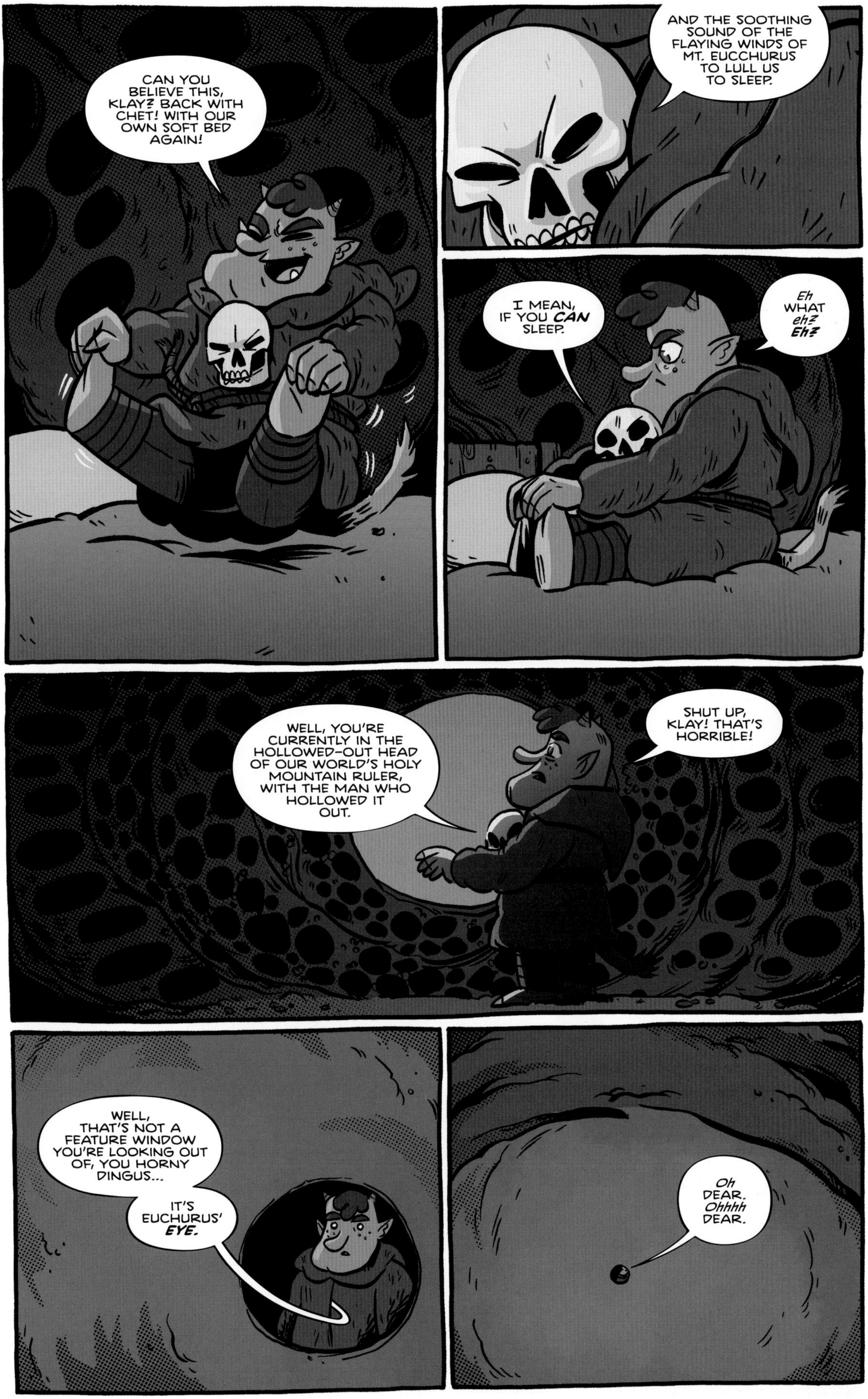
CAN YOU BELIEVE THIS, KLAY? BACK WITH CHET! WITH OUR OWN SOFT BED AGAIN!
AND THE SOOTHING SOUND OF THE FLAYING WINDS OF MT. EUCCHURUS TO LULL US TO SLEEP.
I MEAN, IF YOU CAN SLEEP.
Eh WHAT ehz Ehz
WELL, YOU'RE CURRENTLY IN THE HOLLOWED-OUT HEAD OF OUR WORLD'S HOLY MOUNTAIN RULER, WITH THE MAN WHO HOLLOWED IT OUT.
SHUT UP, KLAY! THAT'S HORRIBLE!
WELL, THAT'S NOT A FEATURE WINDOW YOU'RE LOOKING OUT OF, YOU HORNY DINGUS...
IT'S EUCHURUS' EYE.
Oh DEAR. Ohhhh DEAR.

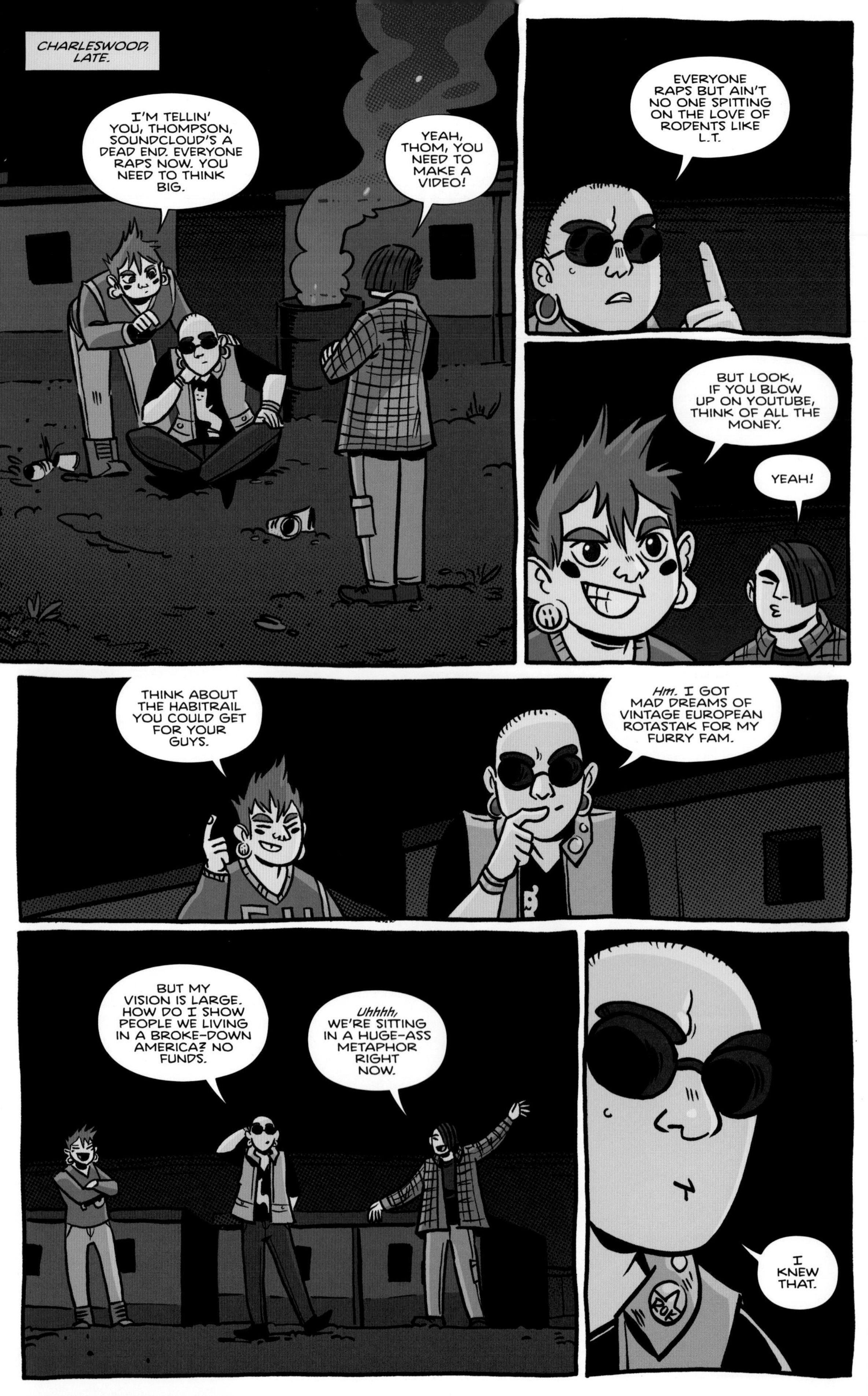
CHARLESWOOD, LATE.
I'M TELLIN' YOU, THOMPSON, SOUNDCLOUD'S A DEAD END. EVERYONE RAPS NOW. YOU NEED TO THINK BIG.
YEAH, THOM, YOU NEED TO MAKE A VIDEO!
EVERYONE RAPS BUT AIN'T NO ONE SPITTING ON THE LOVE OF RODENTS LIKE L.T.
BUT LOOK, IF YOU BLOW UP ON YOUTUBE, THINK OF ALL THE MONEY.
YEAH!
THINK ABOUT THE HABITRAIL YOU COULD GET FOR YOUR GUYS.
Hm. I GOT MAD DREAMS OF VINTAGE EUROPEAN ROTASTAK FOR MY FURRY FAM.
BUT MY VISION IS LARGE. HOW DO I SHOW PEOPLE WE LIVING IN A BROKE-DOWN AMERICA? NO FUNDS.
Uhhhh, WE'RE SITTING IN A HUGE-ASS METAPHOR RIGHT NOW.
I KNEW THAT.

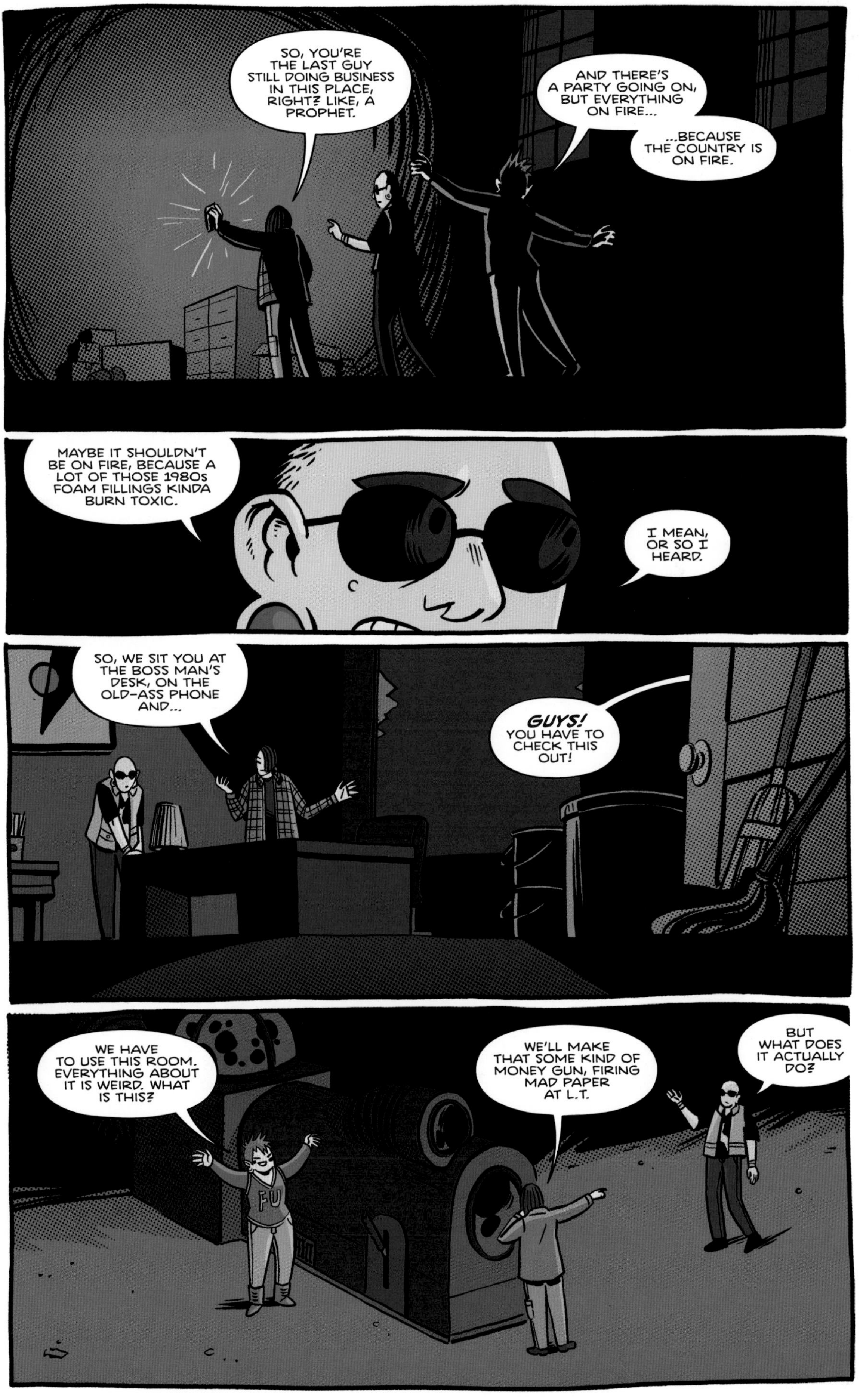
SO, YOU'RE THE LAST GUY STILL DOING BUSINESS IN THIS PLACE, RIGHT? LIKE, A PROPHET.
AND THERE'S A PARTY GOING ON, BUT EVERYTHING ON FIRE...
...BECAUSE THE COUNTRY IS ON FIRE.
MAYBE IT SHOULDN'T BE ON FIRE, BECAUSE A LOT OF THOSE 1980s FOAM FILLINGS KINDA BURN TOXIC.
I MEAN, OR SO I HEARD.
SO, WE SIT YOU AT THE BOSS MAN'S DESK, ON THE OLD-ASS PHONE AND...
GUYS! YOU HAVE TO CHECK THIS OUT!
WE HAVE TO USE THIS ROOM. EVERYTHING ABOUT IT IS WEIRD. WHAT IS THIS?
WE'LL MAKE THAT SOME KIND OF MONEY GUN, FIRING MAD PAPER AT L.T.
BUT WHAT DOES IT ACTUALLY DO?
FU

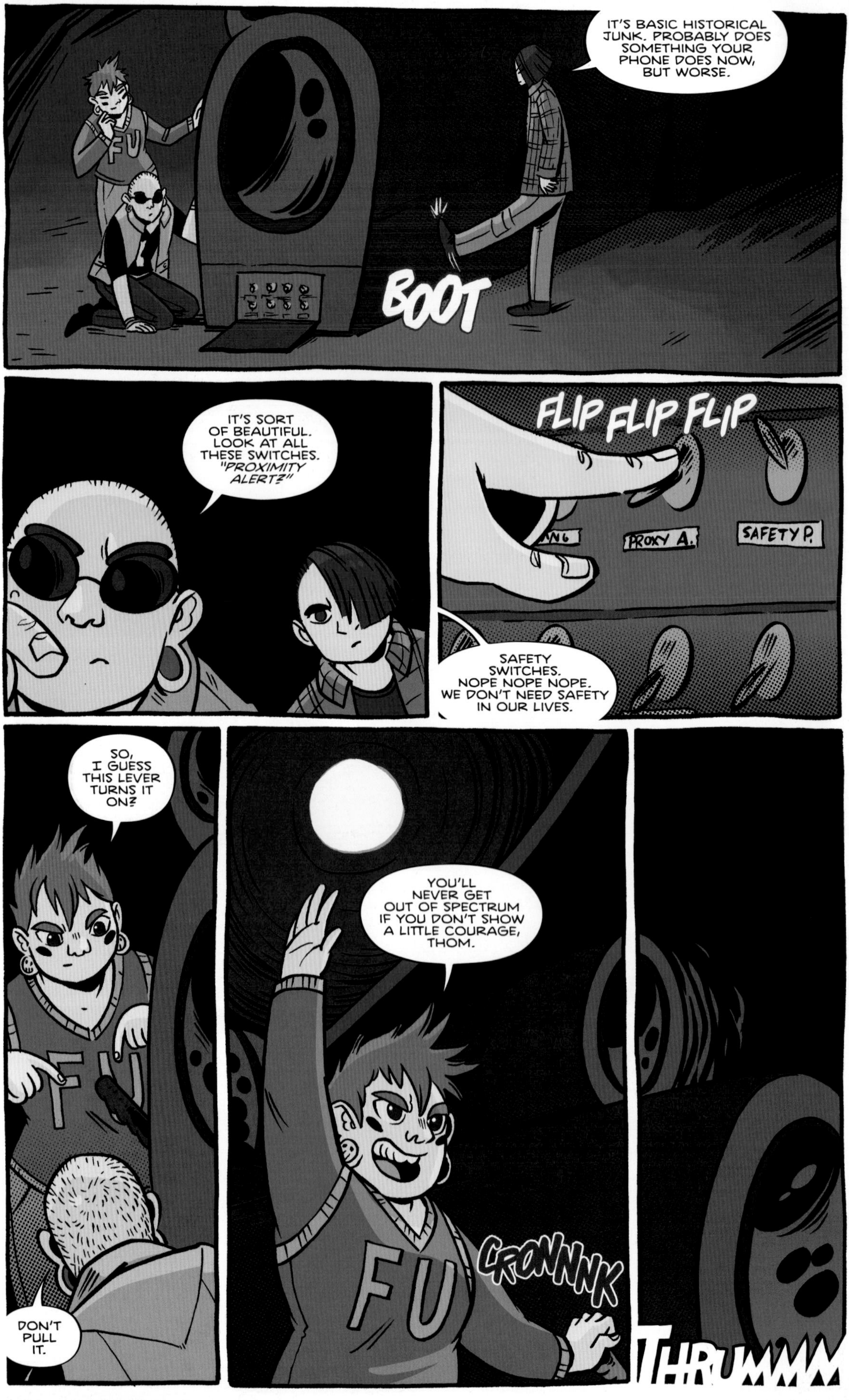
IT'S BASIC HISTORICAL JUNK. PROBABLY DOES SOMETHING YOUR PHONE DOES NOW, BUT WORSE.
BOOT
IT'S SORT OF BEAUTIFUL. LOOK AT ALL THESE SWITCHES. *"PROXIMITY ALERT?"*
FLIP FLIP FLIP
PROXY A.
SAFETY P.
SAFETY SWITCHES. NOPE NOPE NOPE. WE DON'T NEED SAFETY IN OUR LIVES.
SO, I GUESS THIS LEVER TURNS IT ON?
DON'T PULL IT.
YOU'LL NEVER GET OUT OF SPECTRUM IF YOU DON'T SHOW A LITTLE COURAGE, THOM.
CRONNNK
THRUMMM

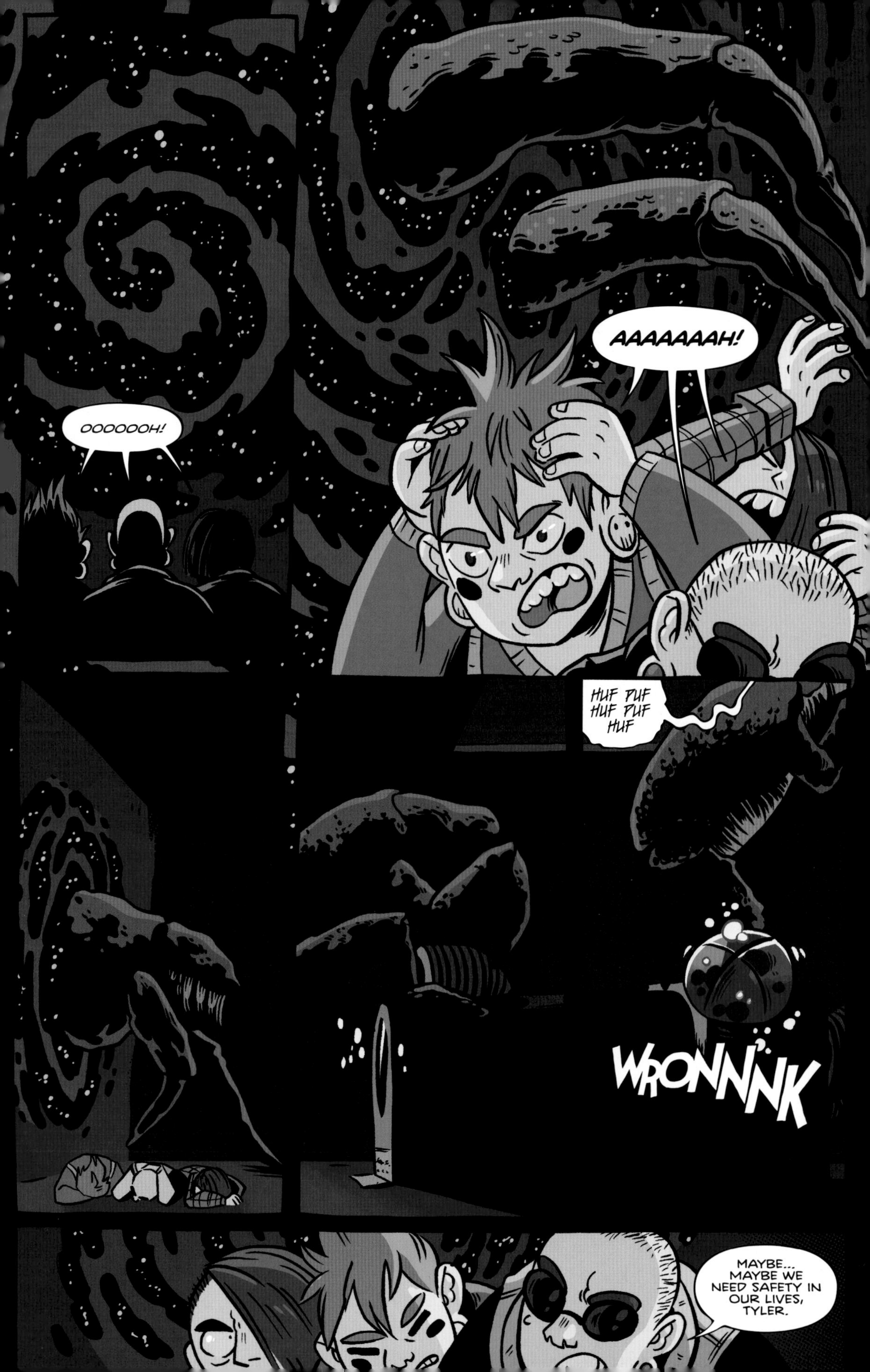
OOOOOOH!
AAAAAAAH!
HUF PUF HUF PUF HUF
WRONNNK
MAYBE... MAYBE WE NEED SAFETY IN OUR LIVES, TYLER.

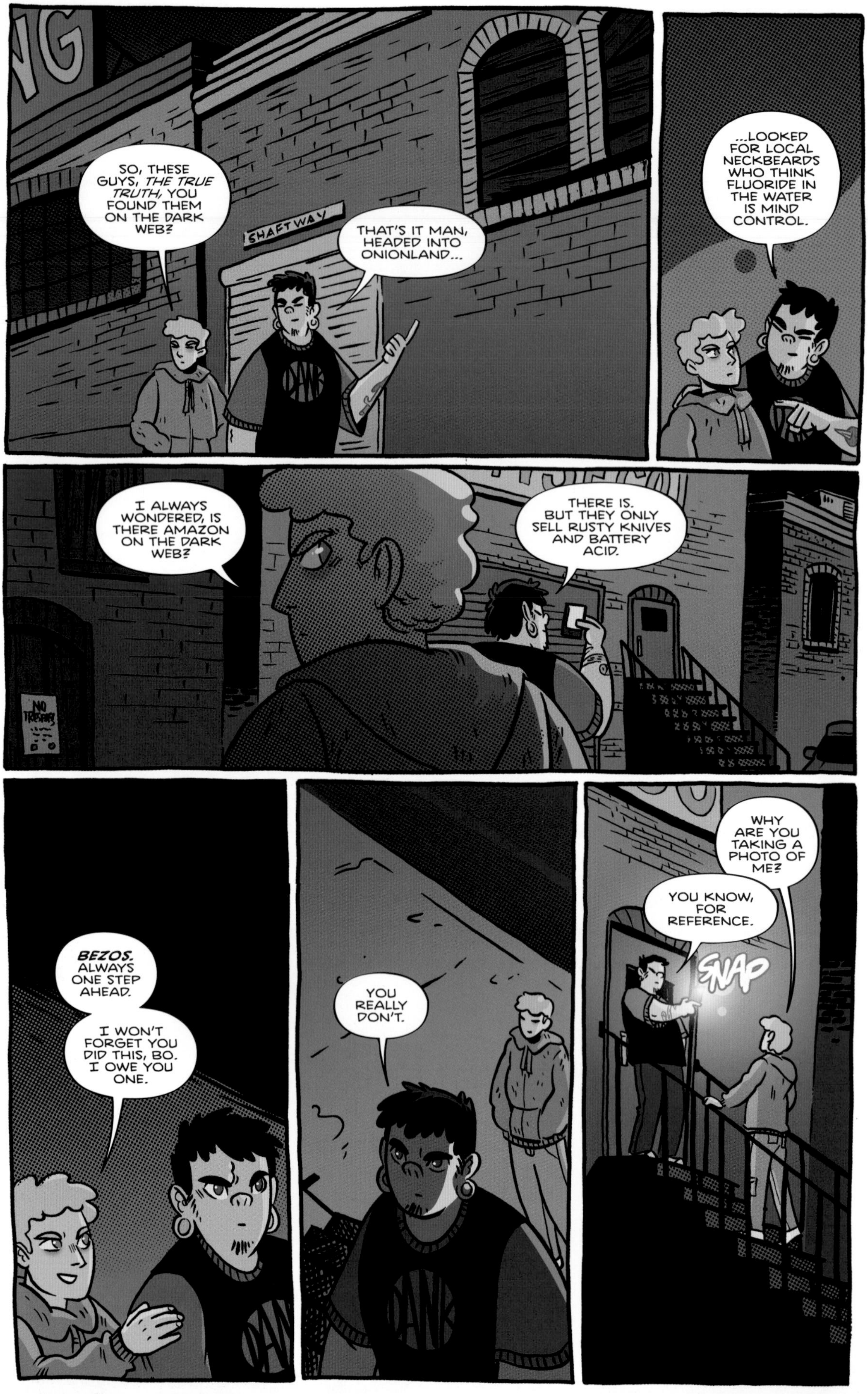

SO, THESE GUYS, *THE TRUE TRUTH*, YOU FOUND THEM ON THE DARK WEB?
SHAFTWAY
THAT'S IT MAN, HEADED INTO ONIONLAND...
...LOOKED FOR LOCAL NECKBEARDS WHO THINK FLUORIDE IN THE WATER IS MIND CONTROL.
I ALWAYS WONDERED, IS THERE AMAZON ON THE DARK WEB?
THERE IS. BUT THEY ONLY SELL RUSTY KNIVES AND BATTERY ACID.
NO TRESPASSING
BEZOS. ALWAYS ONE STEP AHEAD.
I WON'T FORGET YOU DID THIS, BO. I OWE YOU ONE.
YOU REALLY DON'T.
WHY ARE YOU TAKING A PHOTO OF ME?
YOU KNOW, FOR REFERENCE.
SNAP

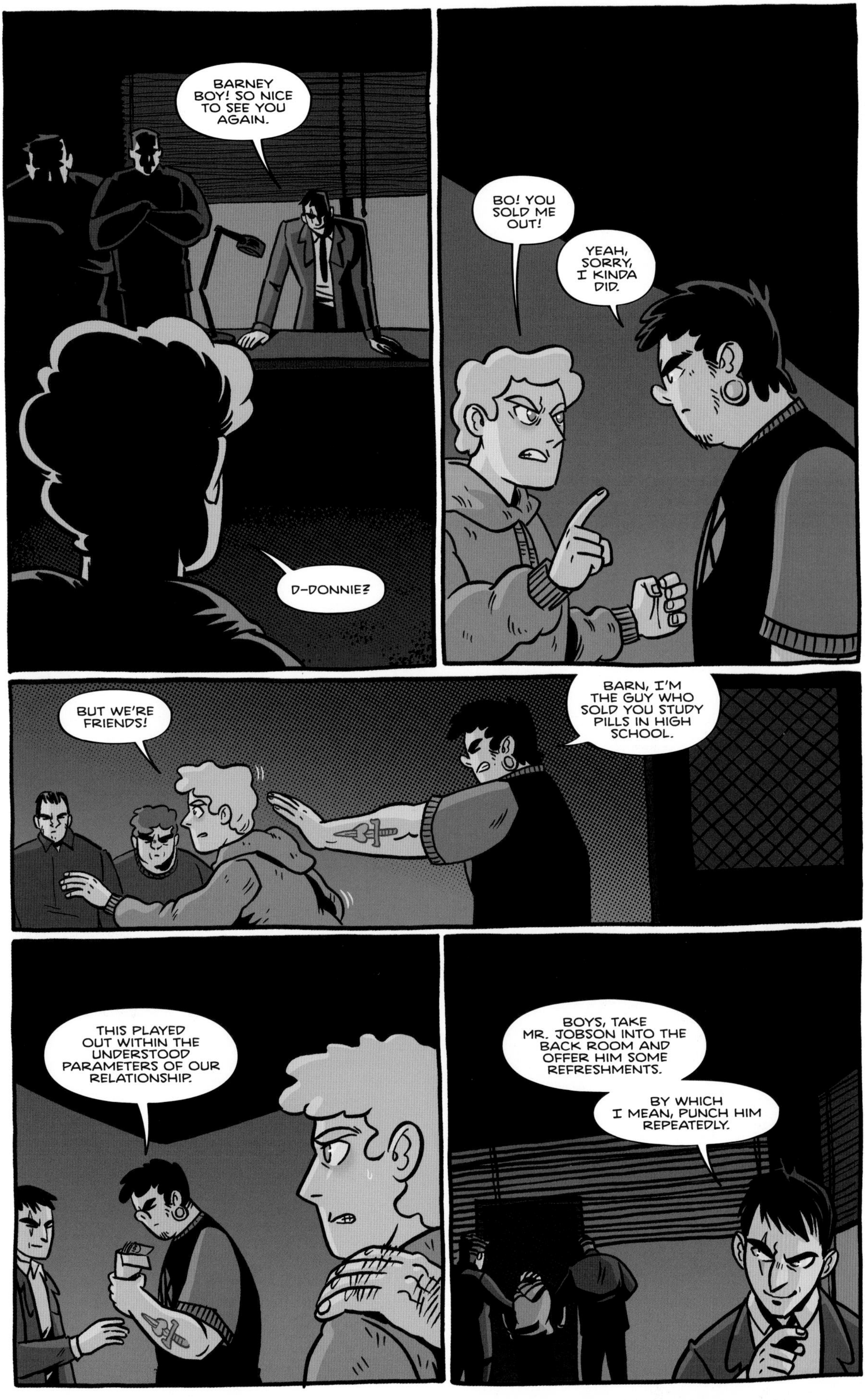
BARNEY BOY! SO NICE TO SEE YOU AGAIN.
D-DONNIE?
BO! YOU SOLD ME OUT!
YEAH, SORRY, I KINDA DID.
BUT WE'RE FRIENDS!
BARN, I'M THE GUY WHO SOLD YOU STUDY PILLS IN HIGH SCHOOL.
THIS PLAYED OUT WITHIN THE UNDERSTOOD PARAMETERS OF OUR RELATIONSHIP.
BOYS, TAKE MR. JOBSON INTO THE BACK ROOM AND OFFER HIM SOME REFRESHMENTS.
BY WHICH I MEAN, PUNCH HIM REPEATEDLY.

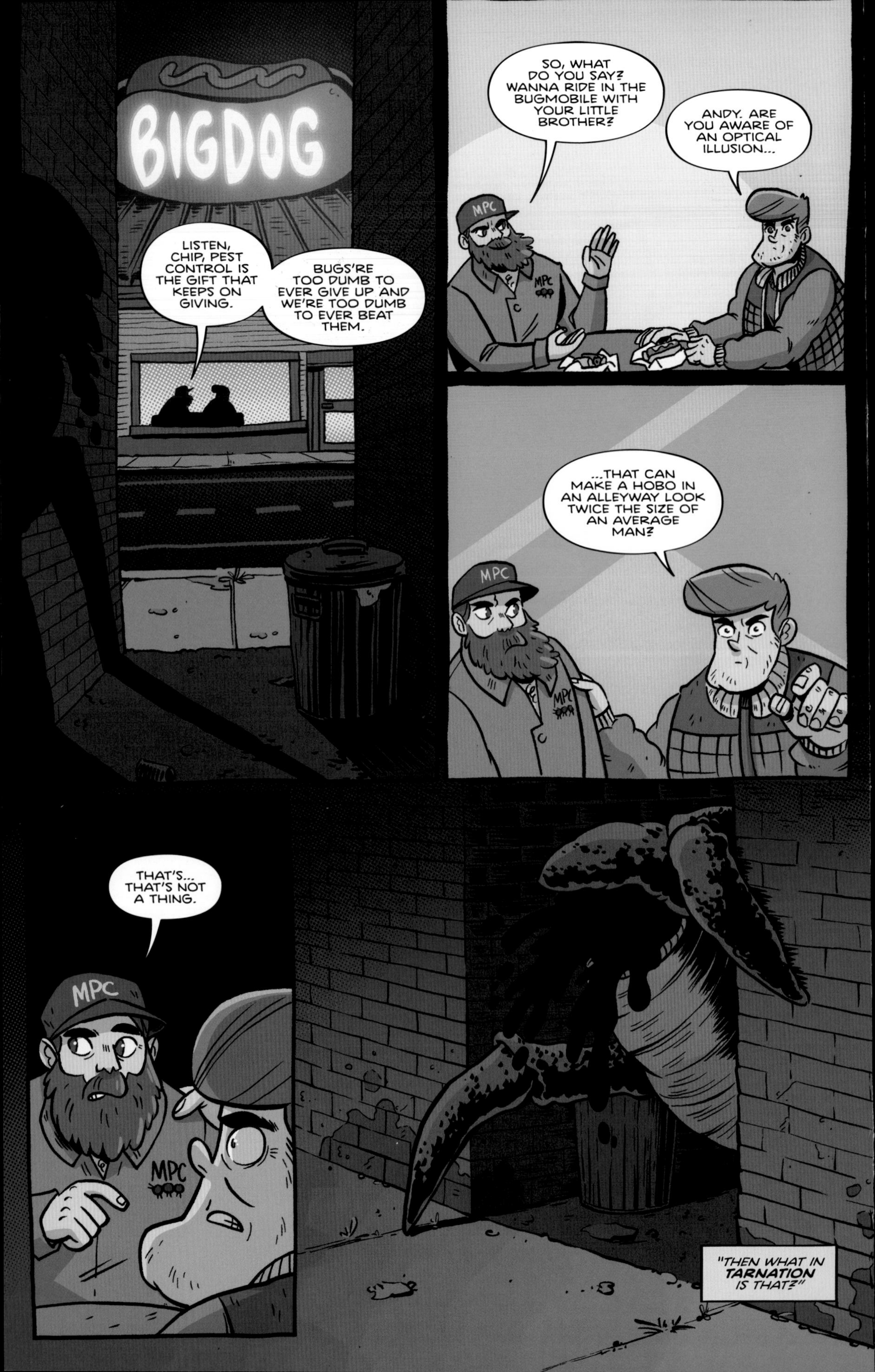
BIGDOG
LISTEN, CHIP, PEST CONTROL IS THE GIFT THAT KEEPS ON GIVING.
BUGS'RE TOO DUMB TO EVER GIVE UP AND WE'RE TOO DUMB TO EVER BEAT THEM.
SO, WHAT DO YOU SAY? WANNA RIDE IN THE BUGMOBILE WITH YOUR LITTLE BROTHER?
ANDY. ARE YOU AWARE OF AN OPTICAL ILLUSION...
...THAT CAN MAKE A HOBO IN AN ALLEYWAY LOOK TWICE THE SIZE OF AN AVERAGE MAN?
THAT'S... THAT'S NOT A THING.
"THEN WHAT IN **TARNATION** IS THAT?"

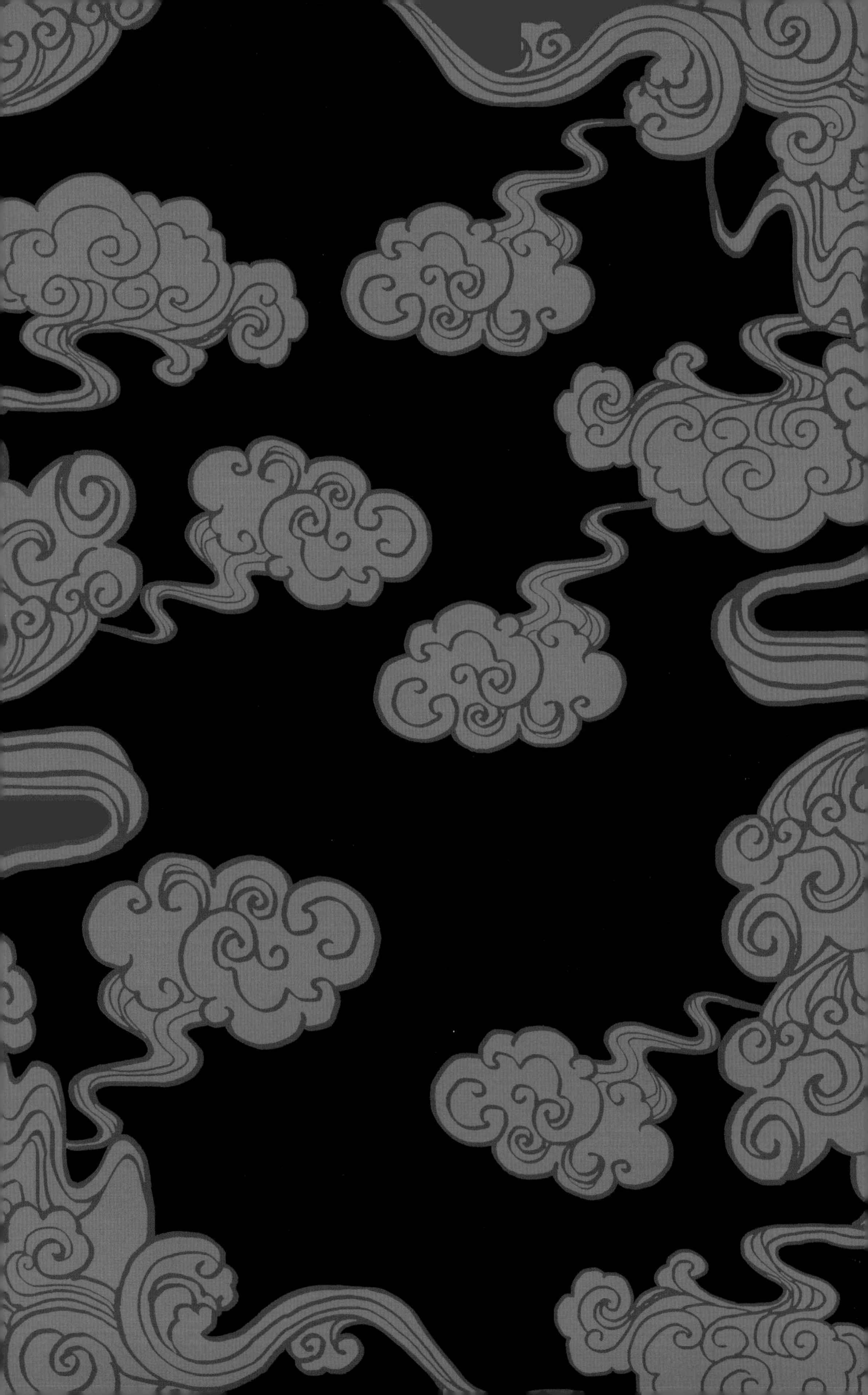

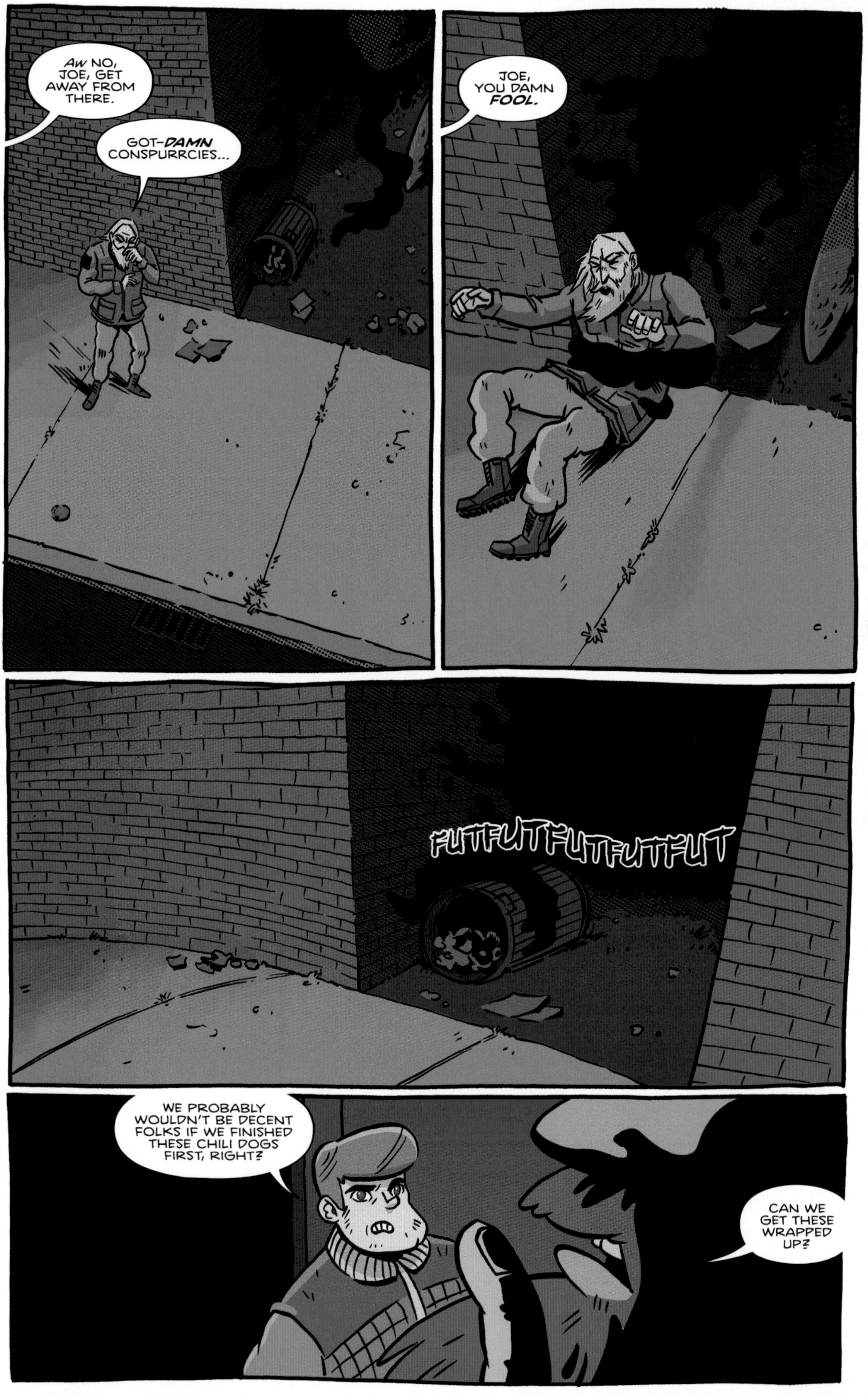
AW NO, JOE, GET AWAY FROM THERE.
GOT-DAMN CONSPURRCIES...
JOE, YOU DAMN FOOL.
FUTFUTFUTFUTFUT
WE PROBABLY WOULDN'T BE DECENT FOLKS IF WE FINISHED THESE CHILI DOGS FIRST, RIGHT?
CAN WE GET THESE WRAPPED UP?

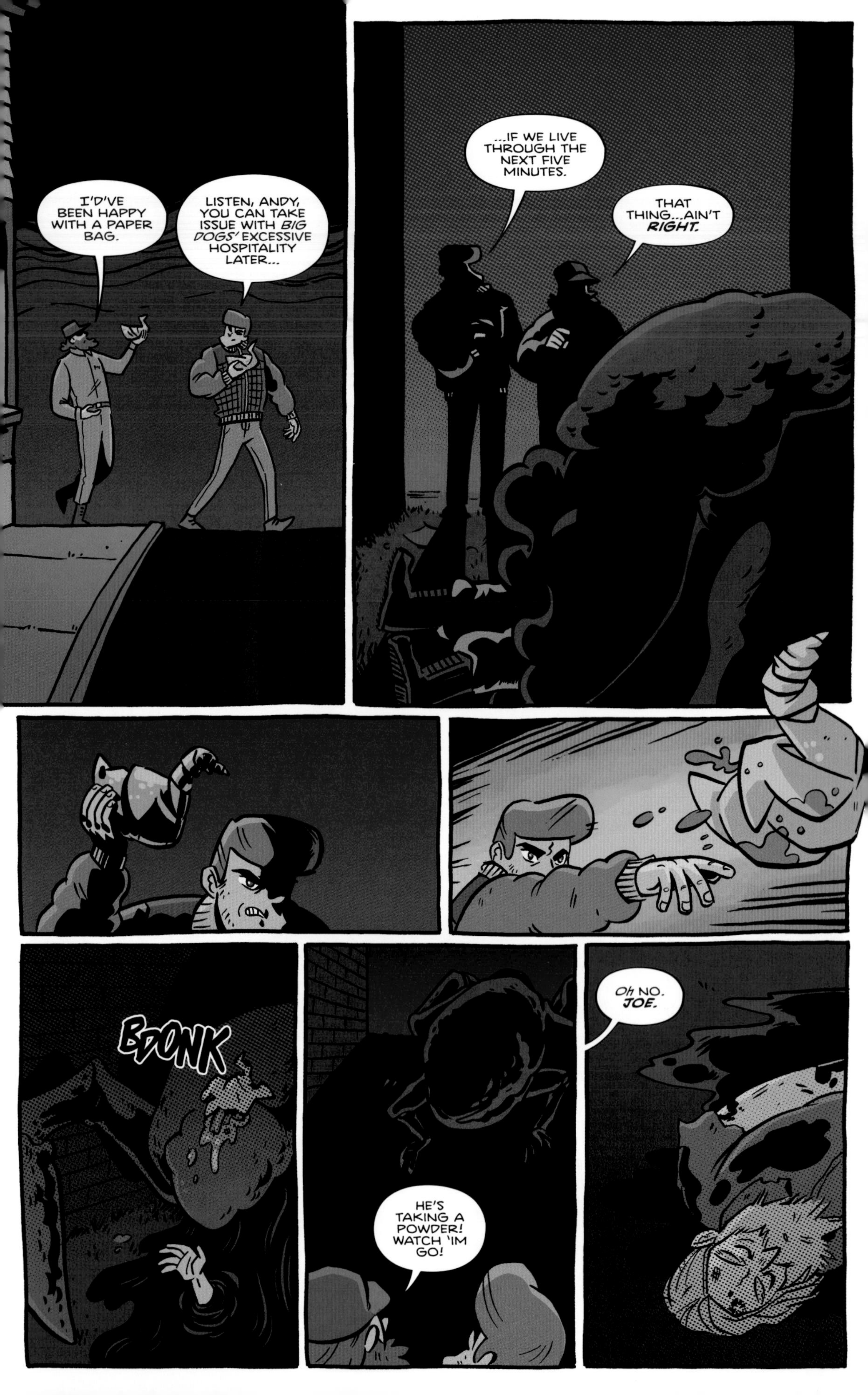

I'D'VE BEEN HAPPY WITH A PAPER BAG.
LISTEN, ANDY, YOU CAN TAKE ISSUE WITH *BIG DOGS'* EXCESSIVE HOSPITALITY LATER...
...IF WE LIVE THROUGH THE NEXT FIVE MINUTES.
THAT THING...AIN'T ***RIGHT.***
BDONK
HE'S TAKING A POWDER! WATCH 'IM GO!
Oh NO. ***JOE.***

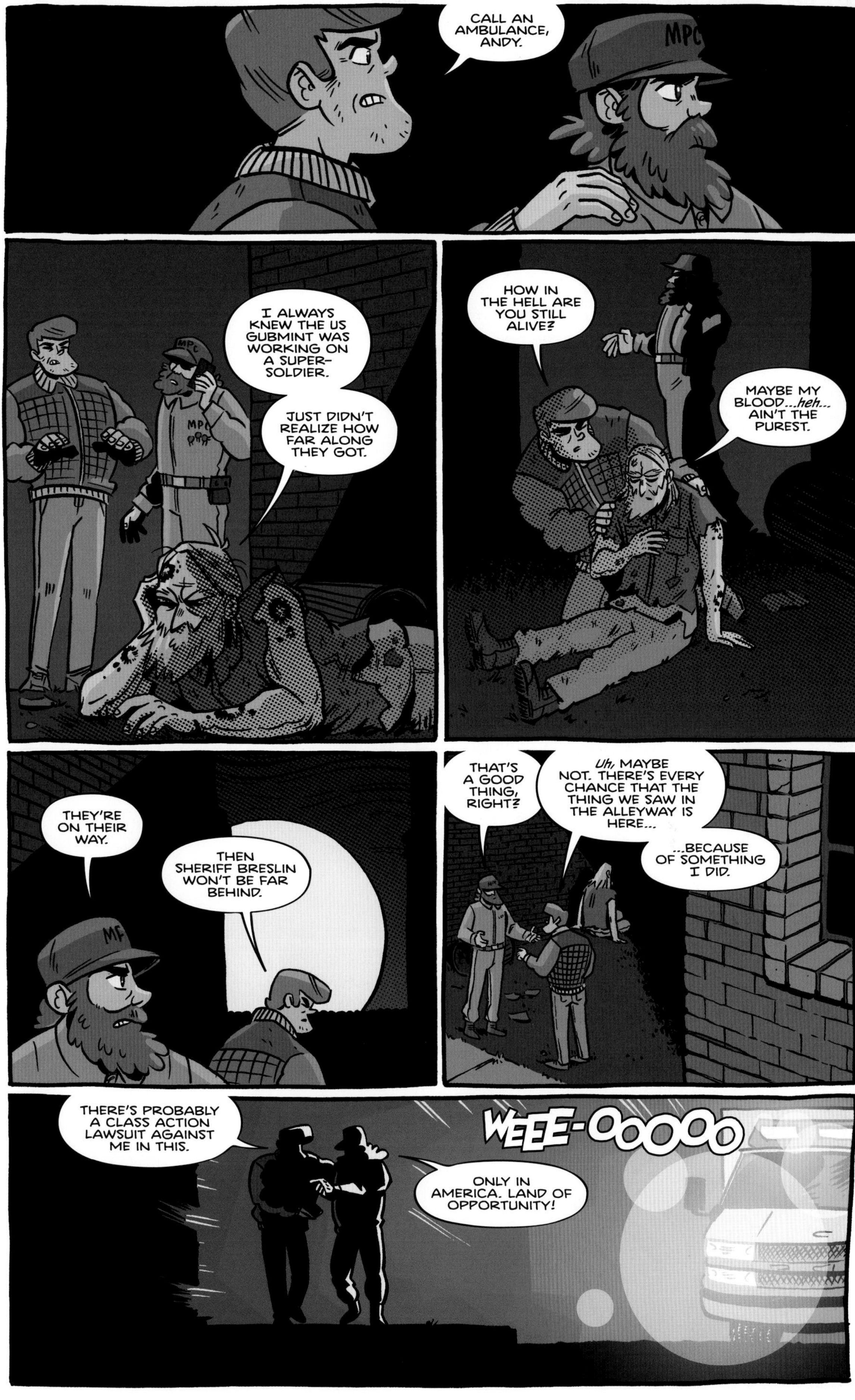
CALL AN AMBULANCE, ANDY.
I ALWAYS KNEW THE US GUBMINT WAS WORKING ON A SUPER-SOLDIER.
JUST DIDN'T REALIZE HOW FAR ALONG THEY GOT.
HOW IN THE HELL ARE YOU STILL ALIVE?
MAYBE MY BLOOD...*heh*... AIN'T THE PUREST.
THEY'RE ON THEIR WAY.
THEN SHERIFF BRESLIN WON'T BE FAR BEHIND.
THAT'S A GOOD THING, RIGHT?
Uh, MAYBE NOT. THERE'S EVERY CHANCE THAT THE THING WE SAW IN THE ALLEYWAY IS HERE...
...BECAUSE OF SOMETHING I DID.
THERE'S PROBABLY A CLASS ACTION LAWSUIT AGAINST ME IN THIS.
WEEE-OOOOO
ONLY IN AMERICA. LAND OF OPPORTUNITY!

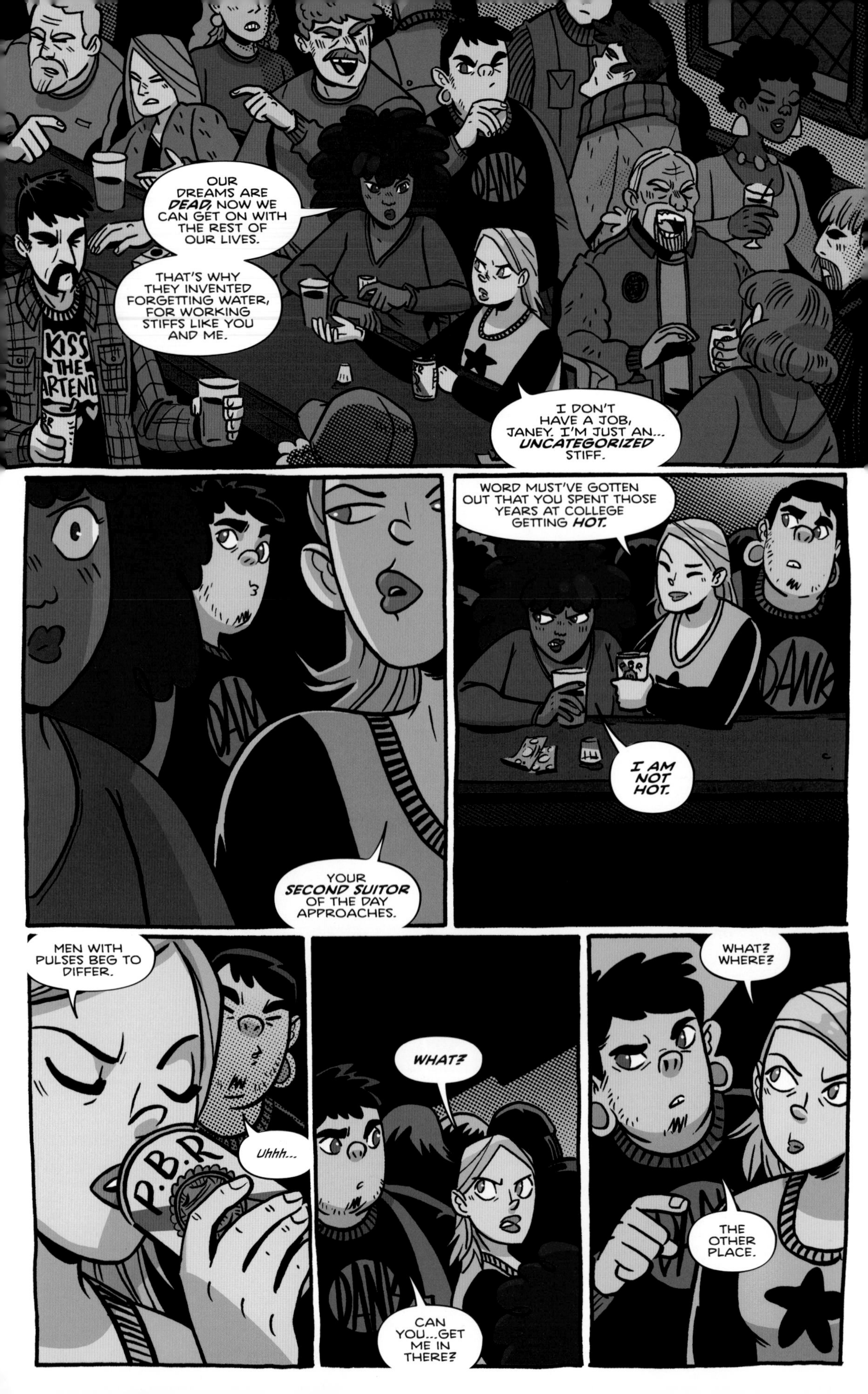
OUR DREAMS ARE *DEAD,* NOW WE CAN GET ON WITH THE REST OF OUR LIVES.
THAT'S WHY THEY INVENTED FORGETTING WATER, FOR WORKING STIFFS LIKE YOU AND ME.
I DON'T HAVE A JOB, JANEY. I'M JUST AN... *UNCATEGORIZED* STIFF.
YOUR *SECOND SUITOR* OF THE DAY APPROACHES.
WORD MUST'VE GOTTEN OUT THAT YOU SPENT THOSE YEARS AT COLLEGE GETTING *HOT.*
I AM NOT HOT.
MEN WITH PULSES BEG TO DIFFER.
Uhhh...
WHAT?
CAN YOU...GET ME IN THERE?
WHAT? WHERE?
THE OTHER PLACE.

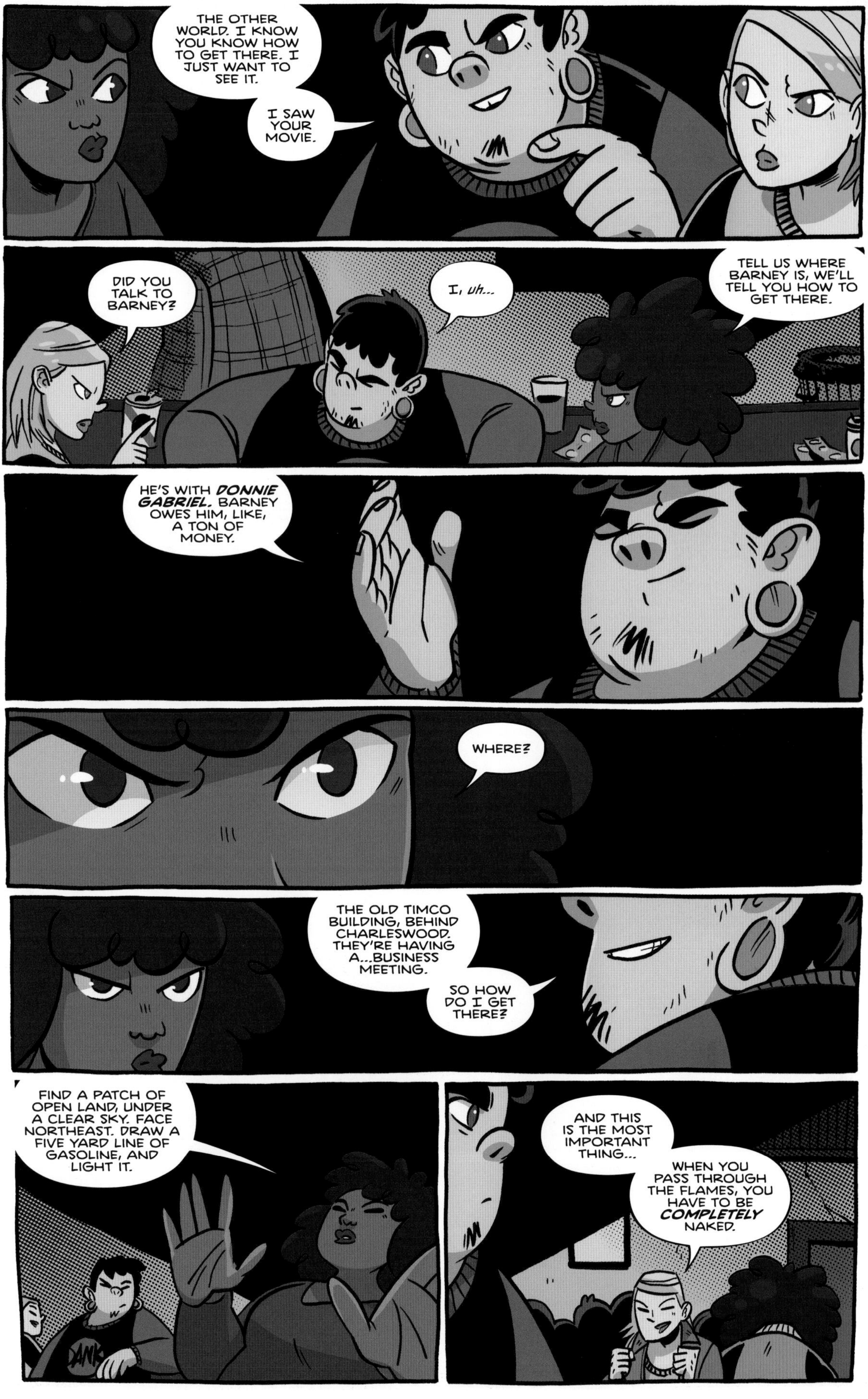
THE OTHER WORLD. I KNOW YOU KNOW HOW TO GET THERE. I JUST WANT TO SEE IT.
I SAW YOUR MOVIE.
DID YOU TALK TO BARNEY?
I, uh...
TELL US WHERE BARNEY IS, WE'LL TELL YOU HOW TO GET THERE.
HE'S WITH *DONNIE GABRIEL.* BARNEY OWES HIM, LIKE, A TON OF MONEY.
WHERE?
THE OLD TIMCO BUILDING, BEHIND CHARLESWOOD. THEY'RE HAVING A...BUSINESS MEETING.
SO HOW DO I GET THERE?
FIND A PATCH OF OPEN LAND, UNDER A CLEAR SKY. FACE NORTHEAST. DRAW A FIVE YARD LINE OF GASOLINE, AND LIGHT IT.
AND THIS IS THE MOST IMPORTANT THING...
WHEN YOU PASS THROUGH THE FLAMES, YOU HAVE TO BE *COMPLETELY* NAKED.
DANK

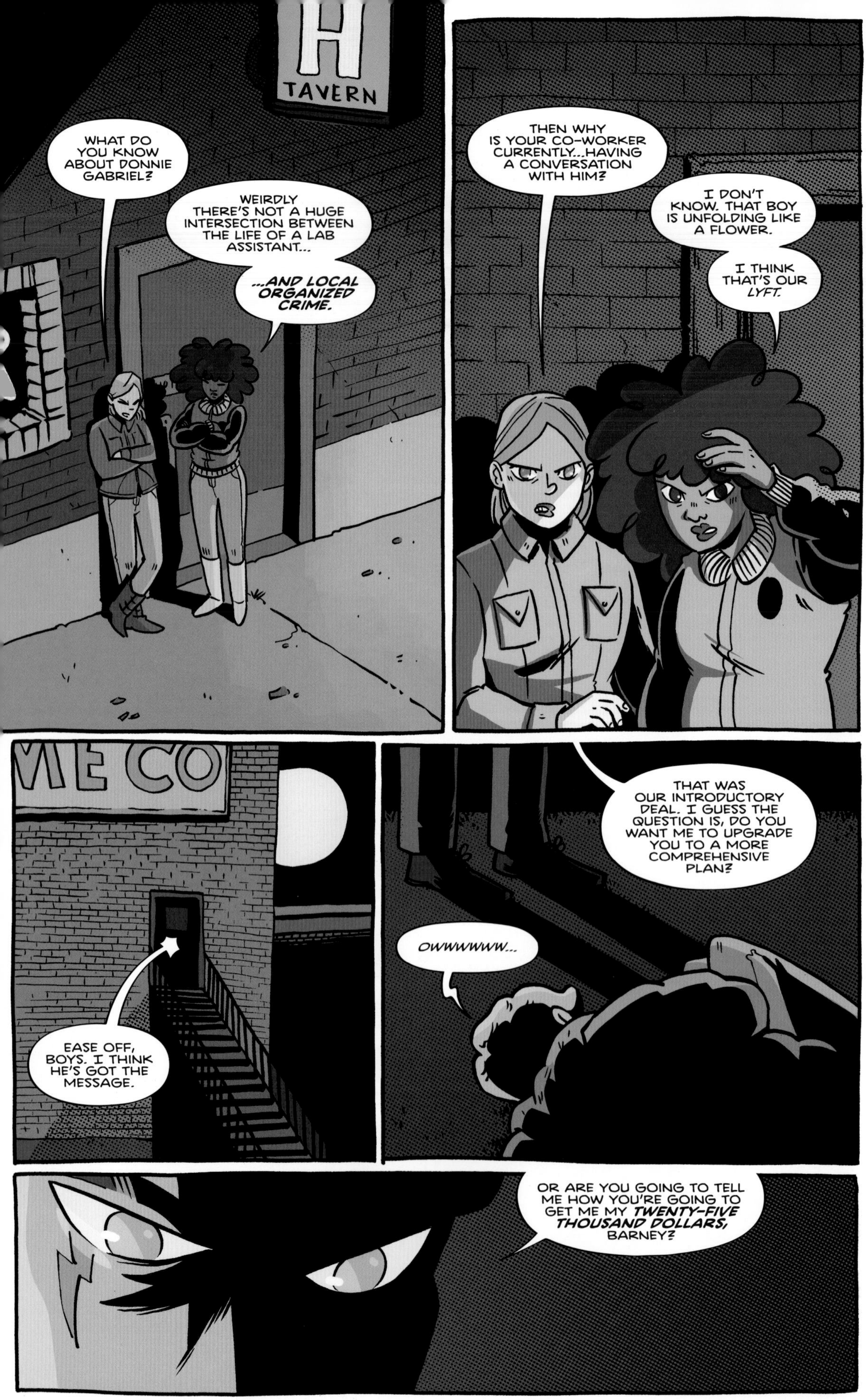
H
TAVERN
WHAT DO YOU KNOW ABOUT DONNIE GABRIEL?
WEIRDLY THERE'S NOT A HUGE INTERSECTION BETWEEN THE LIFE OF A LAB ASSISTANT...
...AND LOCAL ORGANIZED CRIME.
THEN WHY IS YOUR CO-WORKER CURRENTLY...HAVING A CONVERSATION WITH HIM?
I DON'T KNOW. THAT BOY IS UNFOLDING LIKE A FLOWER.
I THINK THAT'S OUR LYFT.
ME CO
EASE OFF, BOYS. I THINK HE'S GOT THE MESSAGE.
THAT WAS OUR INTRODUCTORY DEAL. I GUESS THE QUESTION IS, DO YOU WANT ME TO UPGRADE YOU TO A MORE COMPREHENSIVE PLAN?
OWWWWWW...
OR ARE YOU GOING TO TELL ME HOW YOU'RE GOING TO GET ME MY TWENTY-FIVE THOUSAND DOLLARS, BARNEY?

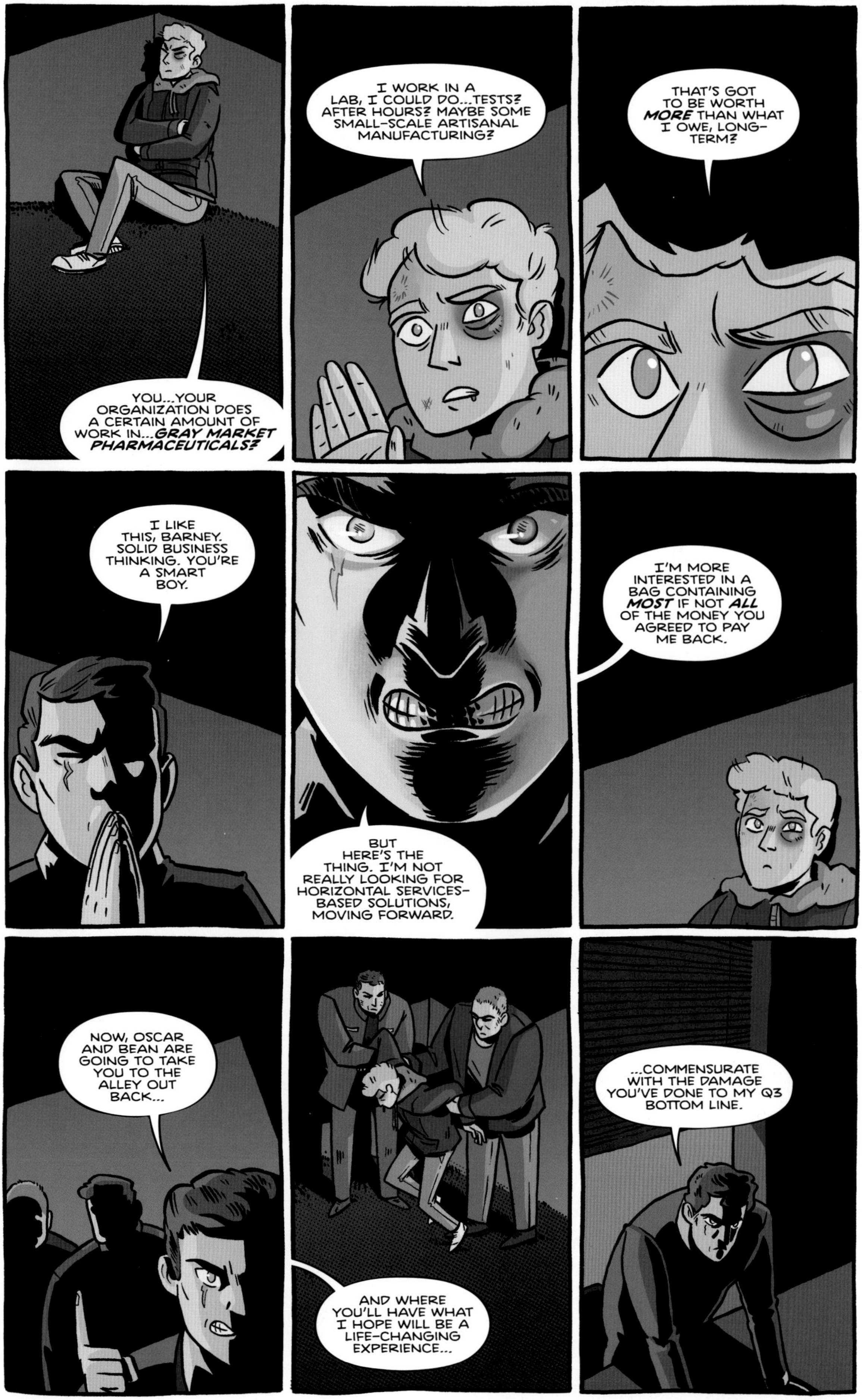
YOU...YOUR ORGANIZATION DOES A CERTAIN AMOUNT OF WORK IN...GRAY MARKET PHARMACEUTICALS?
I WORK IN A LAB, I COULD DO...TESTS? AFTER HOURS? MAYBE SOME SMALL-SCALE ARTISANAL MANUFACTURING?
THAT'S GOT TO BE WORTH MORE THAN WHAT I OWE, LONG-TERM?
I LIKE THIS, BARNEY. SOLID BUSINESS THINKING. YOU'RE A SMART BOY.
BUT HERE'S THE THING. I'M NOT REALLY LOOKING FOR HORIZONTAL SERVICES-BASED SOLUTIONS, MOVING FORWARD.
I'M MORE INTERESTED IN A BAG CONTAINING MOST IF NOT ALL OF THE MONEY YOU AGREED TO PAY ME BACK.
NOW, OSCAR AND BEAN ARE GOING TO TAKE YOU TO THE ALLEY OUT BACK...
AND WHERE YOU'LL HAVE WHAT I HOPE WILL BE A LIFE-CHANGING EXPERIENCE...
...COMMENSURATE WITH THE DAMAGE YOU'VE DONE TO MY Q3 BOTTOM LINE.

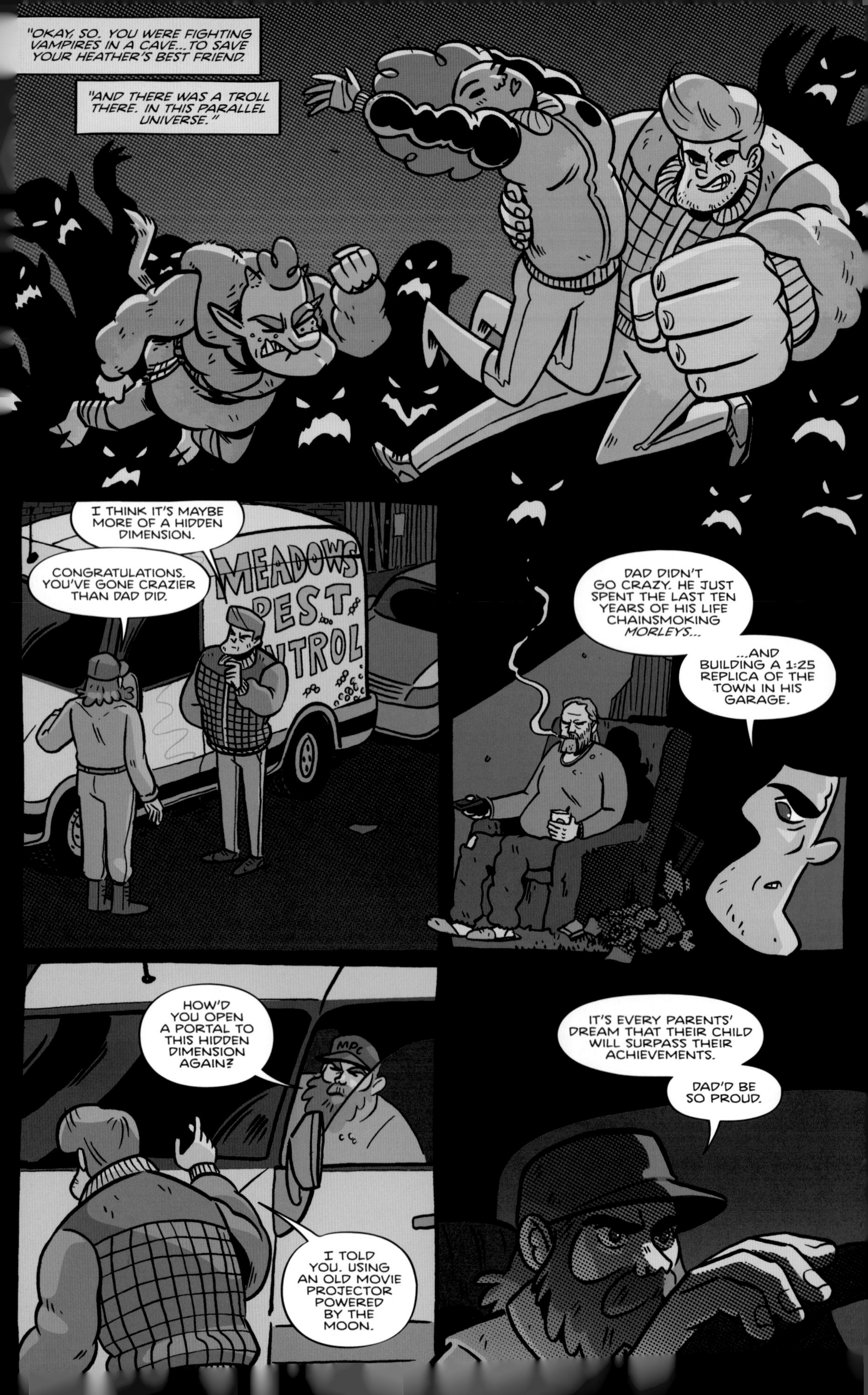
"OKAY, SO. YOU WERE FIGHTING VAMPIRES IN A CAVE...TO SAVE YOUR HEATHER'S BEST FRIEND.
"AND THERE WAS A TROLL THERE. IN THIS PARALLEL UNIVERSE."
I THINK IT'S MAYBE MORE OF A HIDDEN DIMENSION.
CONGRATULATIONS. YOU'VE GONE CRAZIER THAN DAD DID.
MEADOWS PEST NTROL
DAD DIDN'T GO CRAZY. HE JUST SPENT THE LAST TEN YEARS OF HIS LIFE CHAINSMOKING *MORLEYS*...
...AND BUILDING A 1:25 REPLICA OF THE TOWN IN HIS GARAGE.
HOW'D YOU OPEN A PORTAL TO THIS HIDDEN DIMENSION AGAIN?
MPC
I TOLD YOU. USING AN OLD MOVIE PROJECTOR POWERED BY THE MOON.
IT'S EVERY PARENTS' DREAM THAT THEIR CHILD WILL SURPASS THEIR ACHIEVEMENTS.
DAD'D BE SO PROUD.

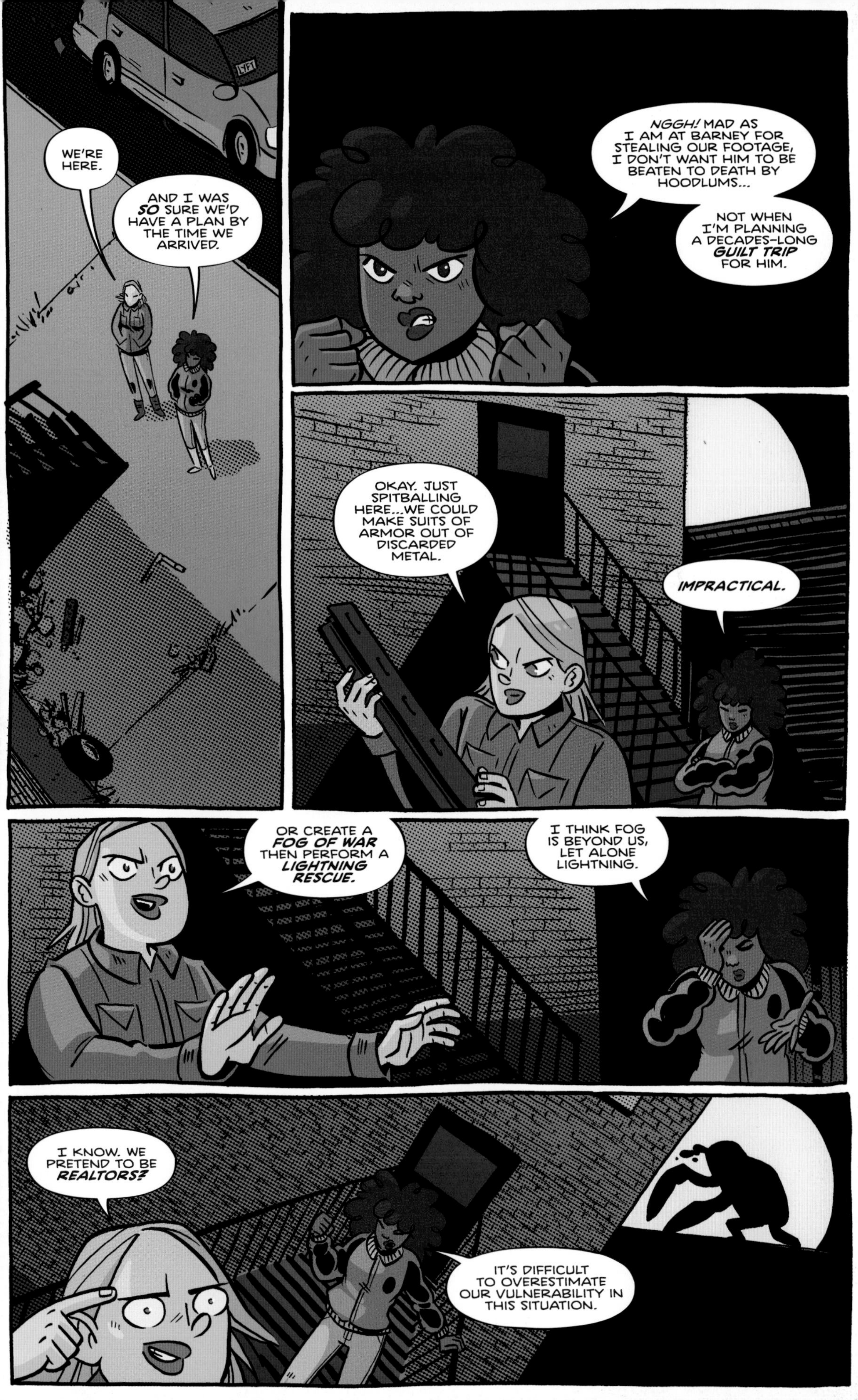
WE'RE HERE.
AND I WAS *SO* SURE WE'D HAVE A PLAN BY THE TIME WE ARRIVED.
NGGH! MAD AS I AM AT BARNEY FOR STEALING OUR FOOTAGE, I DON'T WANT HIM TO BE BEATEN TO DEATH BY HOODLUMS...
NOT WHEN I'M PLANNING A DECADES-LONG ***GUILT TRIP*** FOR HIM.
OKAY. JUST SPITBALLING HERE...WE COULD MAKE SUITS OF ARMOR OUT OF DISCARDED METAL.
IMPRACTICAL.
OR CREATE A ***FOG OF WAR*** THEN PERFORM A ***LIGHTNING RESCUE.***
I THINK FOG IS BEYOND US, LET ALONE LIGHTNING.
I KNOW. WE PRETEND TO BE ***REALTORS?***
IT'S DIFFICULT TO OVERESTIMATE OUR VULNERABILITY IN THIS SITUATION.

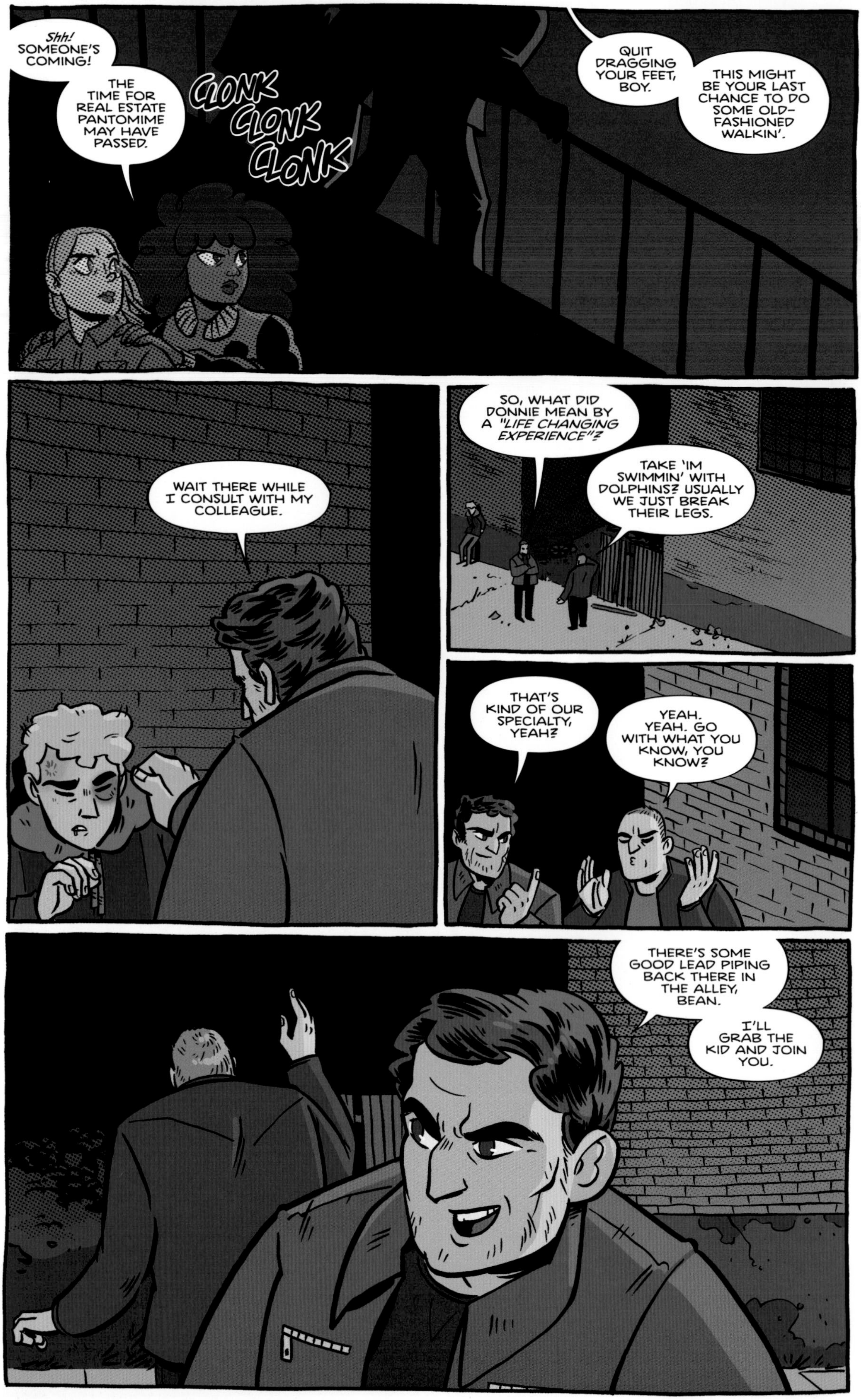

Shh! SOMEONE'S COMING!
THE TIME FOR REAL ESTATE PANTOMIME MAY HAVE PASSED.
CLONK CLONK CLONK
QUIT DRAGGING YOUR FEET, BOY.
THIS MIGHT BE YOUR LAST CHANCE TO DO SOME OLD-FASHIONED WALKIN'.
WAIT THERE WHILE I CONSULT WITH MY COLLEAGUE.
SO, WHAT DID DONNIE MEAN BY A "LIFE CHANGING EXPERIENCE"?
TAKE 'IM SWIMMIN' WITH DOLPHINS? USUALLY WE JUST BREAK THEIR LEGS.
THAT'S KIND OF OUR SPECIALTY, YEAH?
YEAH. YEAH. GO WITH WHAT YOU KNOW, YOU KNOW?
THERE'S SOME GOOD LEAD PIPING BACK THERE IN THE ALLEY, BEAN.
I'LL GRAB THE KID AND JOIN YOU.

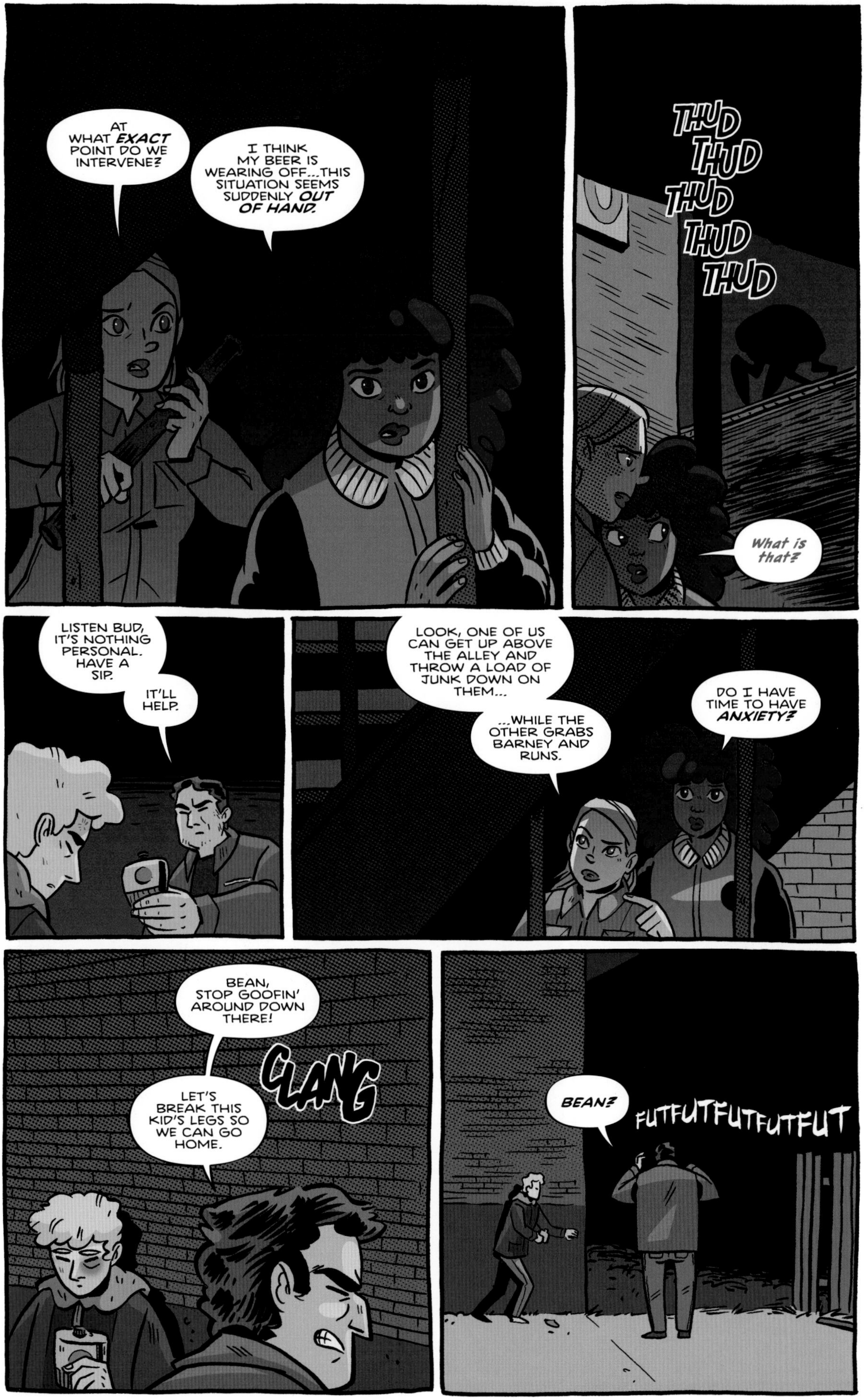

AT WHAT EXACT POINT DO WE INTERVENE?
I THINK MY BEER IS WEARING OFF...THIS SITUATION SEEMS SUDDENLY OUT OF HAND.
THUD THUD THUD THUD THUD
What is that?
LISTEN BUD, IT'S NOTHING PERSONAL. HAVE A SIP.
IT'LL HELP.
LOOK, ONE OF US CAN GET UP ABOVE THE ALLEY AND THROW A LOAD OF JUNK DOWN ON THEM...
...WHILE THE OTHER GRABS BARNEY AND RUNS.
DO I HAVE TIME TO HAVE ANXIETY?
BEAN, STOP GOOFIN' AROUND DOWN THERE!
CLANG
LET'S BREAK THIS KID'S LEGS SO WE CAN GO HOME.
BEAN?
FUTFUTFUTFUTFUT

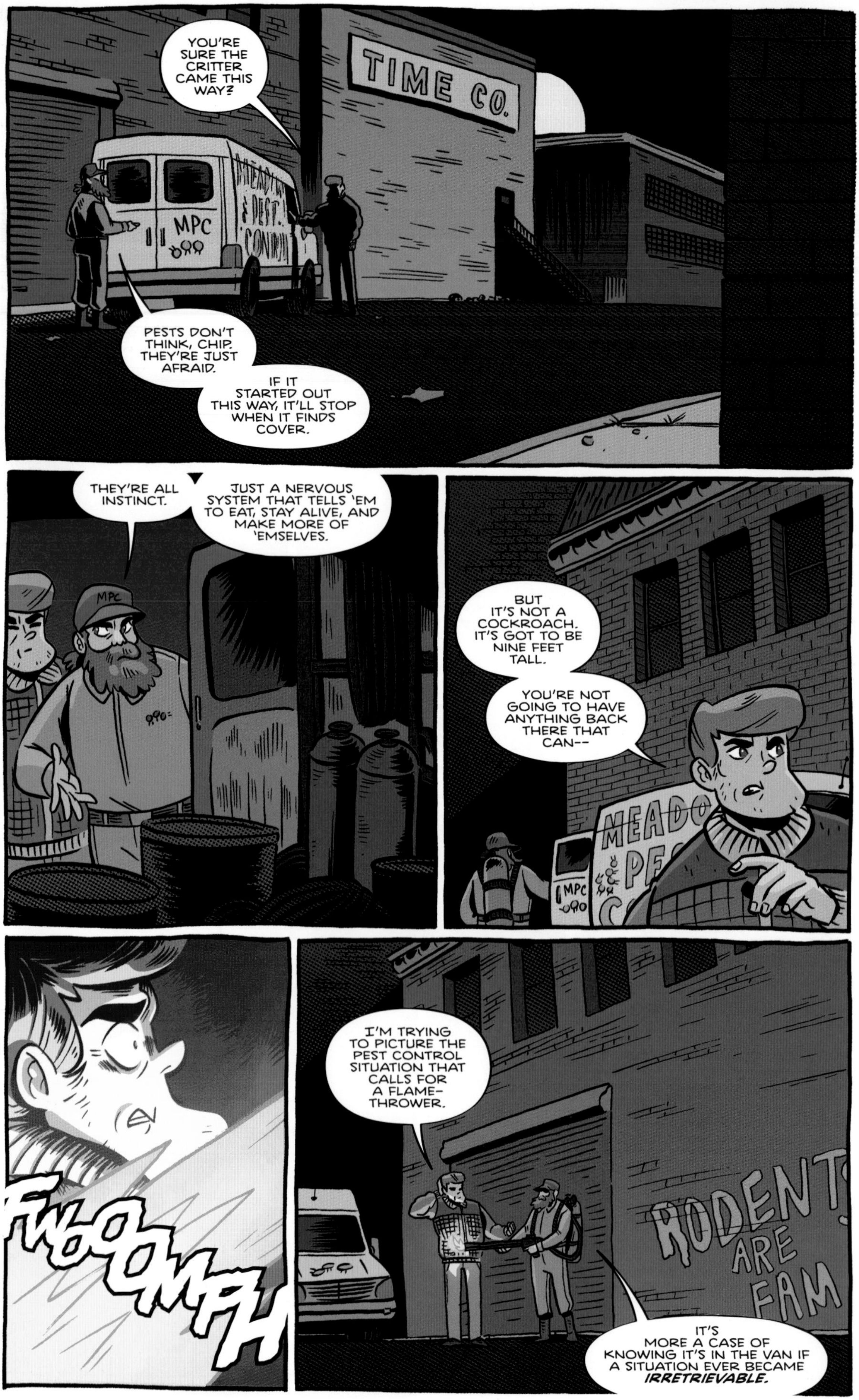
TIME CO.
YOU'RE SURE THE CRITTER CAME THIS WAY?
MEADOW PEST CONTROL
MPC
PESTS DON'T THINK, CHIP. THEY'RE JUST AFRAID.
IF IT STARTED OUT THIS WAY, IT'LL STOP WHEN IT FINDS COVER.
THEY'RE ALL INSTINCT.
JUST A NERVOUS SYSTEM THAT TELLS 'EM TO EAT, STAY ALIVE, AND MAKE MORE OF 'EMSELVES.
MPC
BUT IT'S NOT A COCKROACH. IT'S GOT TO BE NINE FEET TALL.
YOU'RE NOT GOING TO HAVE ANYTHING BACK THERE THAT CAN--
MEADO
MPC
FWOOMPH
I'M TRYING TO PICTURE THE PEST CONTROL SITUATION THAT CALLS FOR A FLAME-THROWER.
RODENTS ARE FAM
IT'S MORE A CASE OF KNOWING IT'S IN THE VAN IF A SITUATION EVER BECAME *IRRETRIEVABLE.*

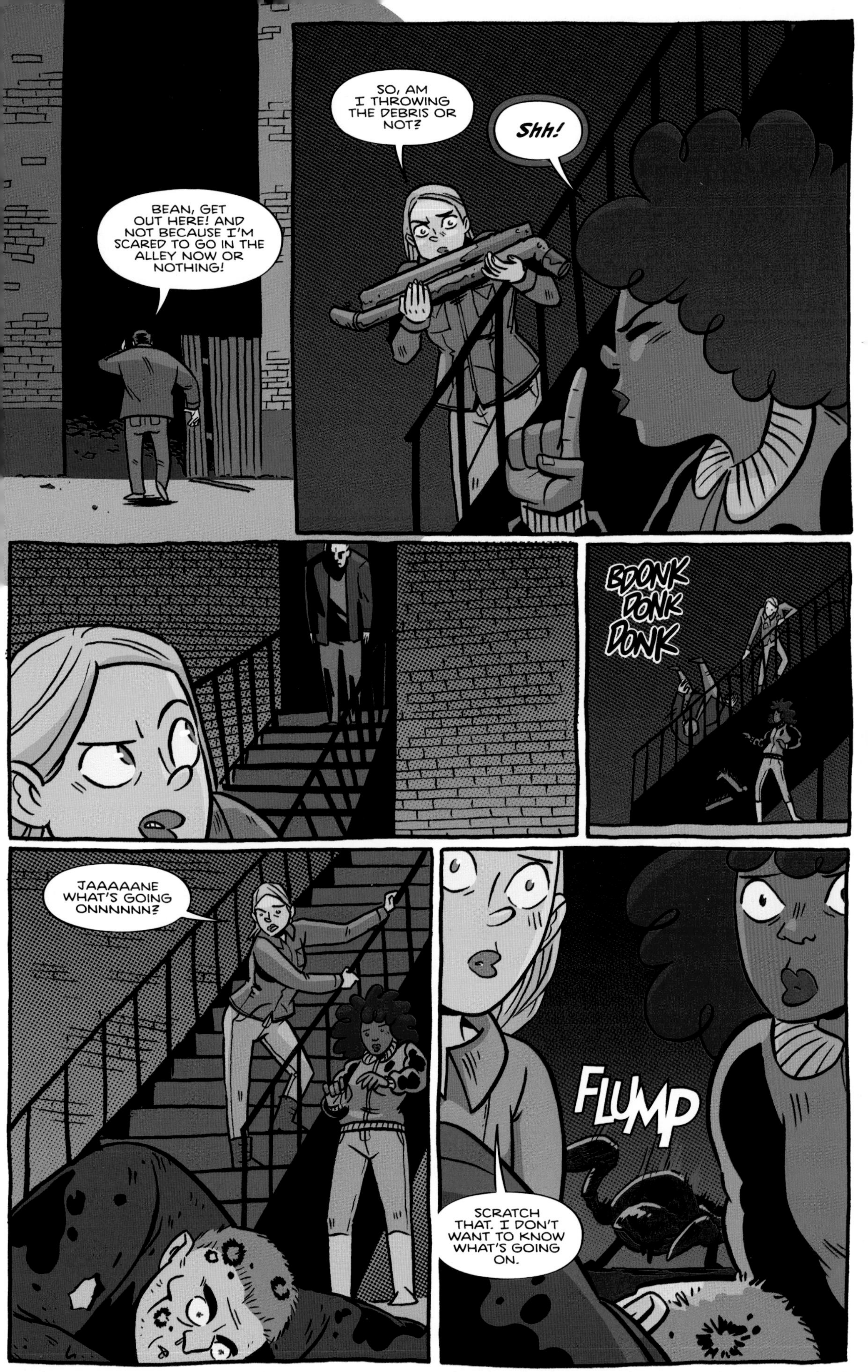
BEAN, GET OUT HERE! AND NOT BECAUSE I'M SCARED TO GO IN THE ALLEY NOW OR NOTHING!
SO, AM I THROWING THE DEBRIS OR NOT?
Shh!
BDONK DONK DONK
JAAAAANE WHAT'S GOING ONNNNNN?
FLUMP
SCRATCH THAT. I DON'T WANT TO KNOW WHAT'S GOING ON.

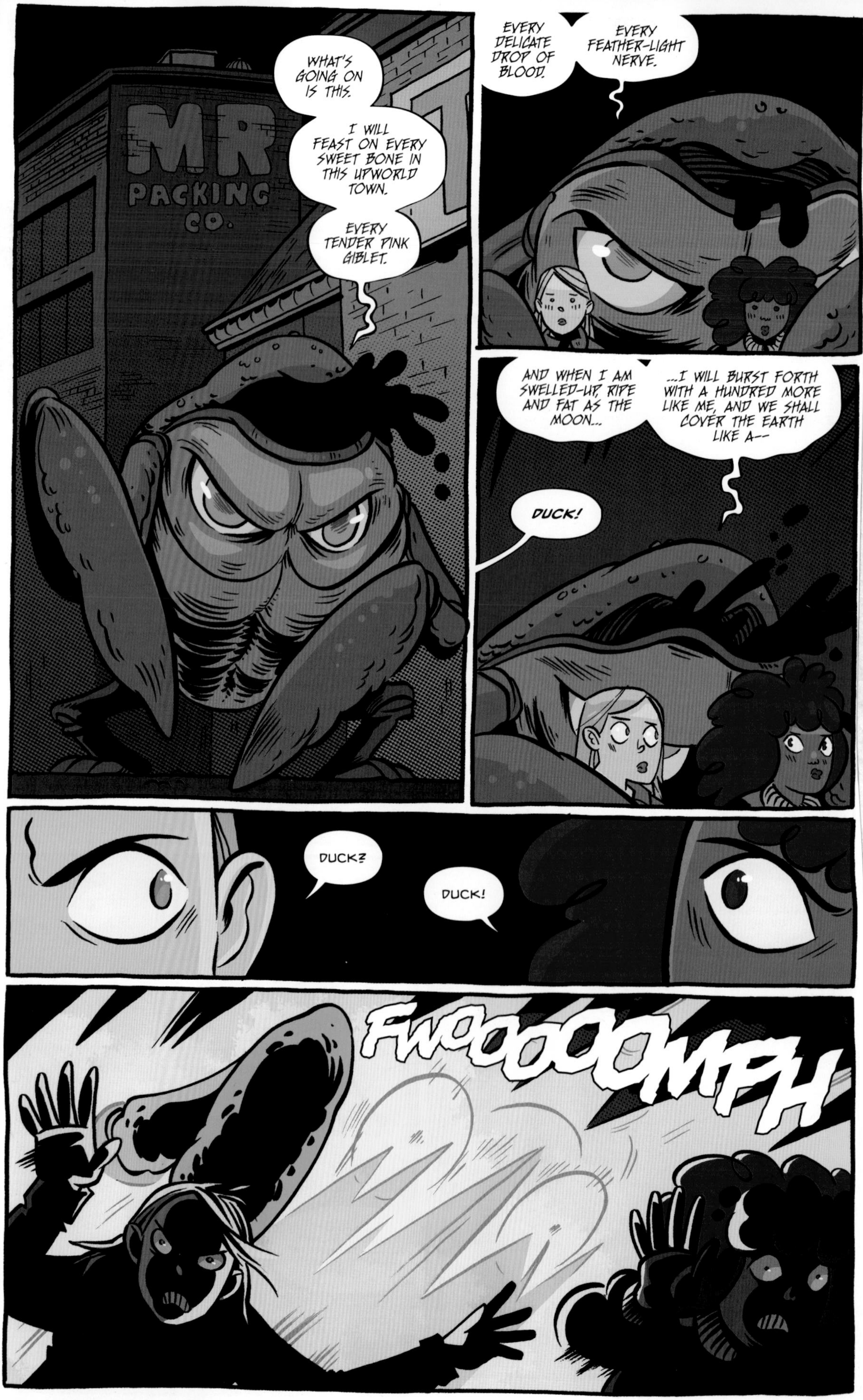
MR
PACKING CO.
WHAT'S GOING ON IS THIS.
I WILL FEAST ON EVERY SWEET BONE IN THIS UPWORLD TOWN.
EVERY TENDER PINK GIBLET.
EVERY DELICATE DROP OF BLOOD.
EVERY FEATHER-LIGHT NERVE.
AND WHEN I AM SWELLED-UP, RIPE AND FAT AS THE MOON...
...I WILL BURST FORTH WITH A HUNDRED MORE LIKE ME, AND WE SHALL COVER THE EARTH LIKE A--
DUCK!
DUCK?
DUCK!
FWOOOOOOMPH

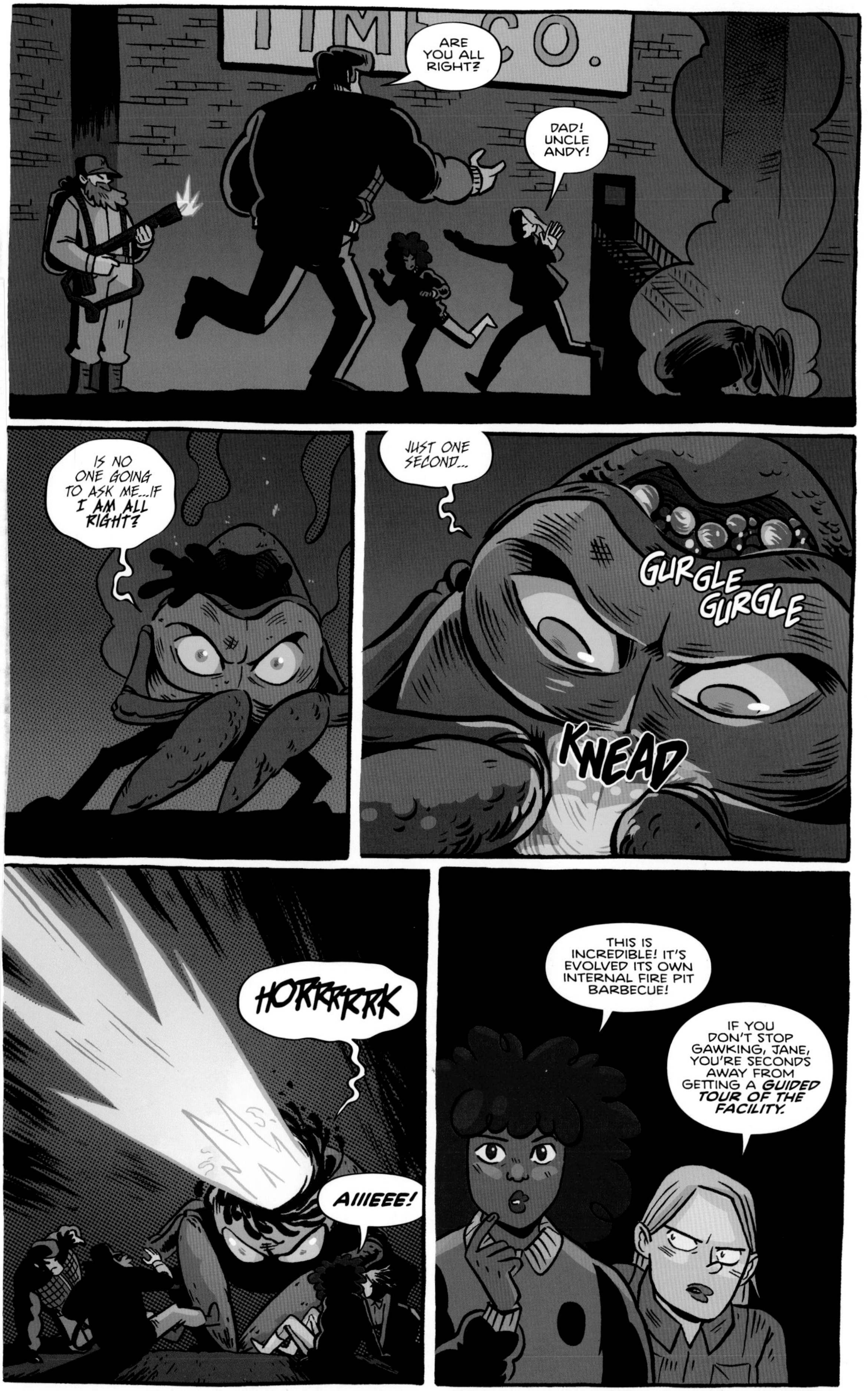
TIME CO.
ARE YOU ALL RIGHT?
DAD! UNCLE ANDY!
IS NO ONE GOING TO ASK ME... IF I AM ALL RIGHT?
JUST ONE SECOND...
GURGLE GURGLE
KNEAD
HORRRRRK
AIIIEEE!
THIS IS INCREDIBLE! IT'S EVOLVED ITS OWN INTERNAL FIRE PIT BARBECUE!
IF YOU DON'T STOP GAWKING, JANE, YOU'RE SECONDS AWAY FROM GETTING A GUIDED TOUR OF THE FACILITY.

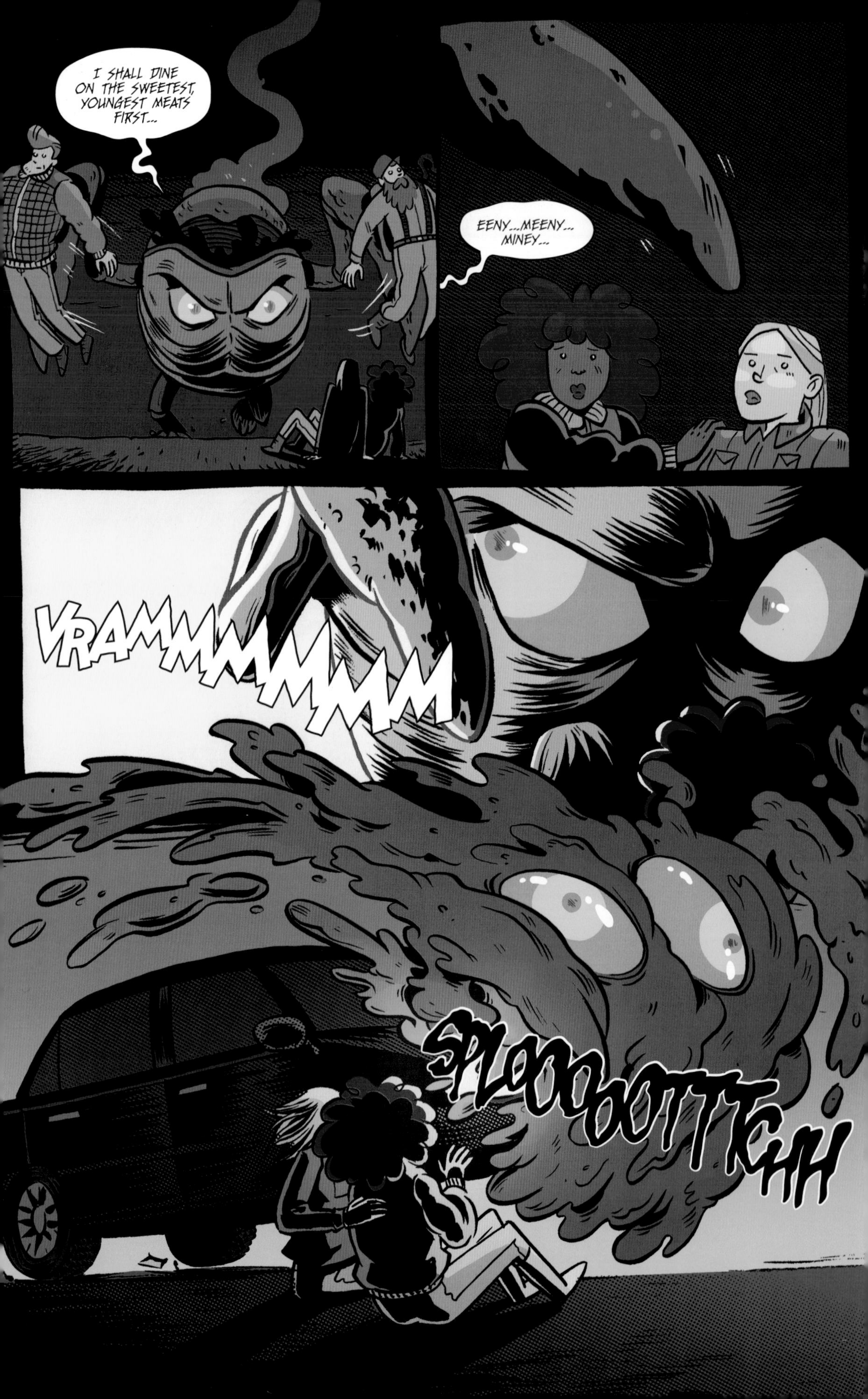
I SHALL DINE ON THE SWEETEST, YOUNGEST MEATS FIRST...
EENY... MEENY... MINEY...
VRAMMMMMMM
SPLOOOOOTTTCHH

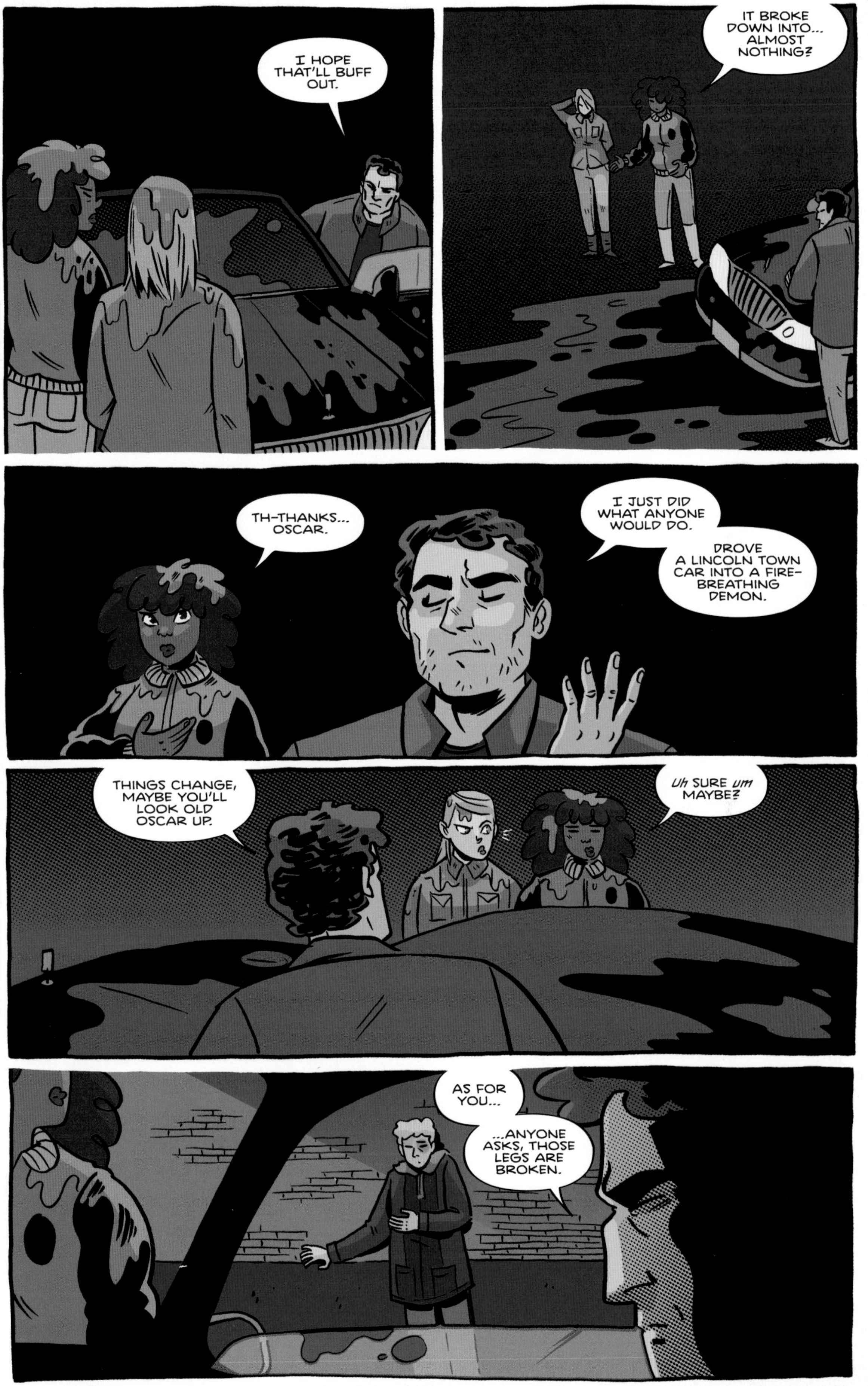
I HOPE THAT'LL BUFF OUT.
IT BROKE DOWN INTO... ALMOST NOTHING?
TH-THANKS... OSCAR.
I JUST DID WHAT ANYONE WOULD DO.
DROVE A LINCOLN TOWN CAR INTO A FIRE-BREATHING DEMON.
THINGS CHANGE, MAYBE YOU'LL LOOK OLD OSCAR UP.
Uh SURE *um* MAYBE?
AS FOR YOU...
...ANYONE ASKS, THOSE LEGS ARE BROKEN.

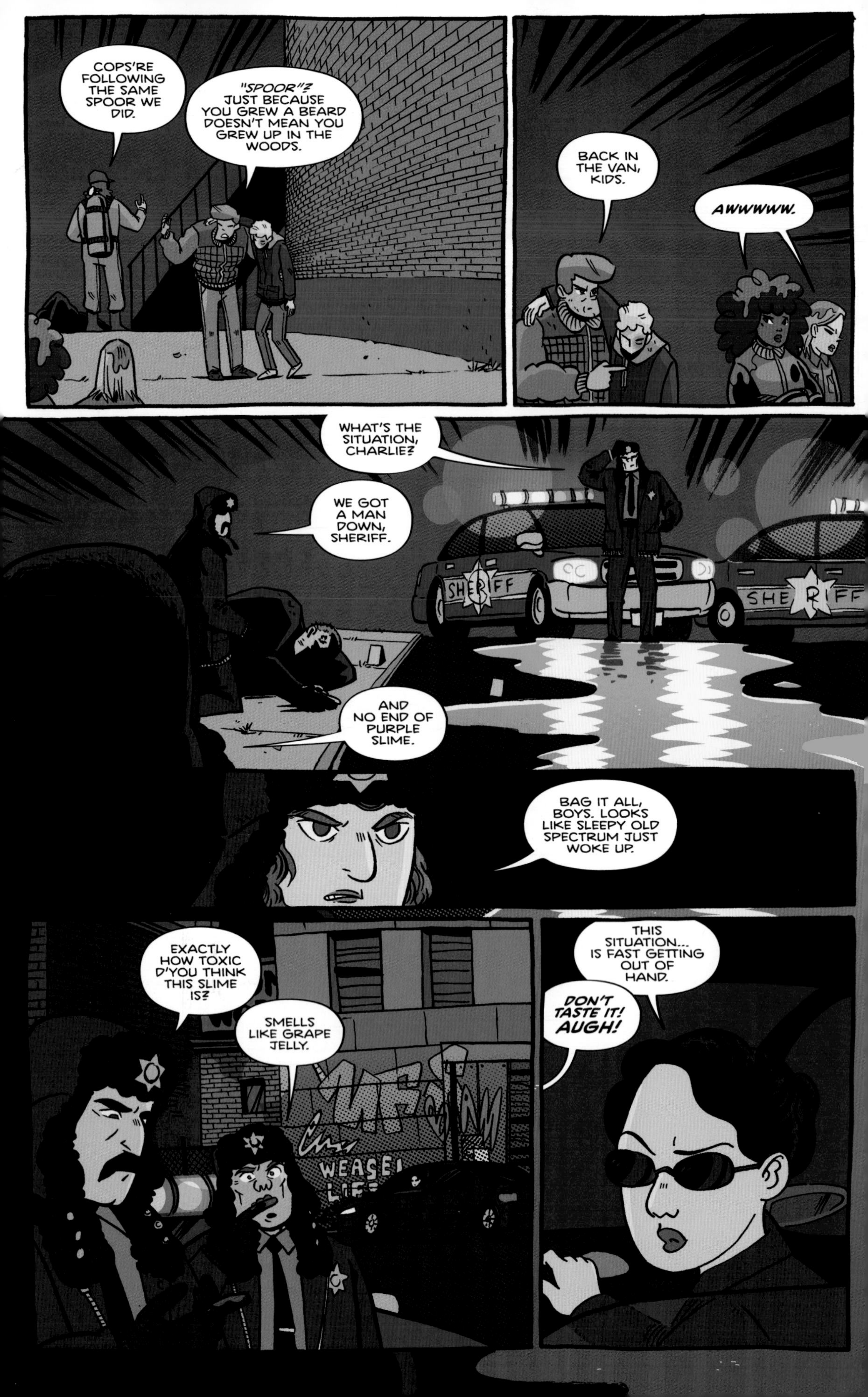
COPS'RE FOLLOWING THE SAME SPOOR WE DID.
"SPOOR"? JUST BECAUSE YOU GREW A BEARD DOESN'T MEAN YOU GREW UP IN THE WOODS.
BACK IN THE VAN, KIDS.
AWWWWW.
WHAT'S THE SITUATION, CHARLIE?
WE GOT A MAN DOWN, SHERIFF.
SHERIFF
SHERIFF
AND NO END OF PURPLE SLIME.
BAG IT ALL, BOYS. LOOKS LIKE SLEEPY OLD SPECTRUM JUST WOKE UP.
EXACTLY HOW TOXIC D'YOU THINK THIS SLIME IS?
SMELLS LIKE GRAPE JELLY.
WEASEL
THIS SITUATION... IS FAST GETTING OUT OF HAND.
DON'T TASTE IT! AUGH!

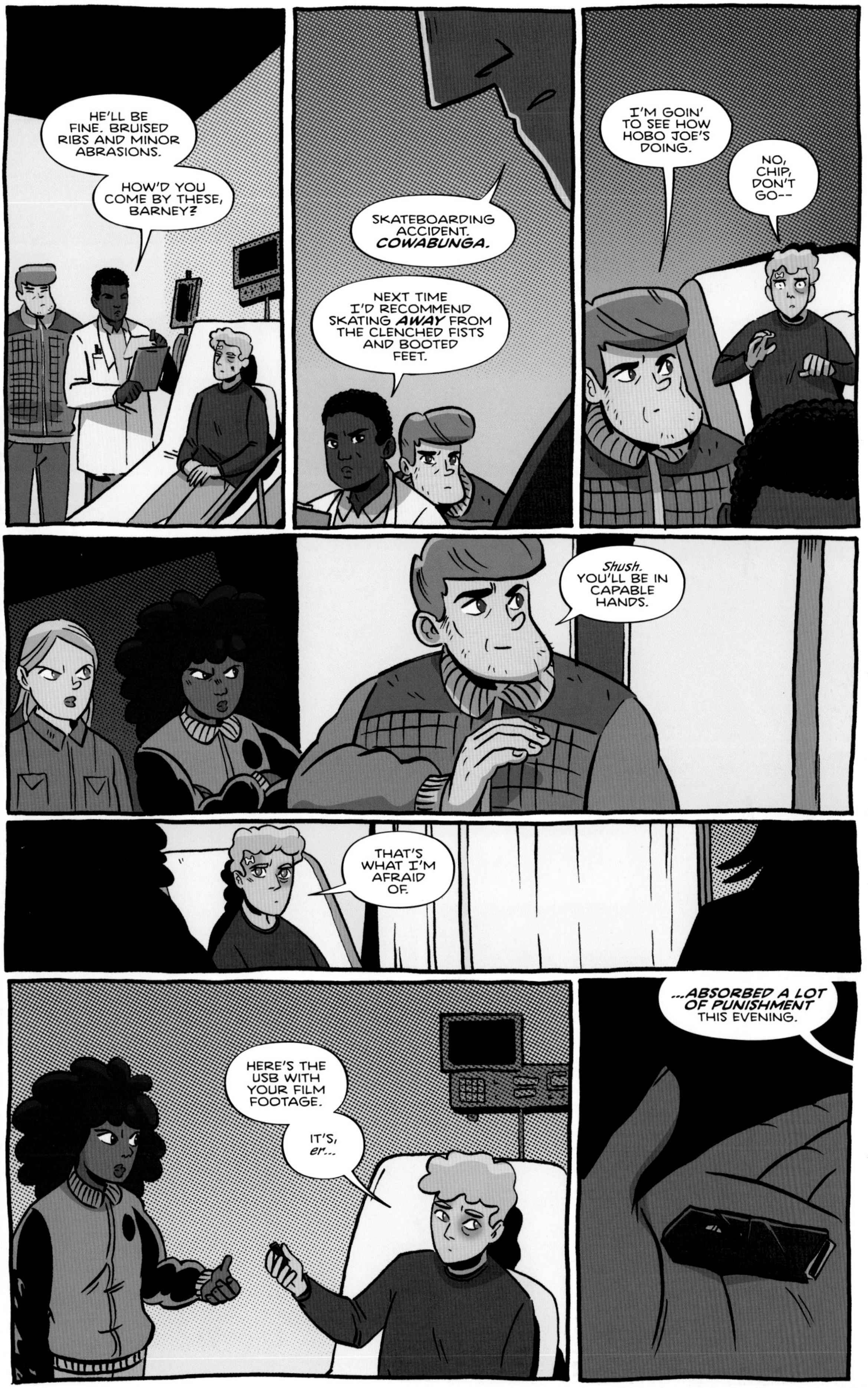
HE'LL BE FINE. BRUISED RIBS AND MINOR ABRASIONS.
HOW'D YOU COME BY THESE, BARNEY?
SKATEBOARDING ACCIDENT. COWABUNGA.
NEXT TIME I'D RECOMMEND SKATING AWAY FROM THE CLENCHED FISTS AND BOOTED FEET.
I'M GOIN' TO SEE HOW HOBO JOE'S DOING.
NO, CHIP, DON'T GO--
Shush. YOU'LL BE IN CAPABLE HANDS.
THAT'S WHAT I'M AFRAID OF.
HERE'S THE USB WITH YOUR FILM FOOTAGE.
IT'S, er...
...ABSORBED A LOT OF PUNISHMENT THIS EVENING.

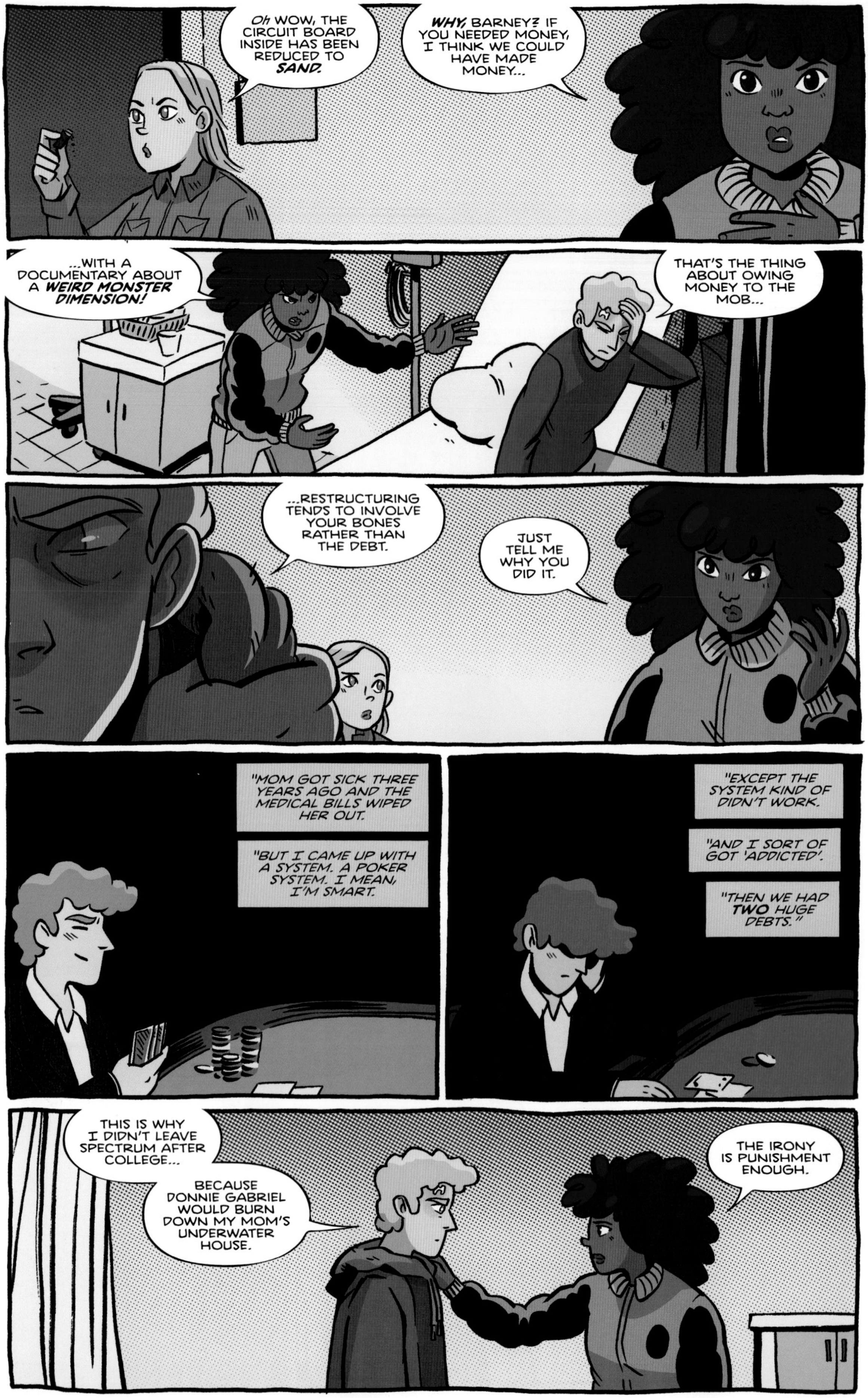
Oh WOW, THE CIRCUIT BOARD INSIDE HAS BEEN REDUCED TO SAND.
WHY, BARNEY? IF YOU NEEDED MONEY, I THINK WE COULD HAVE MADE MONEY...
...WITH A DOCUMENTARY ABOUT A WEIRD MONSTER DIMENSION!
THAT'S THE THING ABOUT OWING MONEY TO THE MOB...
...RESTRUCTURING TENDS TO INVOLVE YOUR BONES RATHER THAN THE DEBT.
JUST TELL ME WHY YOU DID IT.
"MOM GOT SICK THREE YEARS AGO AND THE MEDICAL BILLS WIPED HER OUT.
"BUT I CAME UP WITH A SYSTEM. A POKER SYSTEM. I MEAN, I'M SMART.
"EXCEPT THE SYSTEM KIND OF DIDN'T WORK.
"AND I SORT OF GOT 'ADDICTED'.
"THEN WE HAD TWO HUGE DEBTS."
THIS IS WHY I DIDN'T LEAVE SPECTRUM AFTER COLLEGE...
BECAUSE DONNIE GABRIEL WOULD BURN DOWN MY MOM'S UNDERWATER HOUSE.
THE IRONY IS PUNISHMENT ENOUGH.

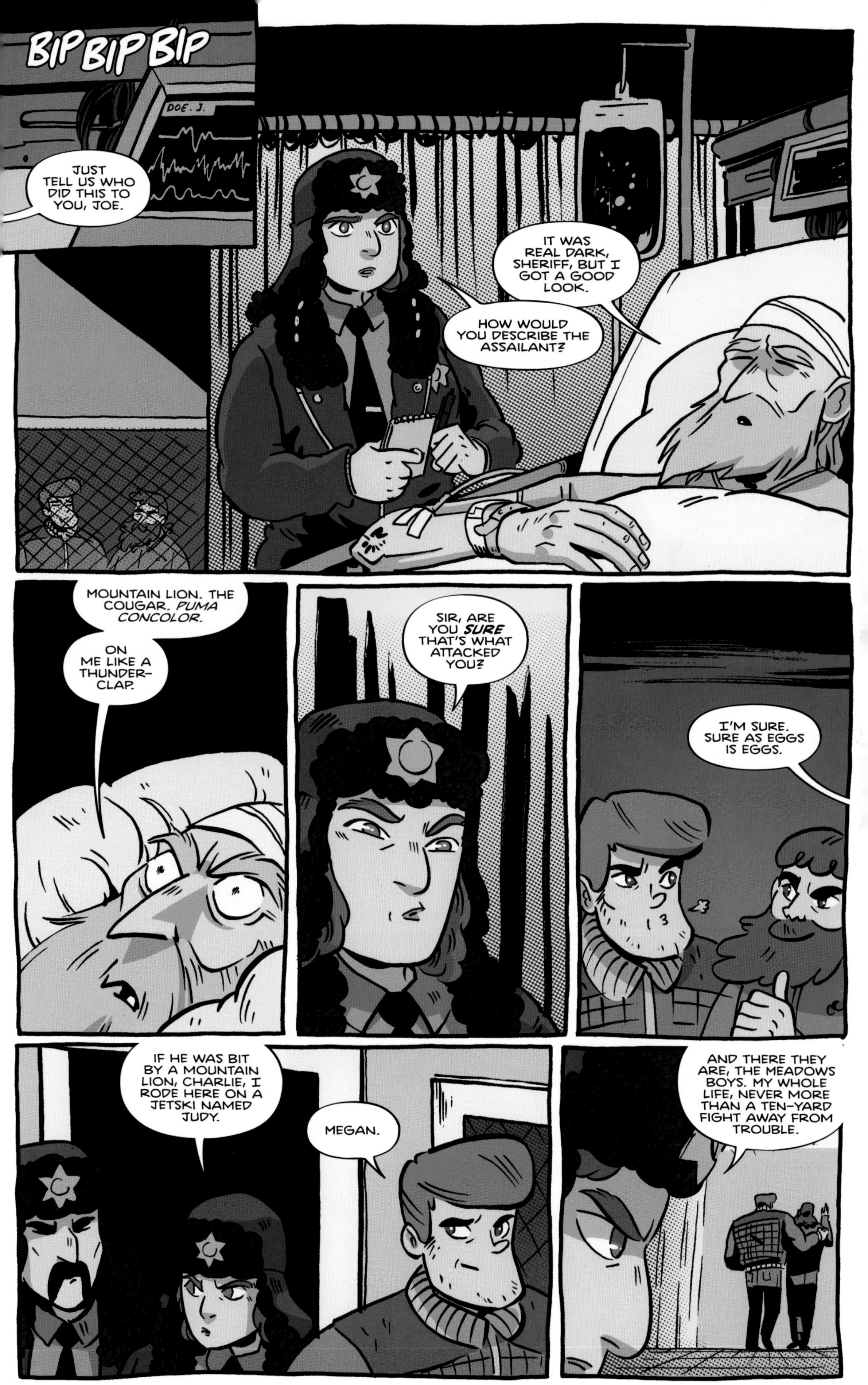
BIP BIP BIP
DOE. J.
JUST TELL US WHO DID THIS TO YOU, JOE.
HOW WOULD YOU DESCRIBE THE ASSAILANT?
IT WAS REAL DARK, SHERIFF, BUT I GOT A GOOD LOOK.
MOUNTAIN LION. THE COUGAR. *PUMA CONCOLOR.*
ON ME LIKE A THUNDER-CLAP.
SIR, ARE YOU ***SURE*** THAT'S WHAT ATTACKED YOU?
I'M SURE. SURE AS EGGS IS EGGS.
IF HE WAS BIT BY A MOUNTAIN LION, CHARLIE, I RODE HERE ON A JETSKI NAMED JUDY.
MEGAN.
AND THERE THEY ARE, THE MEADOWS BOYS. MY WHOLE LIFE, NEVER MORE THAN A TEN-YARD FIGHT AWAY FROM TROUBLE.

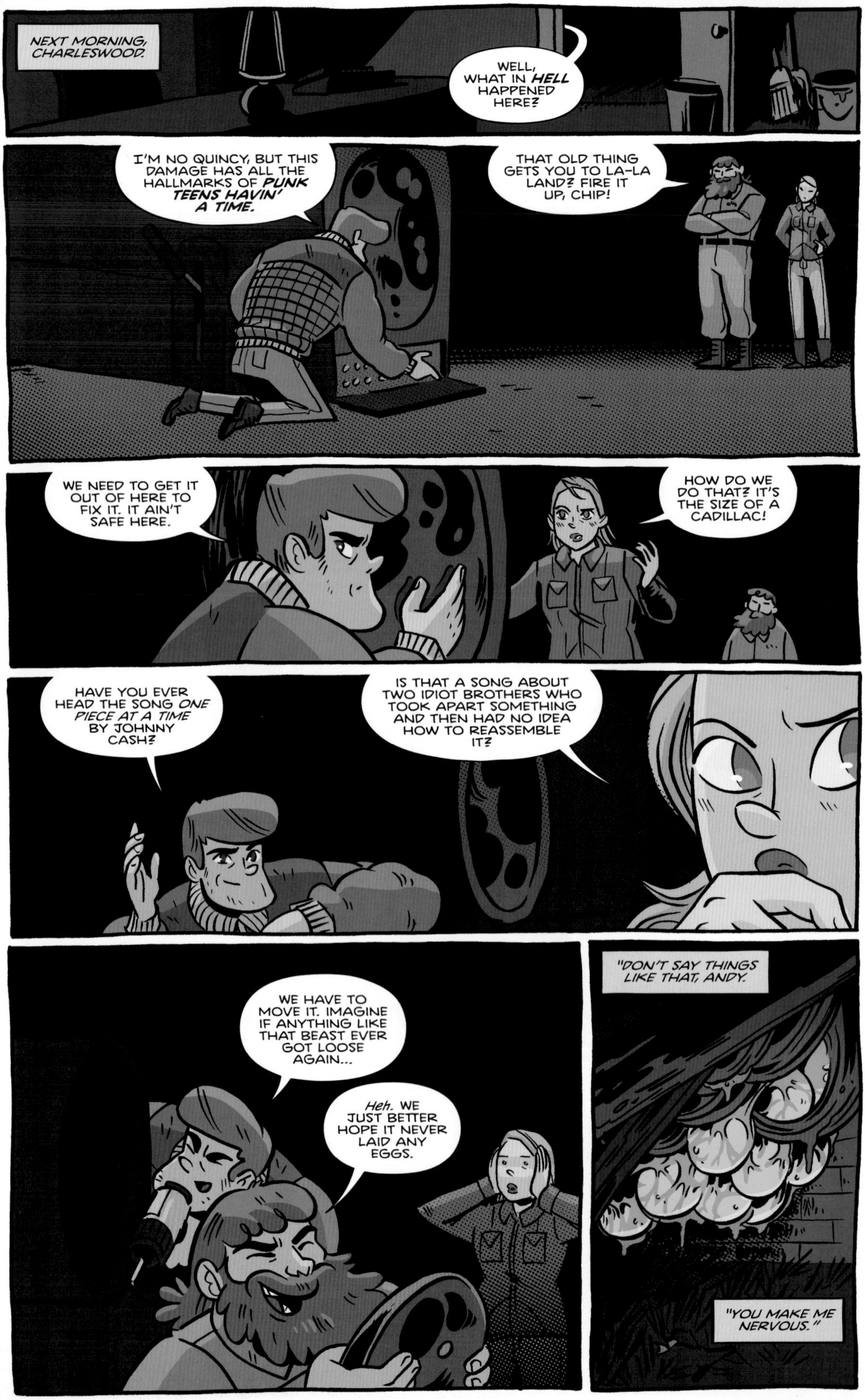

NEXT MORNING, CHARLESWOOD.
WELL, WHAT IN HELL HAPPENED HERE?
I'M NO QUINCY, BUT THIS DAMAGE HAS ALL THE HALLMARKS OF PUNK TEENS HAVIN' A TIME.
THAT OLD THING GETS YOU TO LA-LA LAND? FIRE IT UP, CHIP!
WE NEED TO GET IT OUT OF HERE TO FIX IT. IT AIN'T SAFE HERE.
HOW DO WE DO THAT? IT'S THE SIZE OF A CADILLAC!
HAVE YOU EVER HEAD THE SONG ONE PIECE AT A TIME BY JOHNNY CASH?
IS THAT A SONG ABOUT TWO IDIOT BROTHERS WHO TOOK APART SOMETHING AND THEN HAD NO IDEA HOW TO REASSEMBLE IT?
WE HAVE TO MOVE IT. IMAGINE IF ANYTHING LIKE THAT BEAST EVER GOT LOOSE AGAIN...
Heh. WE JUST BETTER HOPE IT NEVER LAID ANY EGGS.
"DON'T SAY THINGS LIKE THAT, ANDY.
"YOU MAKE ME NERVOUS."

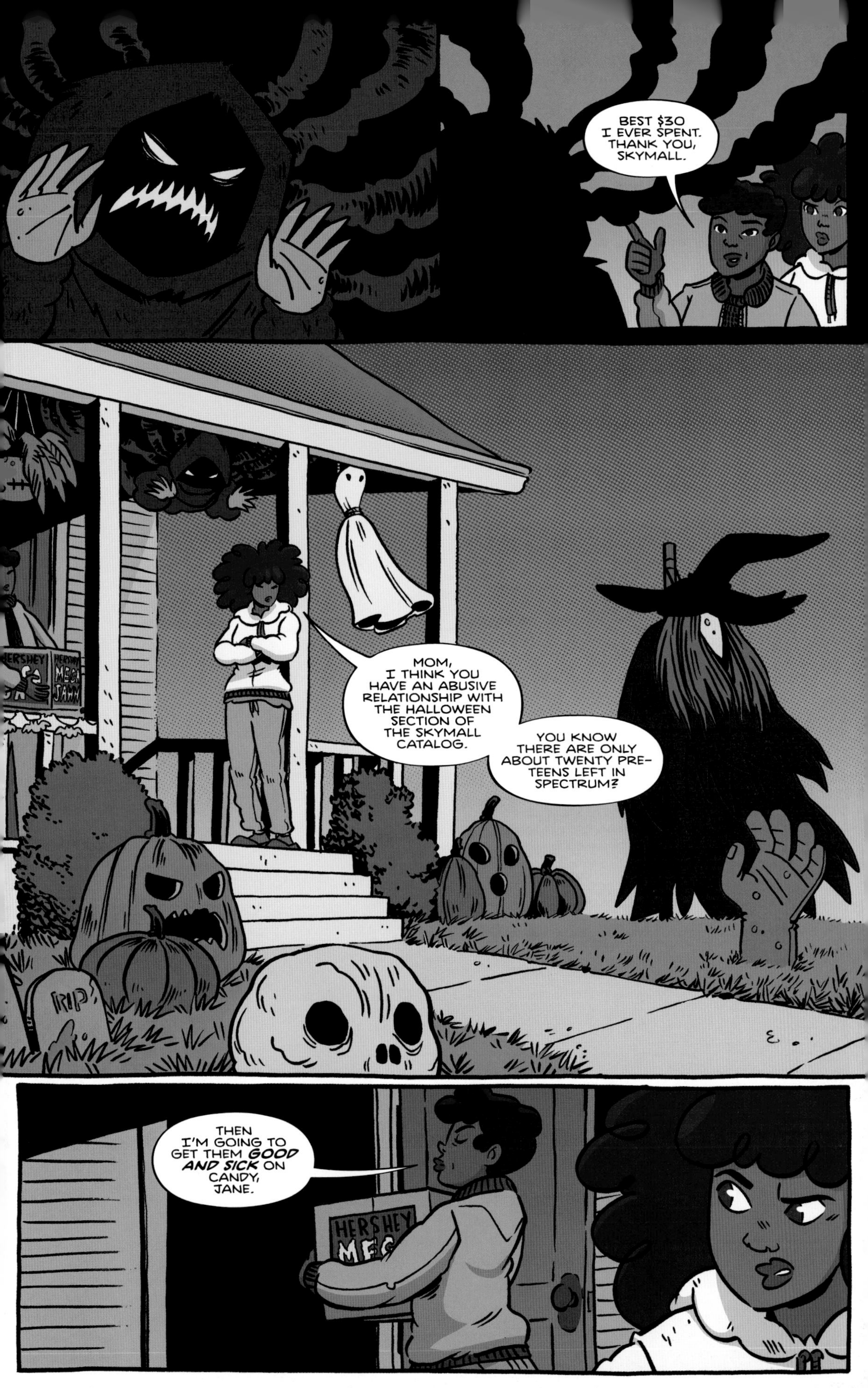
BEST $30 I EVER SPENT. THANK YOU, SKYMALL.
MOM, I THINK YOU HAVE AN ABUSIVE RELATIONSHIP WITH THE HALLOWEEN SECTION OF THE SKYMALL CATALOG.
YOU KNOW THERE ARE ONLY ABOUT TWENTY PRE-TEENS LEFT IN SPECTRUM?
THEN I'M GOING TO GET THEM GOOD AND SICK ON CANDY, JANE.
HERSHEY MEGA

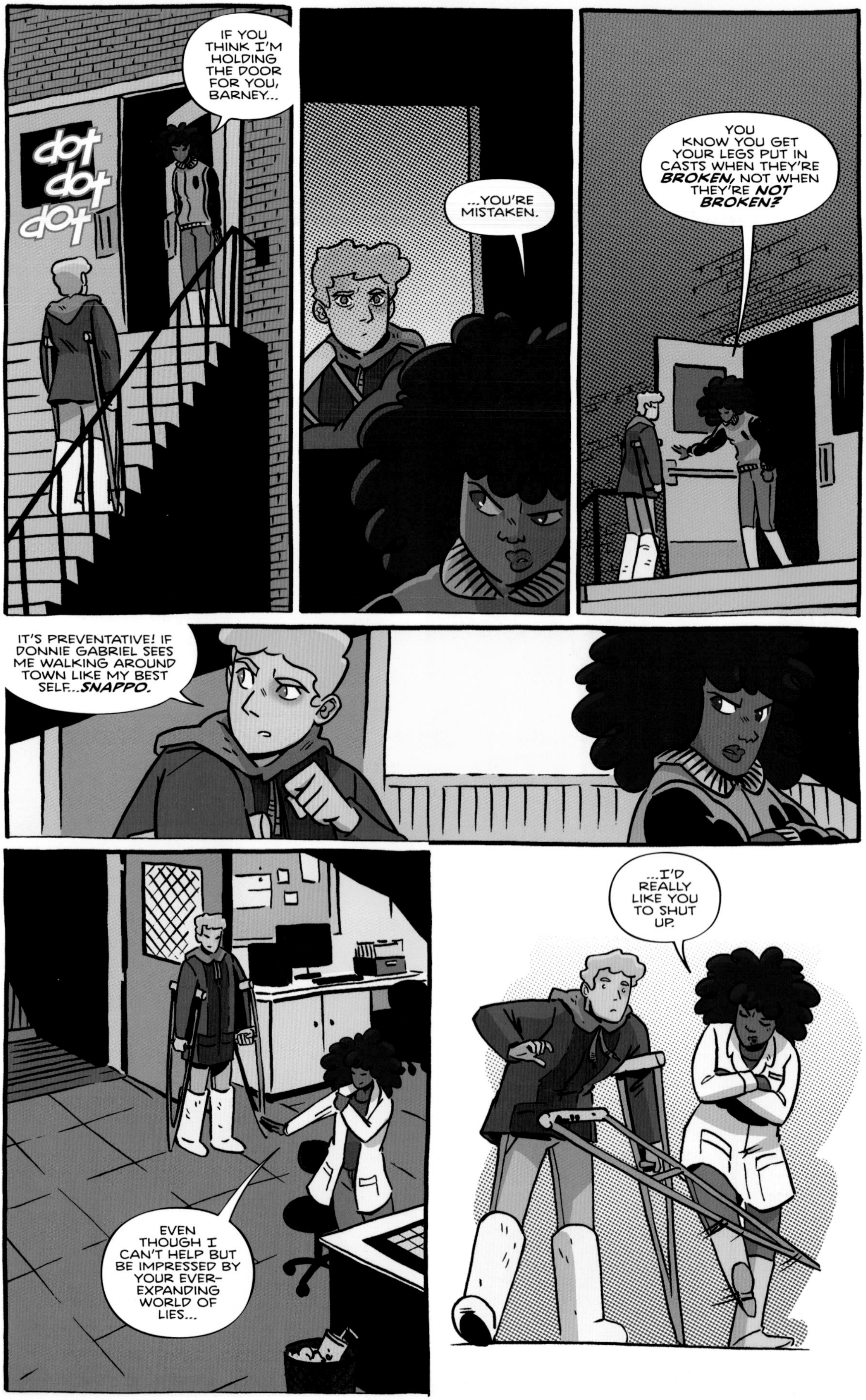
dot dot dot
IF YOU THINK I'M HOLDING THE DOOR FOR YOU, BARNEY...
...YOU'RE MISTAKEN.
YOU KNOW YOU GET YOUR LEGS PUT IN CASTS WHEN THEY'RE BROKEN, NOT WHEN THEY'RE NOT BROKEN?
IT'S PREVENTATIVE! IF DONNIE GABRIEL SEES ME WALKING AROUND TOWN LIKE MY BEST SELF...SNAPPO.
EVEN THOUGH I CAN'T HELP BUT BE IMPRESSED BY YOUR EVER-EXPANDING WORLD OF LIES...
...I'D REALLY LIKE YOU TO SHUT UP.

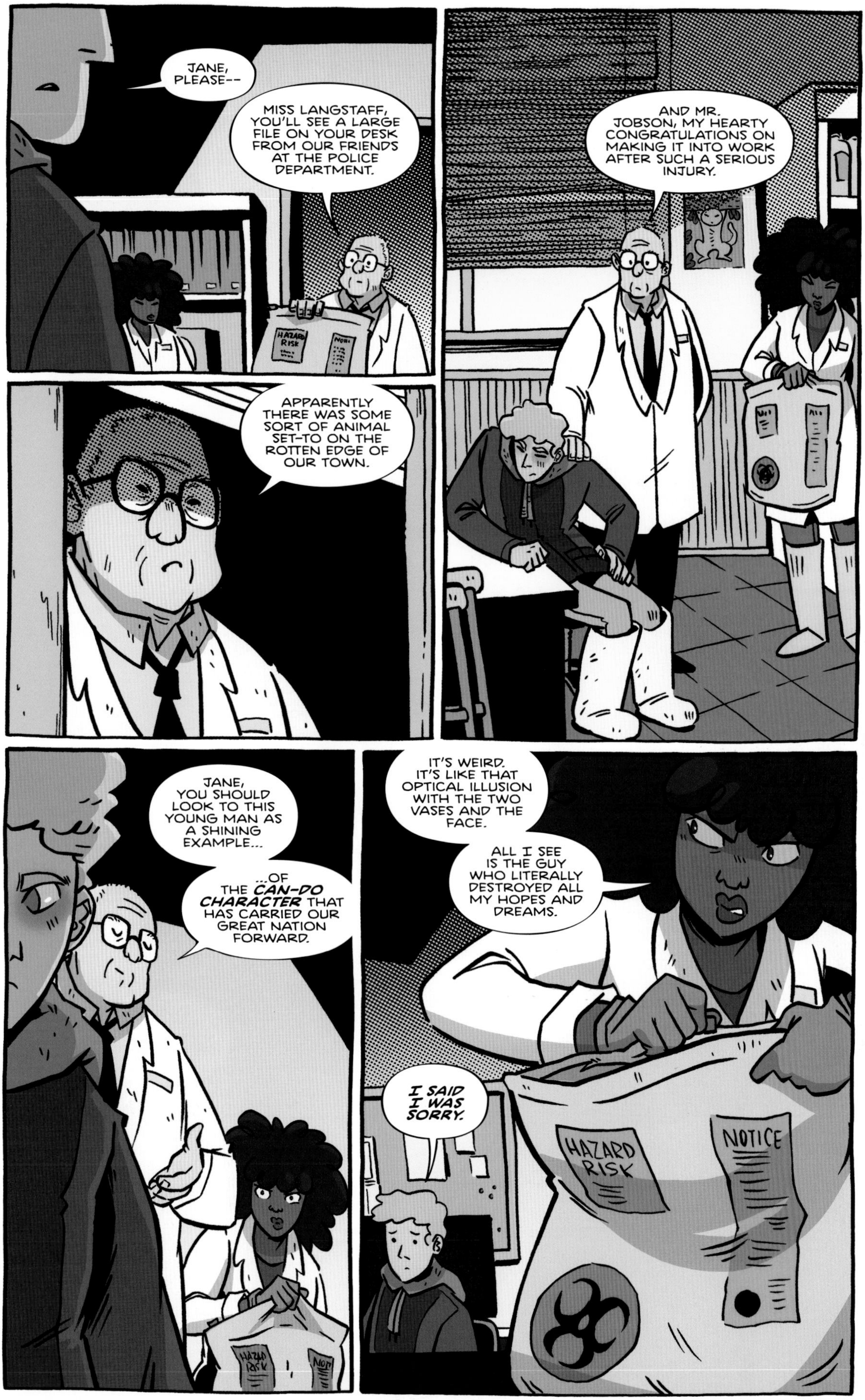
JANE, PLEASE--
MISS LANGSTAFF, YOU'LL SEE A LARGE FILE ON YOUR DESK FROM OUR FRIENDS AT THE POLICE DEPARTMENT.
HAZARD RISK
AND MR. JOBSON, MY HEARTY CONGRATULATIONS ON MAKING IT INTO WORK AFTER SUCH A SERIOUS INJURY.
APPARENTLY THERE WAS SOME SORT OF ANIMAL SET-TO ON THE ROTTEN EDGE OF OUR TOWN.
JANE, YOU SHOULD LOOK TO THIS YOUNG MAN AS A SHINING EXAMPLE...
...OF THE ***CAN-DO CHARACTER*** THAT HAS CARRIED OUR GREAT NATION FORWARD.
IT'S WEIRD. IT'S LIKE THAT OPTICAL ILLUSION WITH THE TWO VASES AND THE FACE.
ALL I SEE IS THE GUY WHO LITERALLY DESTROYED ALL MY HOPES AND DREAMS.
I SAID I WAS SORRY.
HAZARD RISK
NOTICE

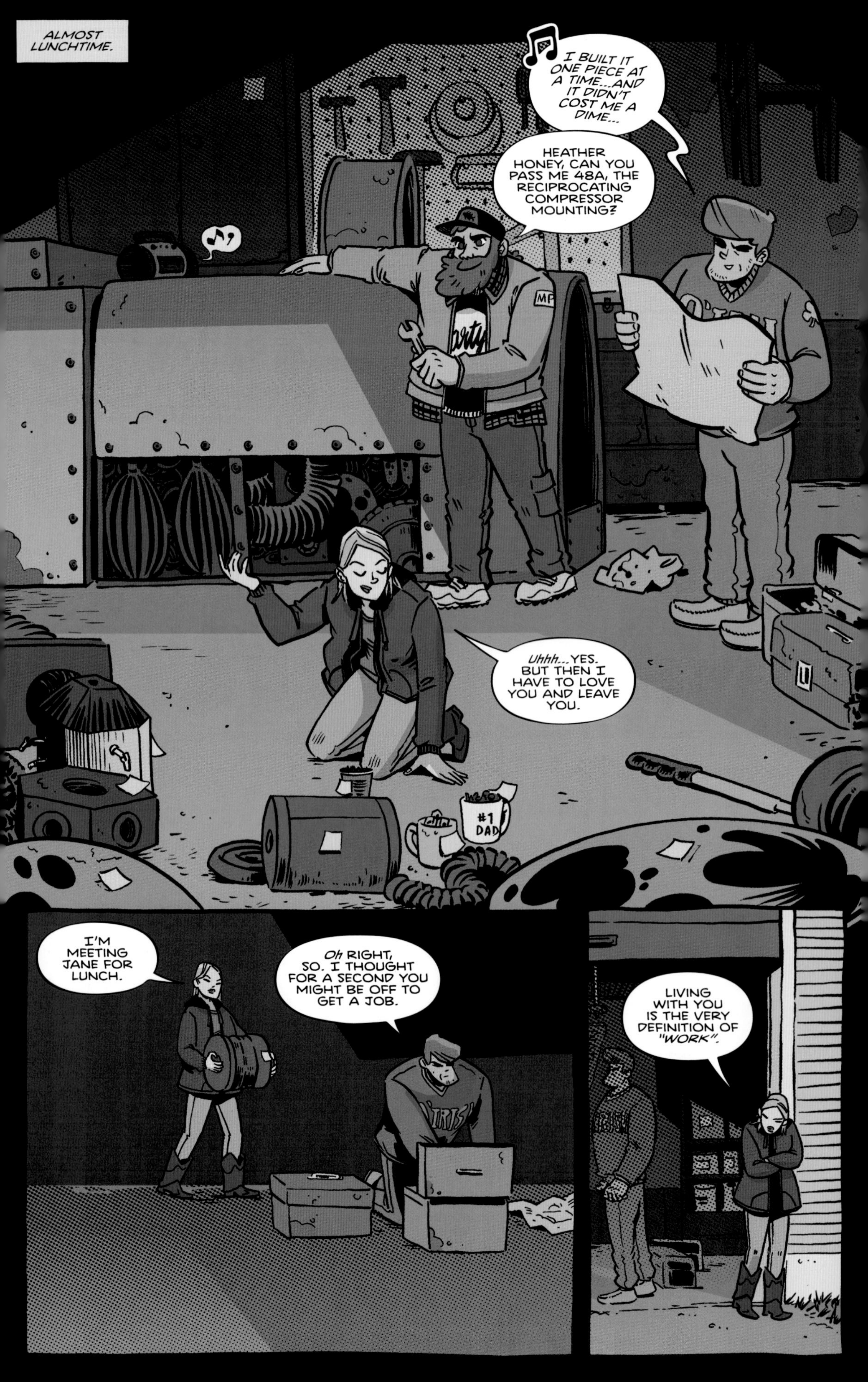
ALMOST LUNCHTIME.
I BUILT IT ONE PIECE AT A TIME...AND IT DIDN'T COST ME A DIME...
HEATHER HONEY, CAN YOU PASS ME 48A, THE RECIPROCATING COMPRESSOR MOUNTING?
Uhhh...YES. BUT THEN I HAVE TO LOVE YOU AND LEAVE YOU.
#1 DAD
I'M MEETING JANE FOR LUNCH.
Oh RIGHT, SO. I THOUGHT FOR A SECOND YOU MIGHT BE OFF TO GET A JOB.
LIVING WITH YOU IS THE VERY DEFINITION OF "WORK".

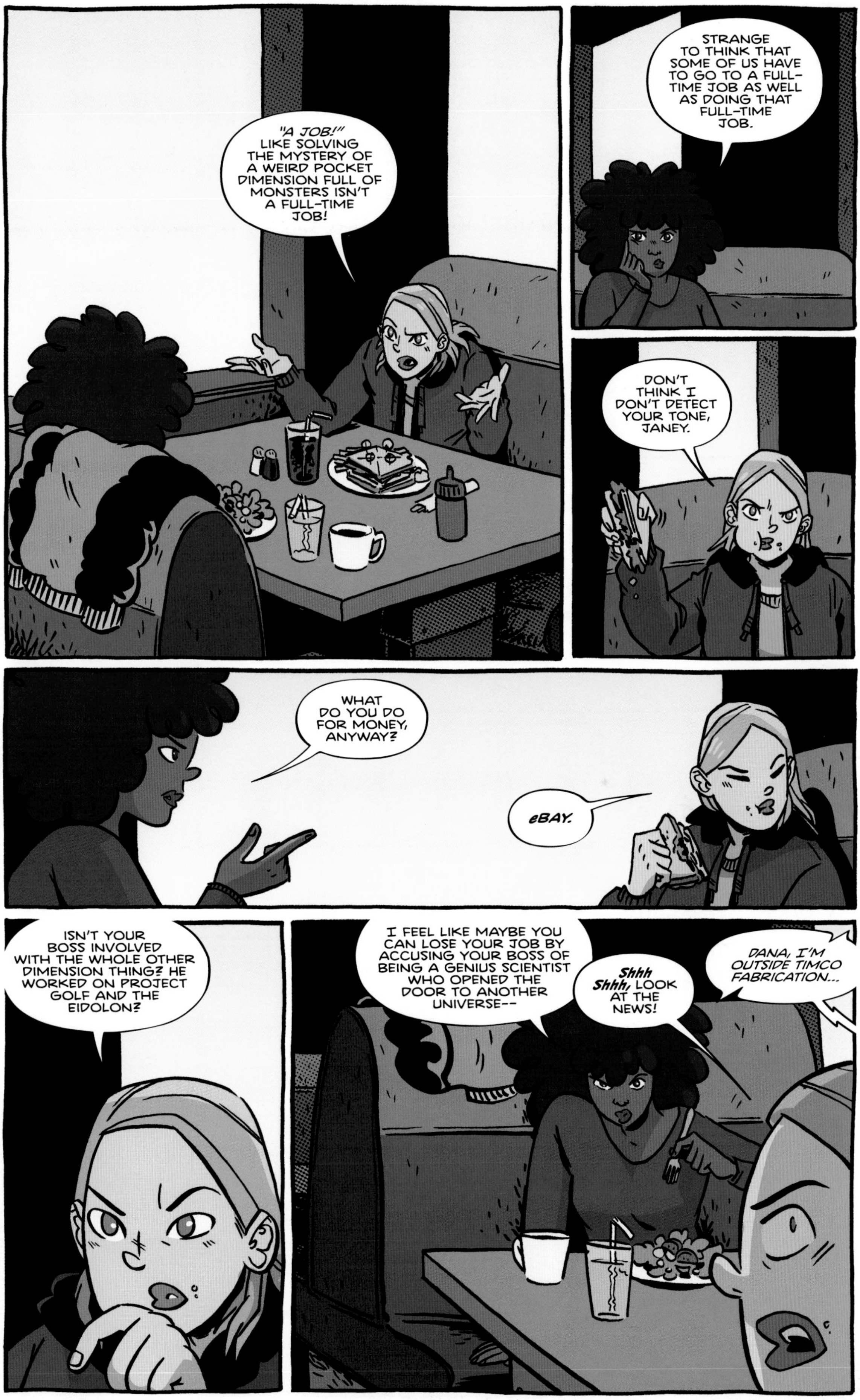
"A JOB!" LIKE SOLVING THE MYSTERY OF A WEIRD POCKET DIMENSION FULL OF MONSTERS ISN'T A FULL-TIME JOB!
STRANGE TO THINK THAT SOME OF US HAVE TO GO TO A FULL-TIME JOB AS WELL AS DOING THAT FULL-TIME JOB.
DON'T THINK I DON'T DETECT YOUR TONE, JANEY.
WHAT DO YOU DO FOR MONEY, ANYWAY?
eBAY.
ISN'T YOUR BOSS INVOLVED WITH THE WHOLE OTHER DIMENSION THING? HE WORKED ON PROJECT GOLF AND THE EIDOLON?
I FEEL LIKE MAYBE YOU CAN LOSE YOUR JOB BY ACCUSING YOUR BOSS OF BEING A GENIUS SCIENTIST WHO OPENED THE DOOR TO ANOTHER UNIVERSE--
Shhh Shhh, LOOK AT THE NEWS!
DANA, I'M OUTSIDE TIMCO FABRICATION...

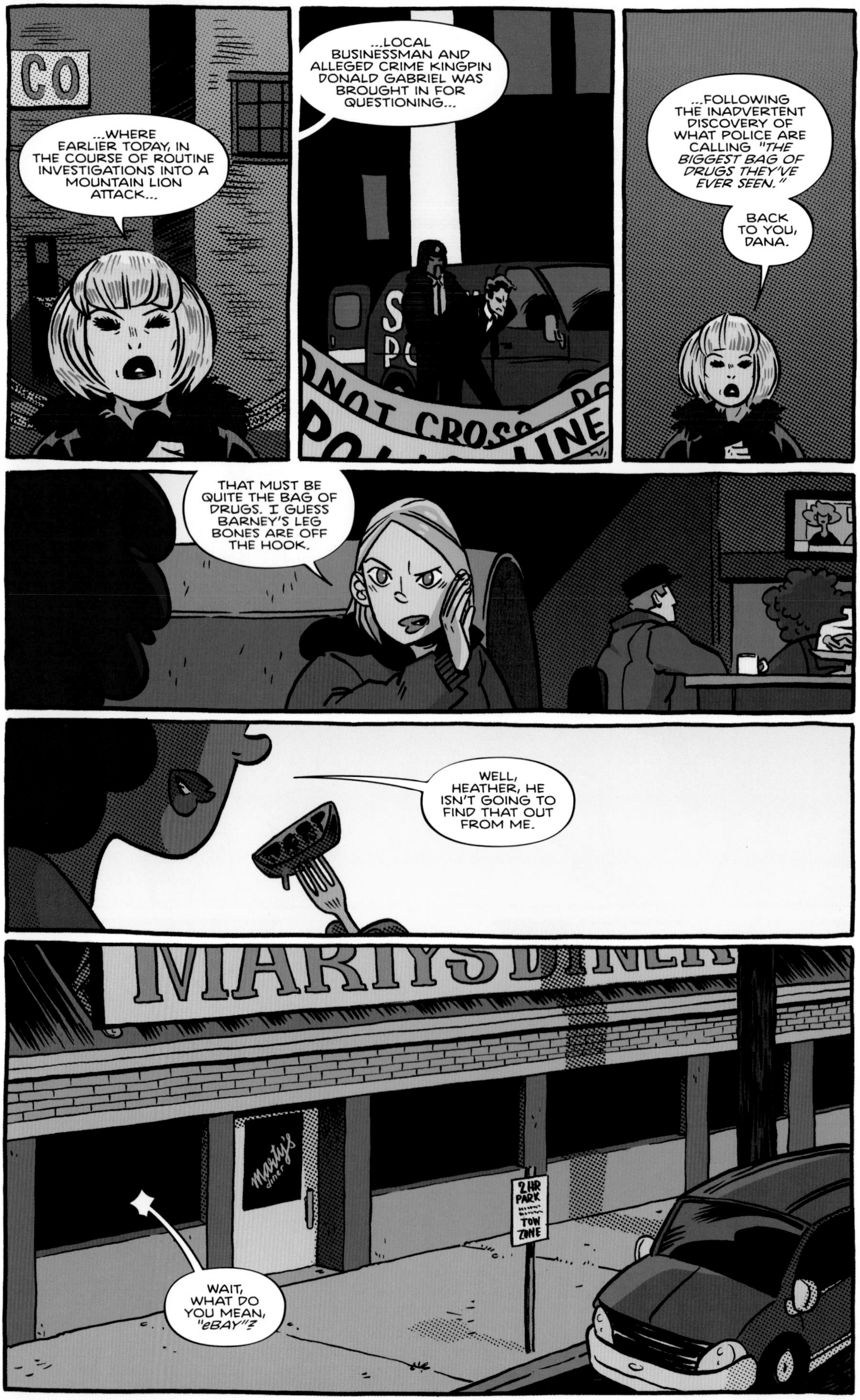
CO
...WHERE EARLIER TODAY, IN THE COURSE OF ROUTINE INVESTIGATIONS INTO A MOUNTAIN LION ATTACK...
...LOCAL BUSINESSMAN AND ALLEGED CRIME KINGPIN DONALD GABRIEL WAS BROUGHT IN FOR QUESTIONING...
...FOLLOWING THE INADVERTENT DISCOVERY OF WHAT POLICE ARE CALLING *"THE BIGGEST BAG OF DRUGS THEY'VE EVER SEEN."*
BACK TO YOU, DANA.
THAT MUST BE QUITE THE BAG OF DRUGS. I GUESS BARNEY'S LEG BONES ARE OFF THE HOOK.
WELL, HEATHER, HE ISN'T GOING TO FIND THAT OUT FROM ME.
MARTY'S DINER
Marty's diner
2 HR PARK
TOW ZONE
WAIT, WHAT DO YOU MEAN, *"eBAY"*?

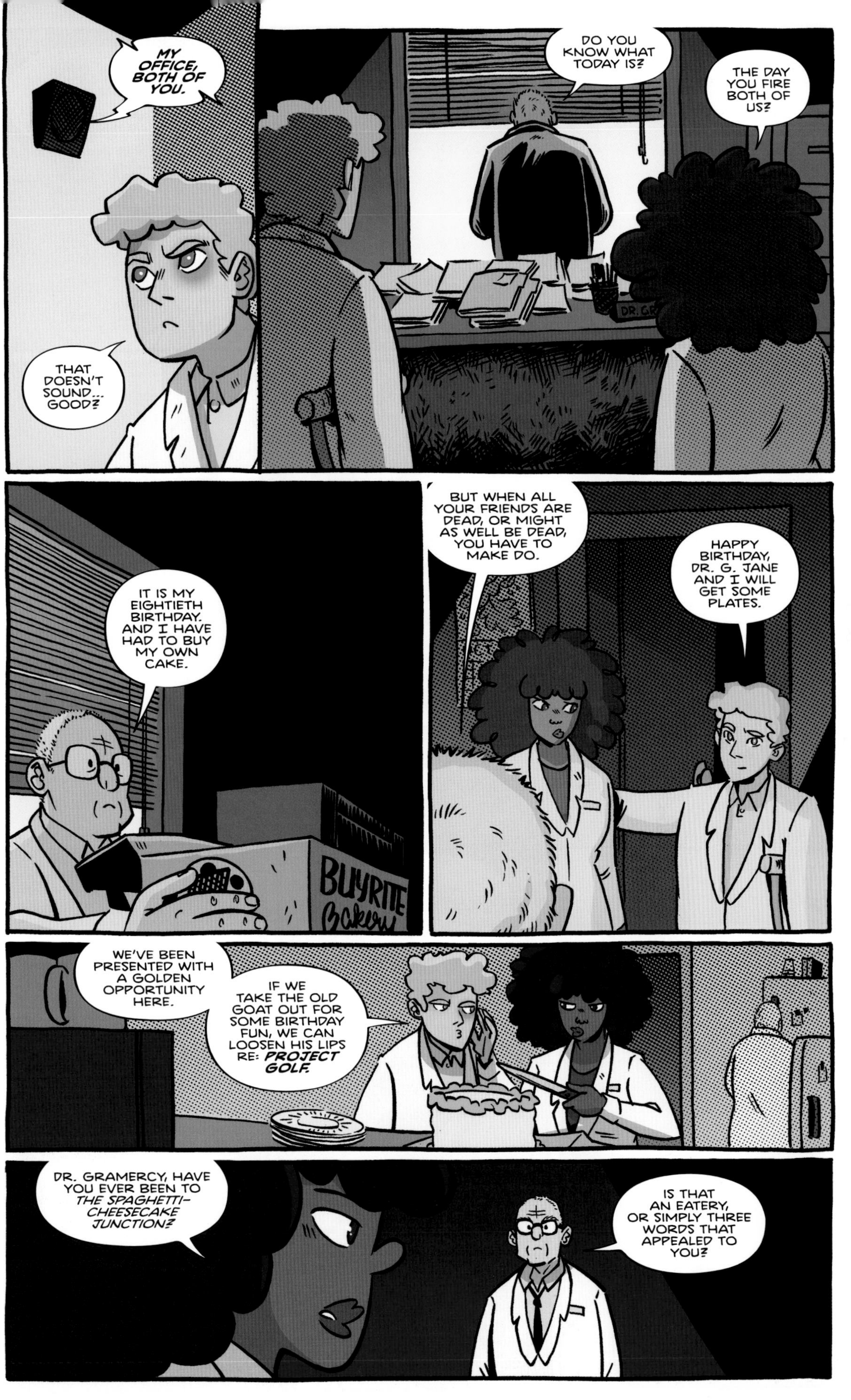
MY OFFICE, BOTH OF YOU.
THAT DOESN'T SOUND... GOOD?
DO YOU KNOW WHAT TODAY IS?
THE DAY YOU FIRE BOTH OF US?
DR. GR
IT IS MY EIGHTIETH BIRTHDAY. AND I HAVE HAD TO BUY MY OWN CAKE.
BUYRITE Bakery
BUT WHEN ALL YOUR FRIENDS ARE DEAD, OR MIGHT AS WELL BE DEAD, YOU HAVE TO MAKE DO.
HAPPY BIRTHDAY, DR. G. JANE AND I WILL GET SOME PLATES.
WE'VE BEEN PRESENTED WITH A GOLDEN OPPORTUNITY HERE.
IF WE TAKE THE OLD GOAT OUT FOR SOME BIRTHDAY FUN, WE CAN LOOSEN HIS LIPS RE: PROJECT GOLF.
DR. GRAMERCY, HAVE YOU EVER BEEN TO THE SPAGHETTI-CHEESECAKE JUNCTION?
IS THAT AN EATERY, OR SIMPLY THREE WORDS THAT APPEALED TO YOU?

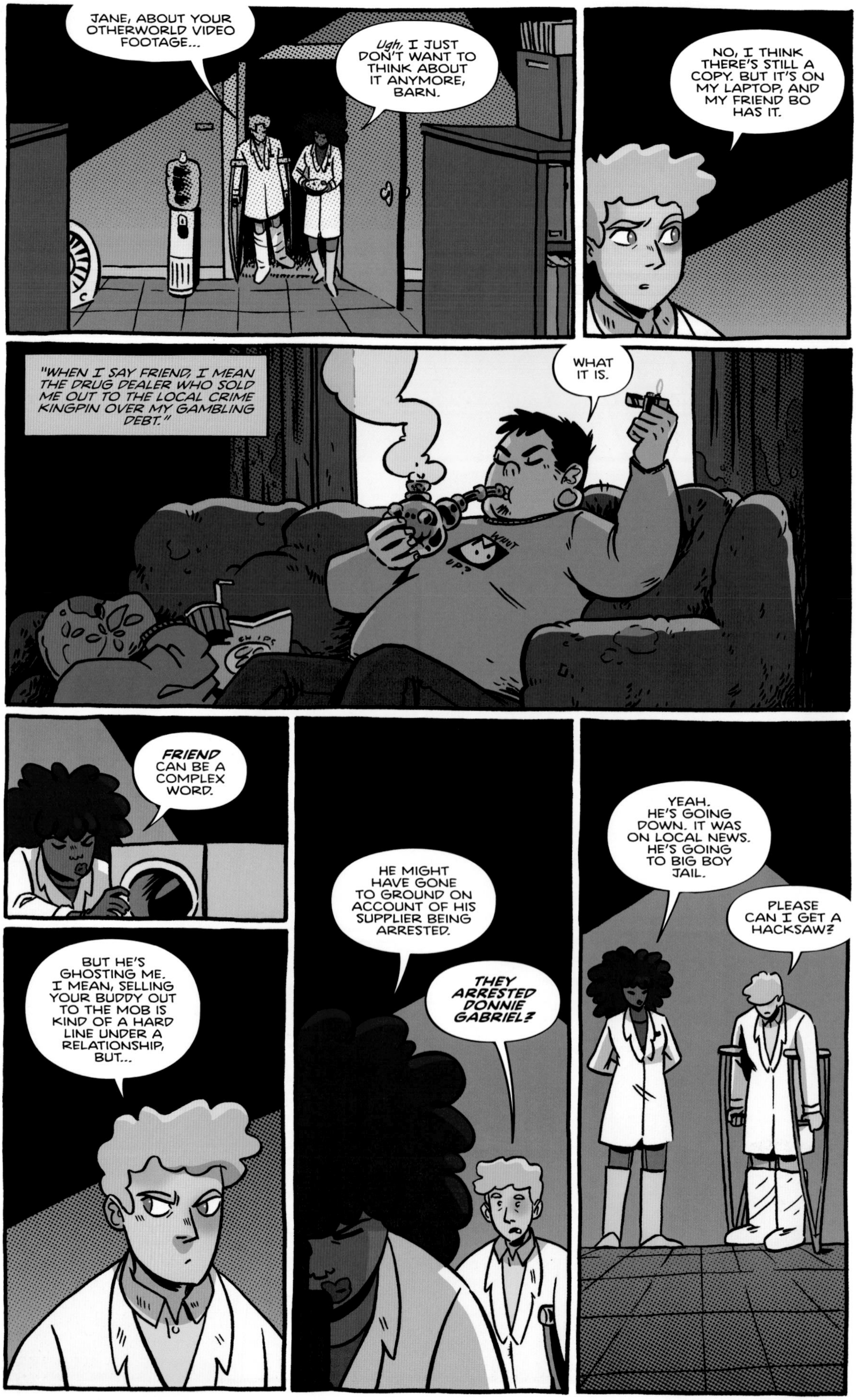
JANE, ABOUT YOUR OTHERWORLD VIDEO FOOTAGE...
Ugh, I JUST DON'T WANT TO THINK ABOUT IT ANYMORE, BARN.
NO, I THINK THERE'S STILL A COPY. BUT IT'S ON MY LAPTOP, AND MY FRIEND BO HAS IT.
"WHEN I SAY FRIEND, I MEAN THE DRUG DEALER WHO SOLD ME OUT TO THE LOCAL CRIME KINGPIN OVER MY GAMBLING DEBT."
WHAT IT IS.
FRIEND CAN BE A COMPLEX WORD.
BUT HE'S GHOSTING ME. I MEAN, SELLING YOUR BUDDY OUT TO THE MOB IS KIND OF A HARD LINE UNDER A RELATIONSHIP, BUT...
HE MIGHT HAVE GONE TO GROUND ON ACCOUNT OF HIS SUPPLIER BEING ARRESTED.
THEY ARRESTED DONNIE GABRIEL?
YEAH. HE'S GOING DOWN. IT WAS ON LOCAL NEWS. HE'S GOING TO BIG BOY JAIL.
PLEASE CAN I GET A HACKSAW?

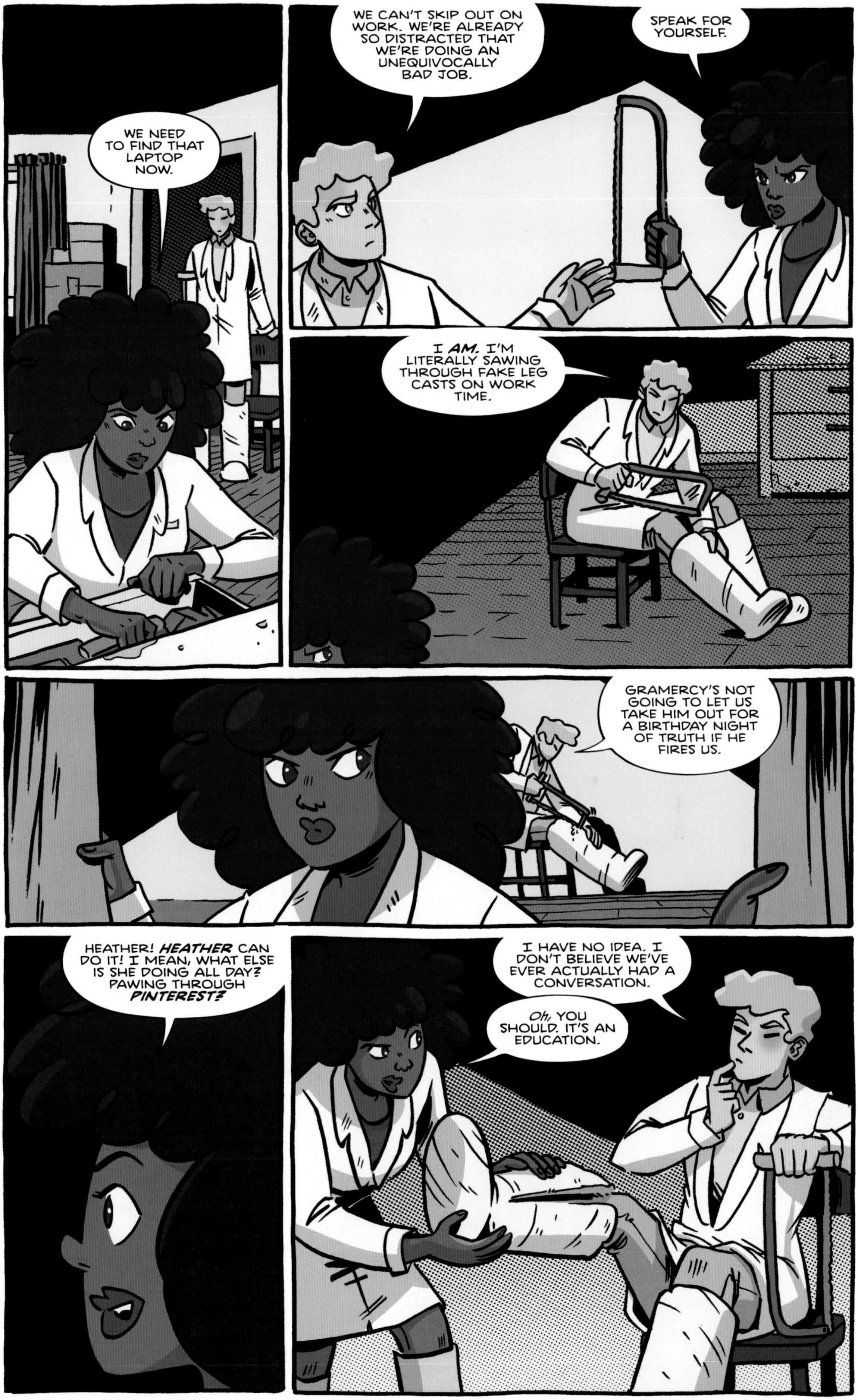
WE NEED TO FIND THAT LAPTOP NOW.
WE CAN'T SKIP OUT ON WORK. WE'RE ALREADY SO DISTRACTED THAT WE'RE DOING AN UNEQUIVOCALLY BAD JOB.
SPEAK FOR YOURSELF.
I *AM.* I'M LITERALLY SAWING THROUGH FAKE LEG CASTS ON WORK TIME.
GRAMERCY'S NOT GOING TO LET US TAKE HIM OUT FOR A BIRTHDAY NIGHT OF TRUTH IF HE FIRES US.
HEATHER! ***HEATHER*** CAN DO IT! I MEAN, WHAT ELSE IS SHE DOING ALL DAY? PAWING THROUGH ***PINTEREST?***
I HAVE NO IDEA. I DON'T BELIEVE WE'VE EVER ACTUALLY HAD A CONVERSATION.
Oh, YOU SHOULD. IT'S AN EDUCATION.

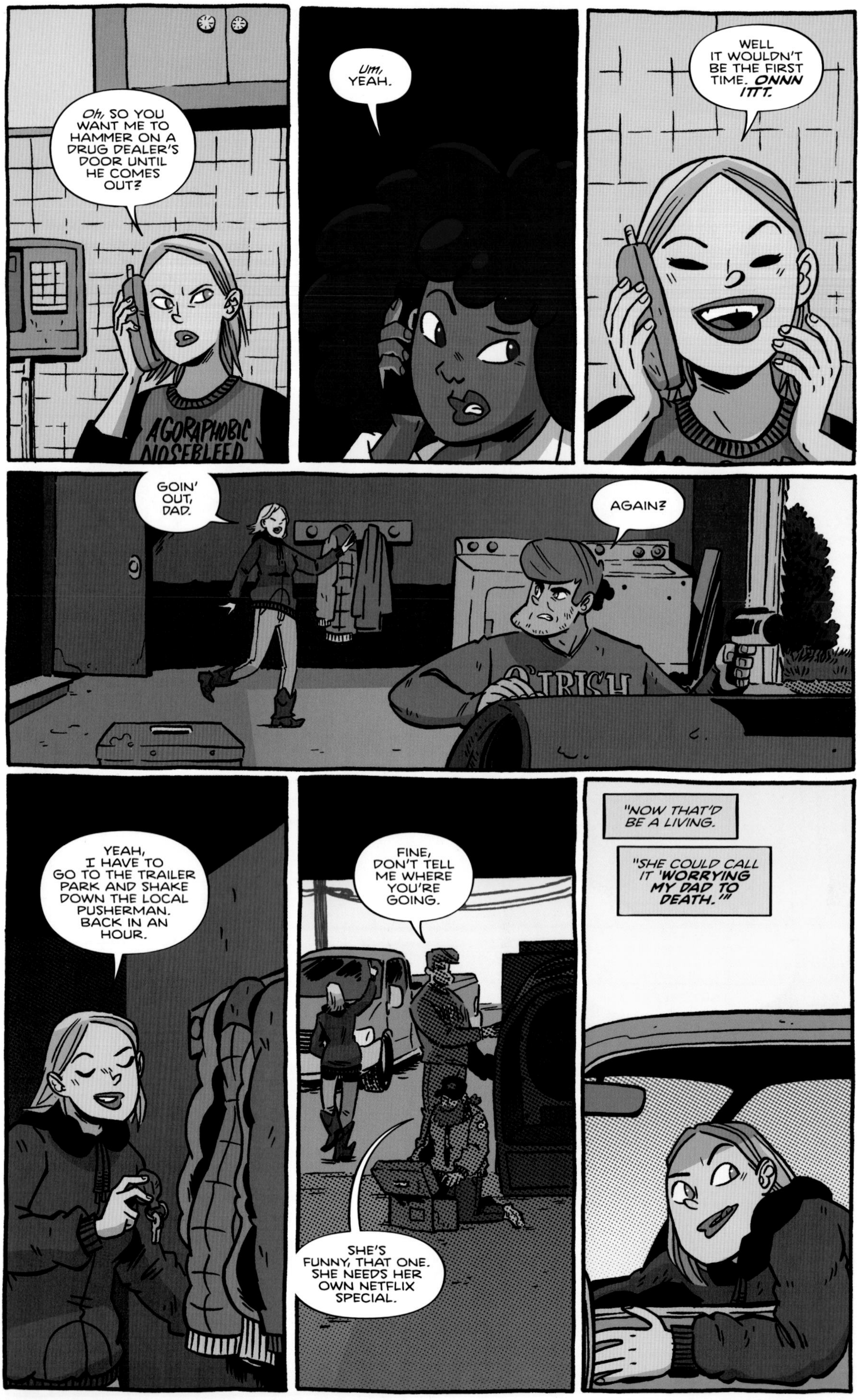
Oh, SO YOU WANT ME TO HAMMER ON A DRUG DEALER'S DOOR UNTIL HE COMES OUT?
AGORAPHOBIC NOSEBLEED
Um, YEAH.
WELL IT WOULDN'T BE THE FIRST TIME. ONNN ITTT.
GOIN' OUT, DAD.
AGAIN?
O'TRISH
YEAH, I HAVE TO GO TO THE TRAILER PARK AND SHAKE DOWN THE LOCAL PUSHERMAN. BACK IN AN HOUR.
FINE, DON'T TELL ME WHERE YOU'RE GOING.
SHE'S FUNNY, THAT ONE. SHE NEEDS HER OWN NETFLIX SPECIAL.
"NOW THAT'D BE A LIVING.
"SHE COULD CALL IT 'WORRYING MY DAD TO DEATH.'"

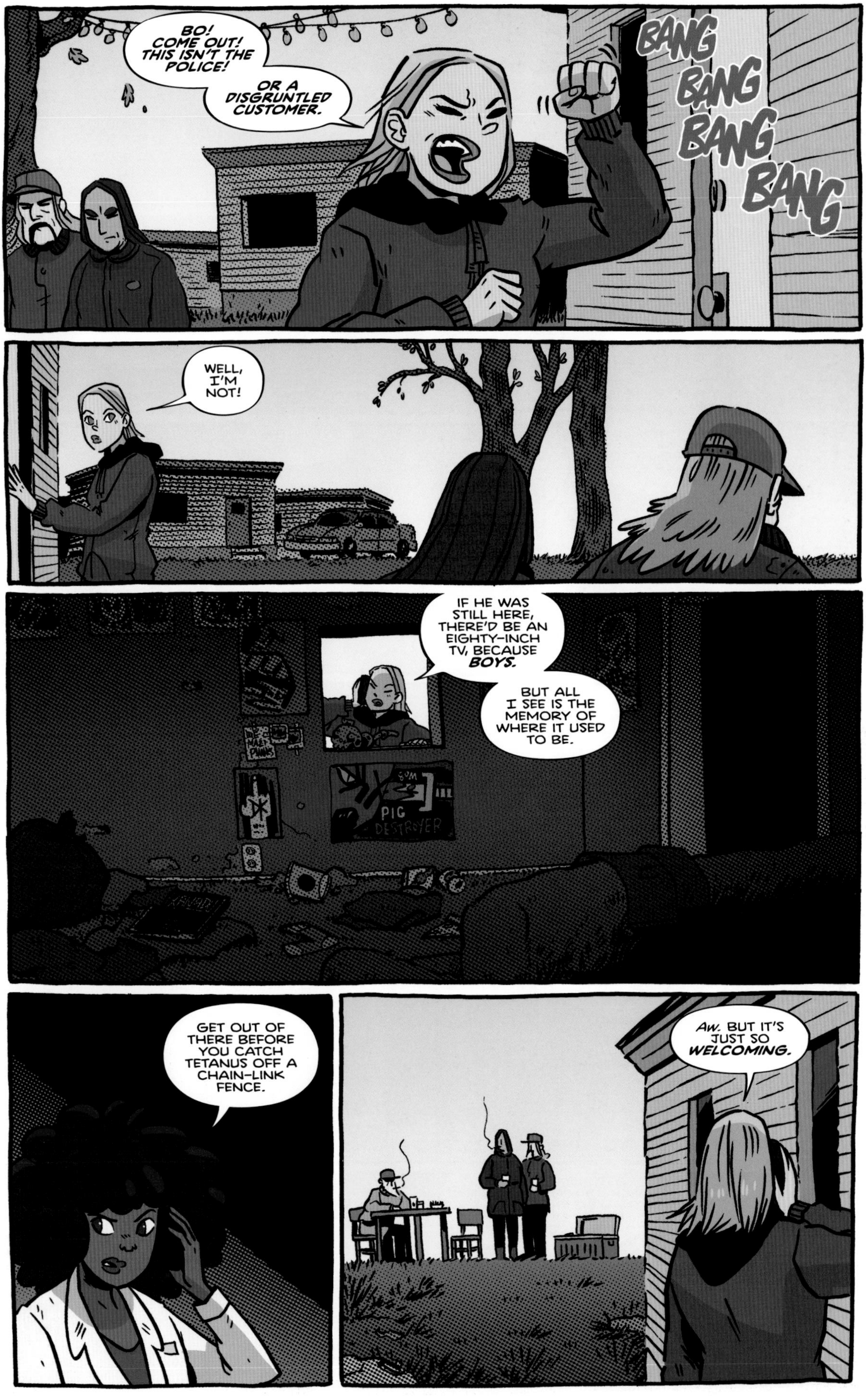
BO! COME OUT! THIS ISN'T THE POLICE!
OR A DISGRUNTLED CUSTOMER.
BANG BANG BANG BANG
WELL, I'M NOT!
IF HE WAS STILL HERE, THERE'D BE AN EIGHTY-INCH TV, BECAUSE BOYS.
BUT ALL I SEE IS THE MEMORY OF WHERE IT USED TO BE.
PIG DESTROYER
GET OUT OF THERE BEFORE YOU CATCH TETANUS OFF A CHAIN-LINK FENCE.
Aw. BUT IT'S JUST SO WELCOMING.

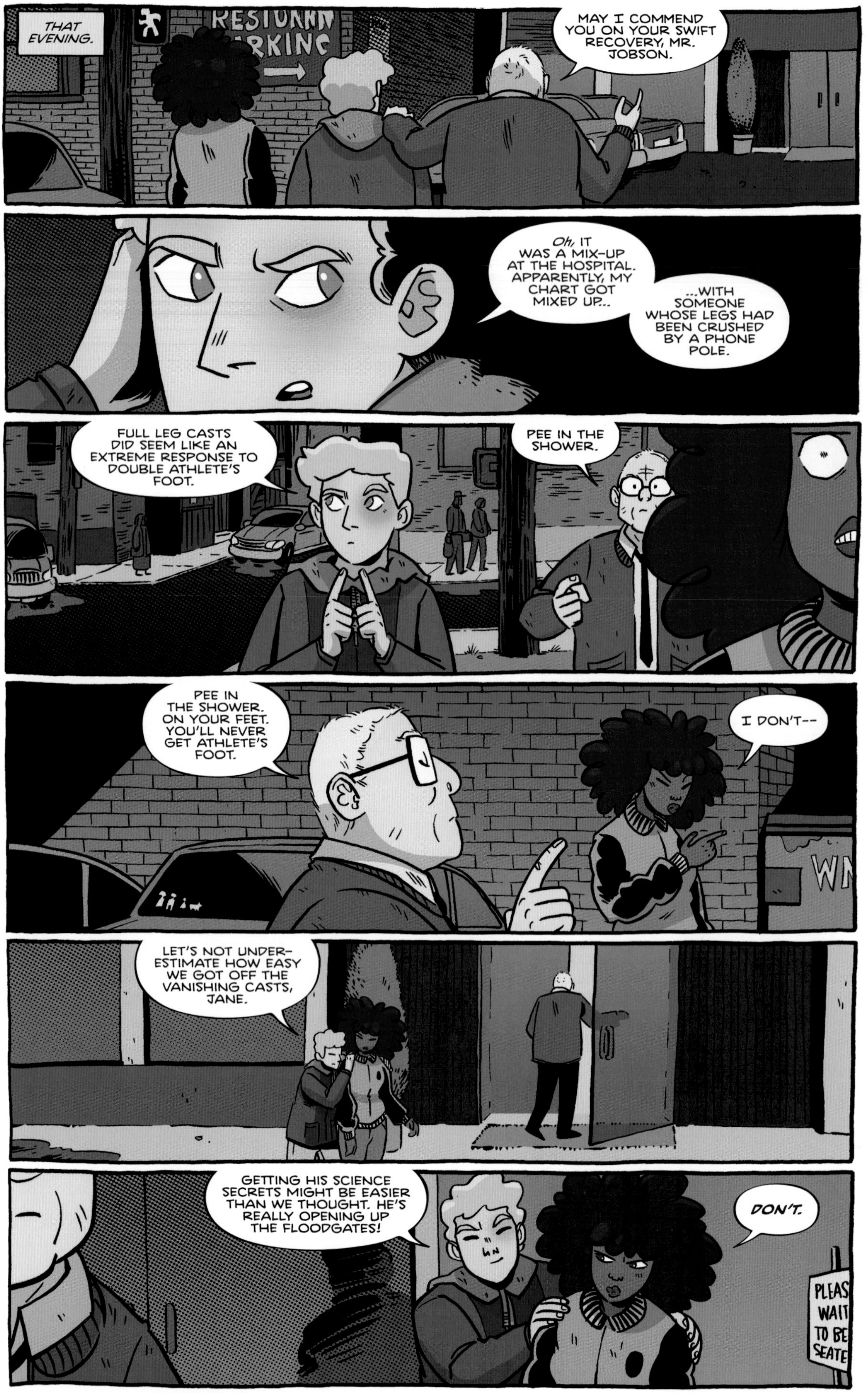
THAT EVENING.
RESTURAN
ARKING
MAY I COMMEND YOU ON YOUR SWIFT RECOVERY, MR. JOBSON.
Oh, IT WAS A MIX-UP AT THE HOSPITAL. APPARENTLY, MY CHART GOT MIXED UP...
...WITH SOMEONE WHOSE LEGS HAD BEEN CRUSHED BY A PHONE POLE.
FULL LEG CASTS DID SEEM LIKE AN EXTREME RESPONSE TO DOUBLE ATHLETE'S FOOT.
PEE IN THE SHOWER.
PEE IN THE SHOWER. ON YOUR FEET. YOU'LL NEVER GET ATHLETE'S FOOT.
I DON'T--
LET'S NOT UNDER-ESTIMATE HOW EASY WE GOT OFF THE VANISHING CASTS, JANE.
GETTING HIS SCIENCE SECRETS MIGHT BE EASIER THAN WE THOUGHT. HE'S REALLY OPENING UP THE FLOODGATES!
DON'T.
PLEAS WAIT TO BE SEATE

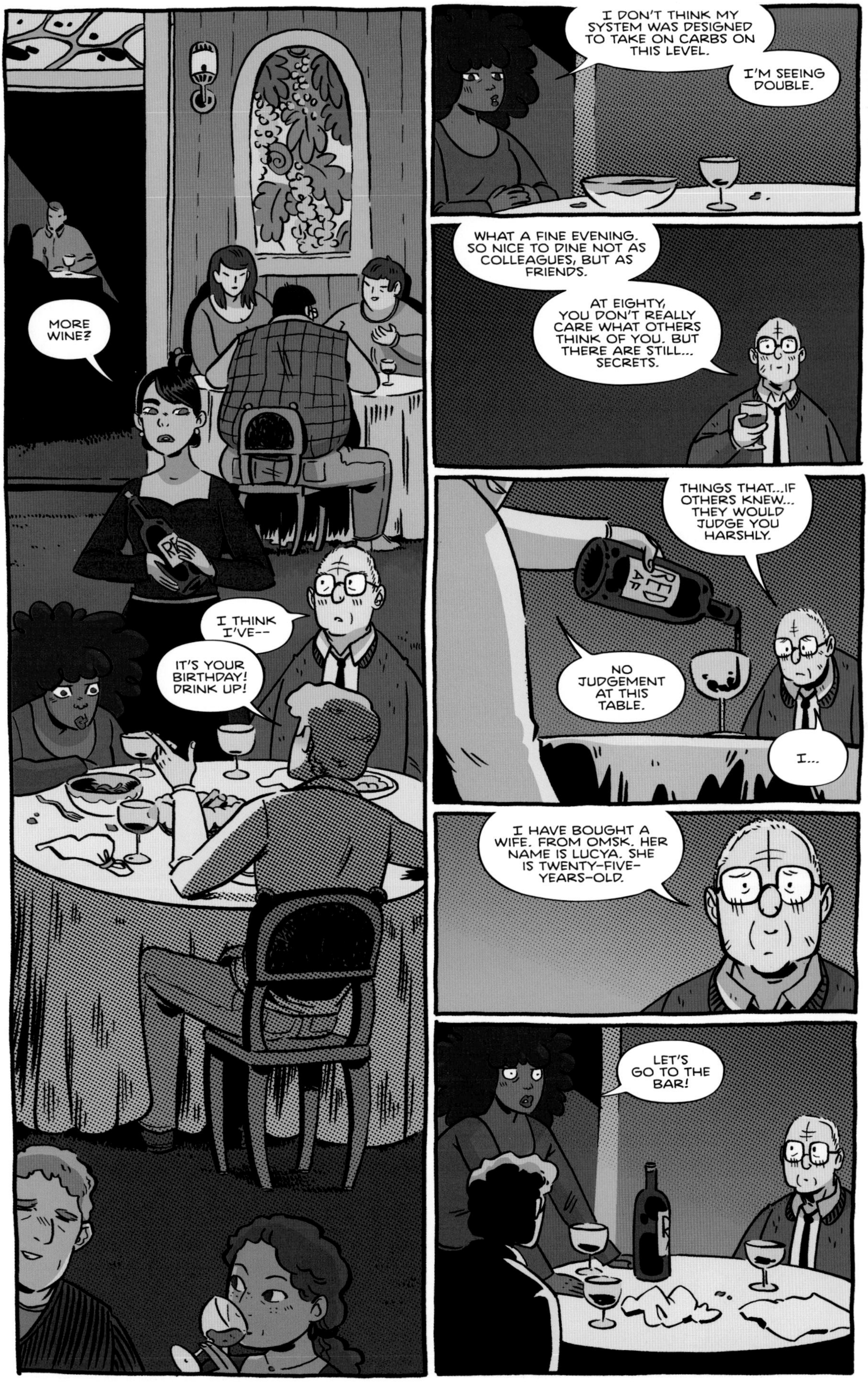
MORE WINE?
I THINK I'VE--
IT'S YOUR BIRTHDAY! DRINK UP!
I DON'T THINK MY SYSTEM WAS DESIGNED TO TAKE ON CARBS ON THIS LEVEL.
I'M SEEING DOUBLE.
WHAT A FINE EVENING. SO NICE TO DINE NOT AS COLLEAGUES, BUT AS FRIENDS.
AT EIGHTY, YOU DON'T REALLY CARE WHAT OTHERS THINK OF YOU. BUT THERE ARE STILL... SECRETS.
THINGS THAT...IF OTHERS KNEW... THEY WOULD JUDGE YOU HARSHLY.
NO JUDGEMENT AT THIS TABLE.
I...
I HAVE BOUGHT A WIFE. FROM OMSK. HER NAME IS LUCYA. SHE IS TWENTY-FIVE-YEARS-OLD.
LET'S GO TO THE BAR!

EVENING, DANNY. THIS IS MY EMPLOYER, DR. GRAMERCY.

WHAT'LL IT BE?

APPROPRIATELY FOR HALLOWEEN, THISH SHALOON IS DEADER THAN A COFFIN NAIL.

SO, uh, DR. GRAMERCY, I WAS WONDERING IF YOU'D EVER HEARD OF...PROJECT GOLF? IT--

♫♪ HAAAPPY BIRTHDAY, MR. PRES-I-DENT...

...HAPPY BIRTHDAY... TO...YOU.

HIPPIES USE SIDE DOOR

TABITHA, YOU KNOW YOU'RE BARRED FROM HERE. COME ON.

schlitz

I DON REP LIS

BUT IT'S...HIS BIRTHDAY.

YOU...CANNOT IMAGINE...HOW THISH COUNTRY OWESH TABITHA LEONE.

COME ON, DEAR.

HAPPY HOUR SPEC

CITY WIDE $5

PBR + FRIE

DRAFT $7 1/2

OIRISH TAVERN

ASHK YOUR MOTHER ABOUT PROJECT GOLF.

BUT--

ASHK YOUR MOTHER!

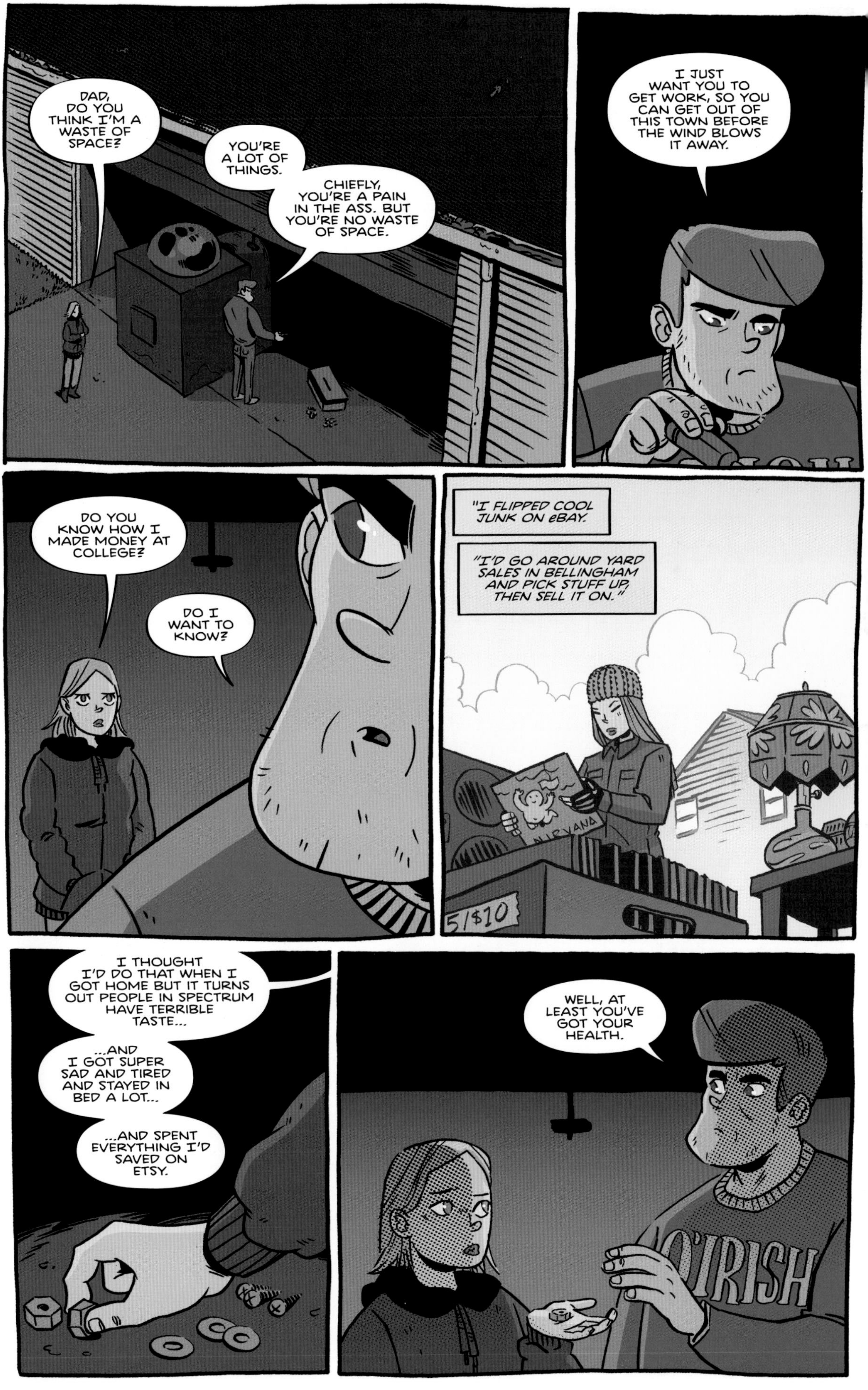
DAD, DO YOU THINK I'M A WASTE OF SPACE?
YOU'RE A LOT OF THINGS.
CHIEFLY, YOU'RE A PAIN IN THE ASS. BUT YOU'RE NO WASTE OF SPACE.
I JUST WANT YOU TO GET WORK, SO YOU CAN GET OUT OF THIS TOWN BEFORE THE WIND BLOWS IT AWAY.
DO YOU KNOW HOW I MADE MONEY AT COLLEGE?
DO I WANT TO KNOW?
"I FLIPPED COOL JUNK ON eBAY.
"I'D GO AROUND YARD SALES IN BELLINGHAM AND PICK STUFF UP, THEN SELL IT ON."
NIRVANA
5/$10
I THOUGHT I'D DO THAT WHEN I GOT HOME BUT IT TURNS OUT PEOPLE IN SPECTRUM HAVE TERRIBLE TASTE...
...AND I GOT SUPER SAD AND TIRED AND STAYED IN BED A LOT...
...AND SPENT EVERYTHING I'D SAVED ON ETSY.
WELL, AT LEAST YOU'VE GOT YOUR HEALTH.
O'IRISH

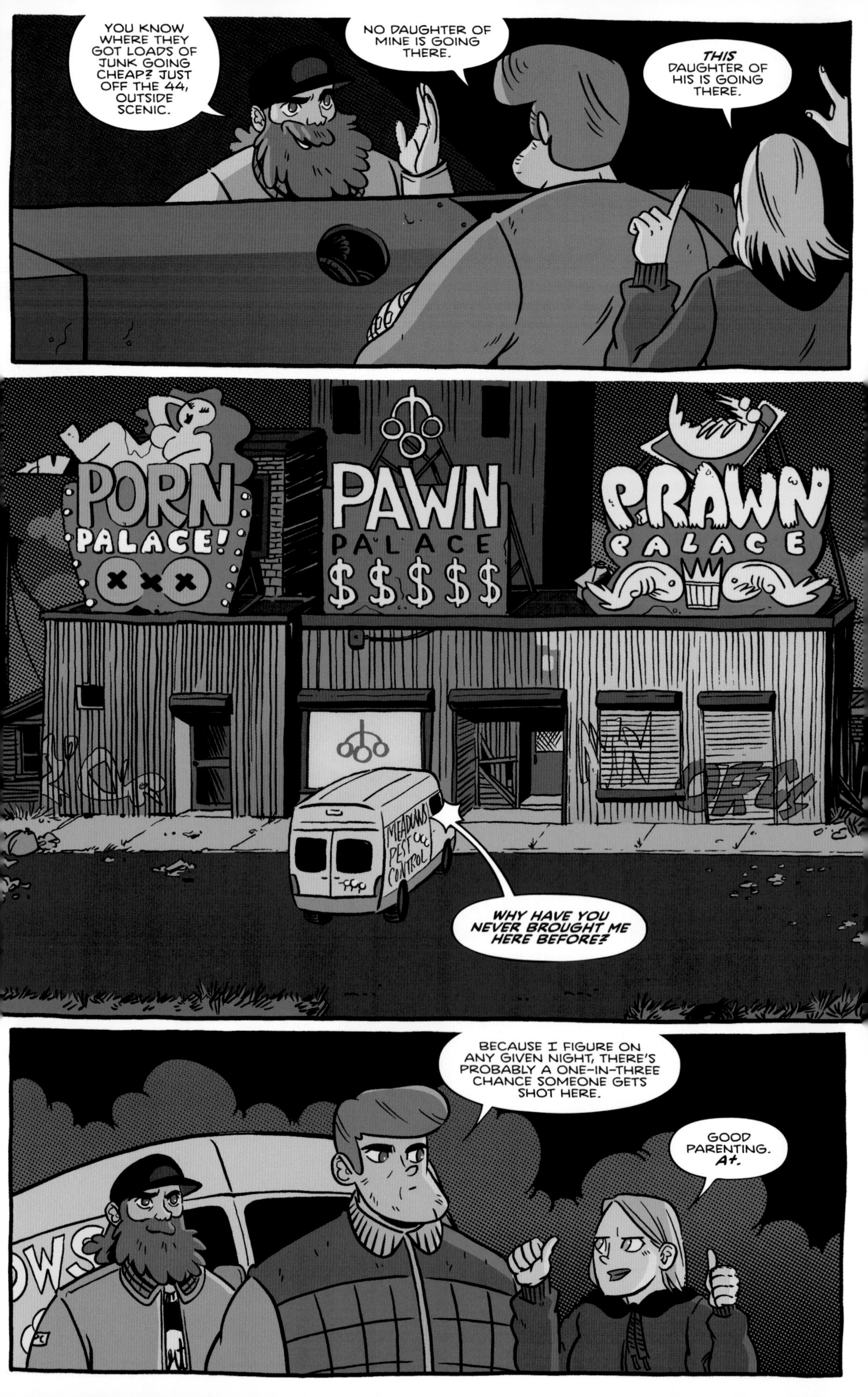
YOU KNOW WHERE THEY GOT LOADS OF JUNK GOING CHEAP? JUST OFF THE 44, OUTSIDE SCENIC.
NO DAUGHTER OF MINE IS GOING THERE.
THIS DAUGHTER OF HIS IS GOING THERE.
PORN PALACE!
PAWN PALACE $$$$$
PRAWN PALACE
MEADOWS PEST CONTROL
WHY HAVE YOU NEVER BROUGHT ME HERE BEFORE?
BECAUSE I FIGURE ON ANY GIVEN NIGHT, THERE'S PROBABLY A ONE-IN-THREE CHANCE SOMEONE GETS SHOT HERE.
GOOD PARENTING. A+.

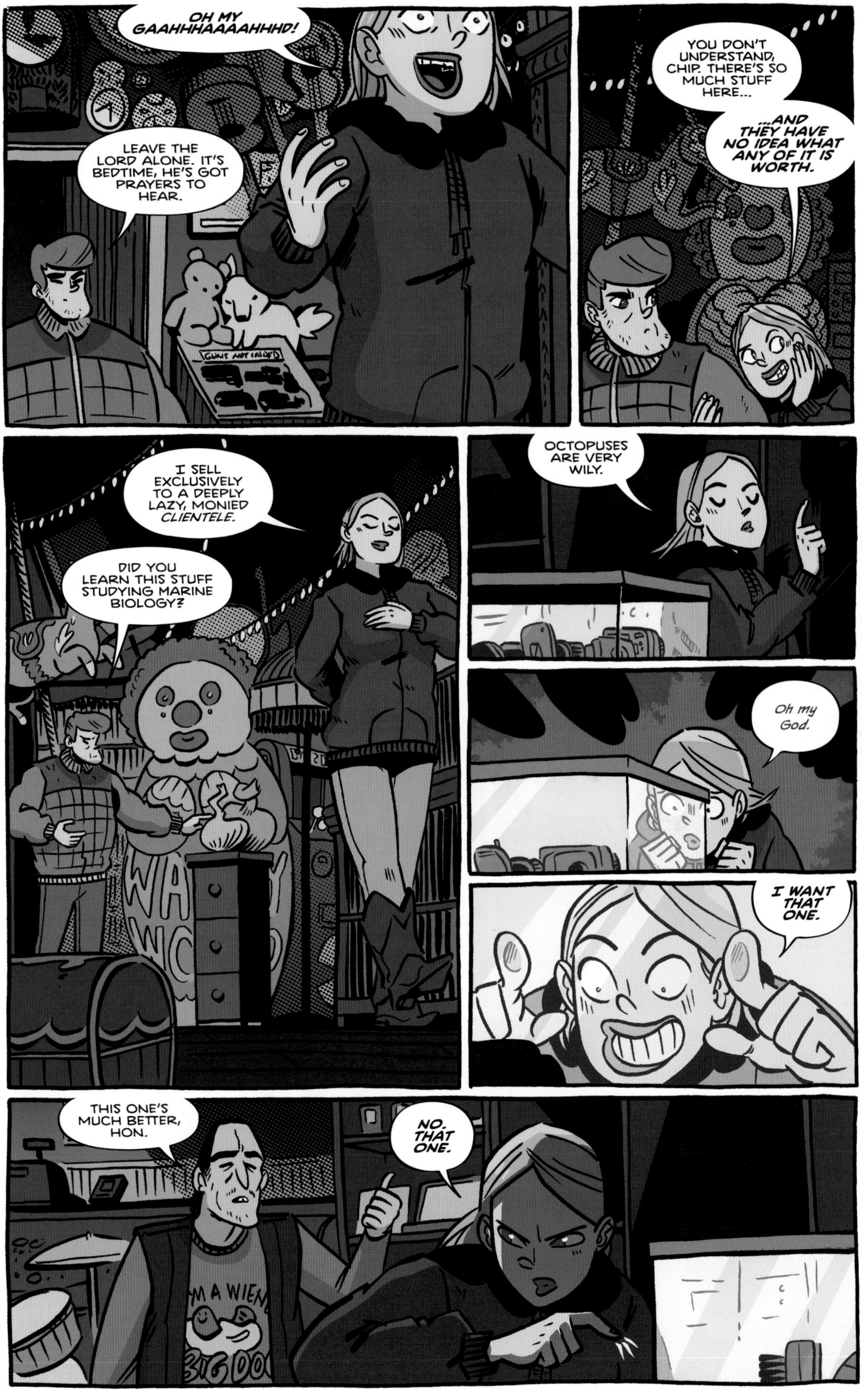

OH MY GAAHHHAAAAHHHD!
LEAVE THE LORD ALONE. IT'S BEDTIME, HE'S GOT PRAYERS TO HEAR.
GUNS NOT LOADED
YOU DON'T UNDERSTAND, CHIP. THERE'S SO MUCH STUFF HERE...
...AND THEY HAVE NO IDEA WHAT ANY OF IT IS WORTH.
I SELL EXCLUSIVELY TO A DEEPLY LAZY, MONIED CLIENTELE.
DID YOU LEARN THIS STUFF STUDYING MARINE BIOLOGY?
OCTOPUSES ARE VERY WILY.
Oh my God.
I WANT THAT ONE.
THIS ONE'S MUCH BETTER, HON.
NO. THAT ONE.

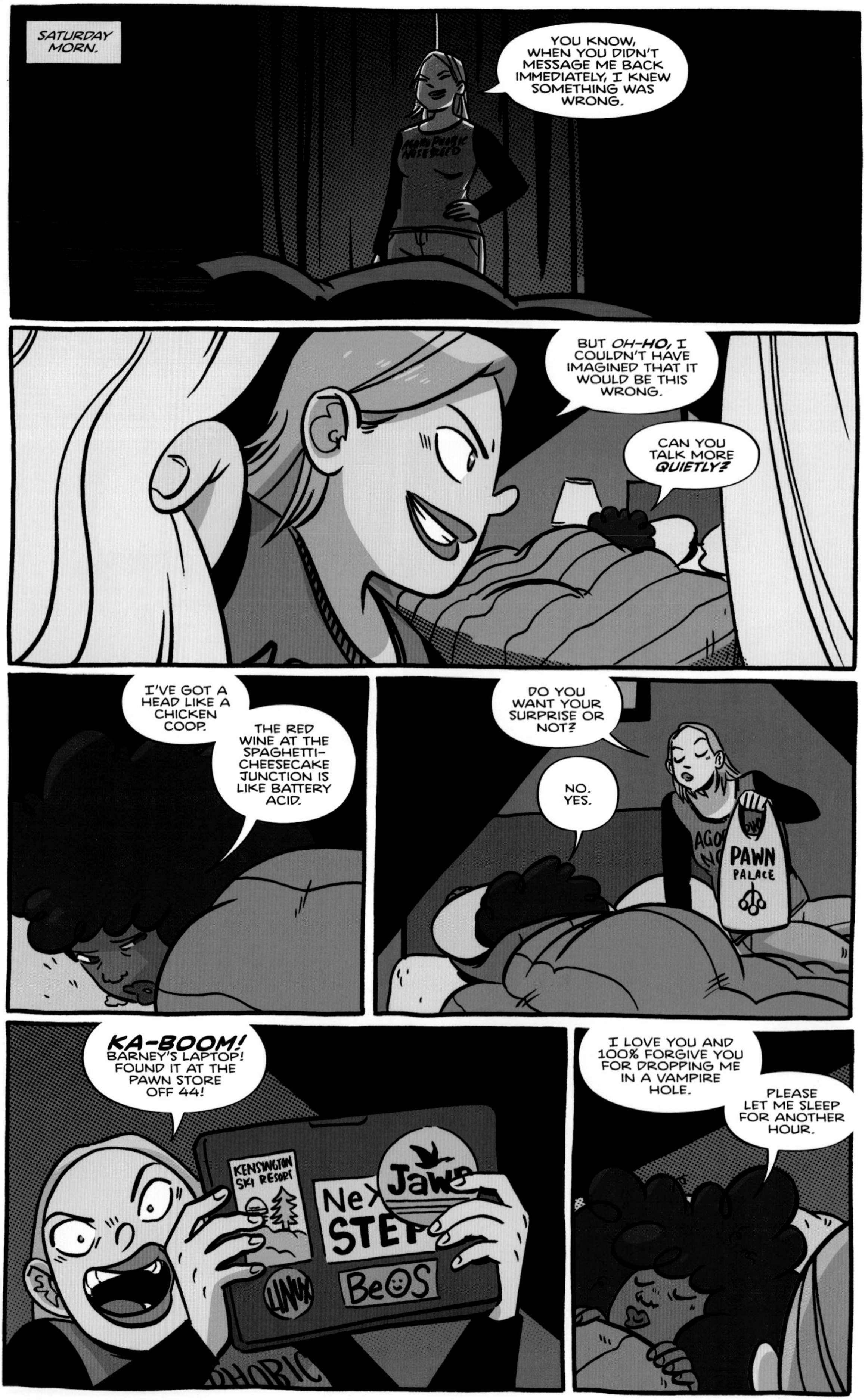
SATURDAY MORN.
YOU KNOW, WHEN YOU DIDN'T MESSAGE ME BACK IMMEDIATELY, I KNEW SOMETHING WAS WRONG.
BUT OH-HO, I COULDN'T HAVE IMAGINED THAT IT WOULD BE THIS WRONG.
CAN YOU TALK MORE QUIETLY?
I'VE GOT A HEAD LIKE A CHICKEN COOP.
THE RED WINE AT THE SPAGHETTI-CHEESECAKE JUNCTION IS LIKE BATTERY ACID.
DO YOU WANT YOUR SURPRISE OR NOT?
NO. YES.
PAWN PALACE
KA-BOOM! BARNEY'S LAPTOP! FOUND IT AT THE PAWN STORE OFF 44!
KENSINGTON SKI RESORT
Jaws
LINUX
BeOS
I LOVE YOU AND 100% FORGIVE YOU FOR DROPPING ME IN A VAMPIRE HOLE.
PLEASE LET ME SLEEP FOR ANOTHER HOUR.

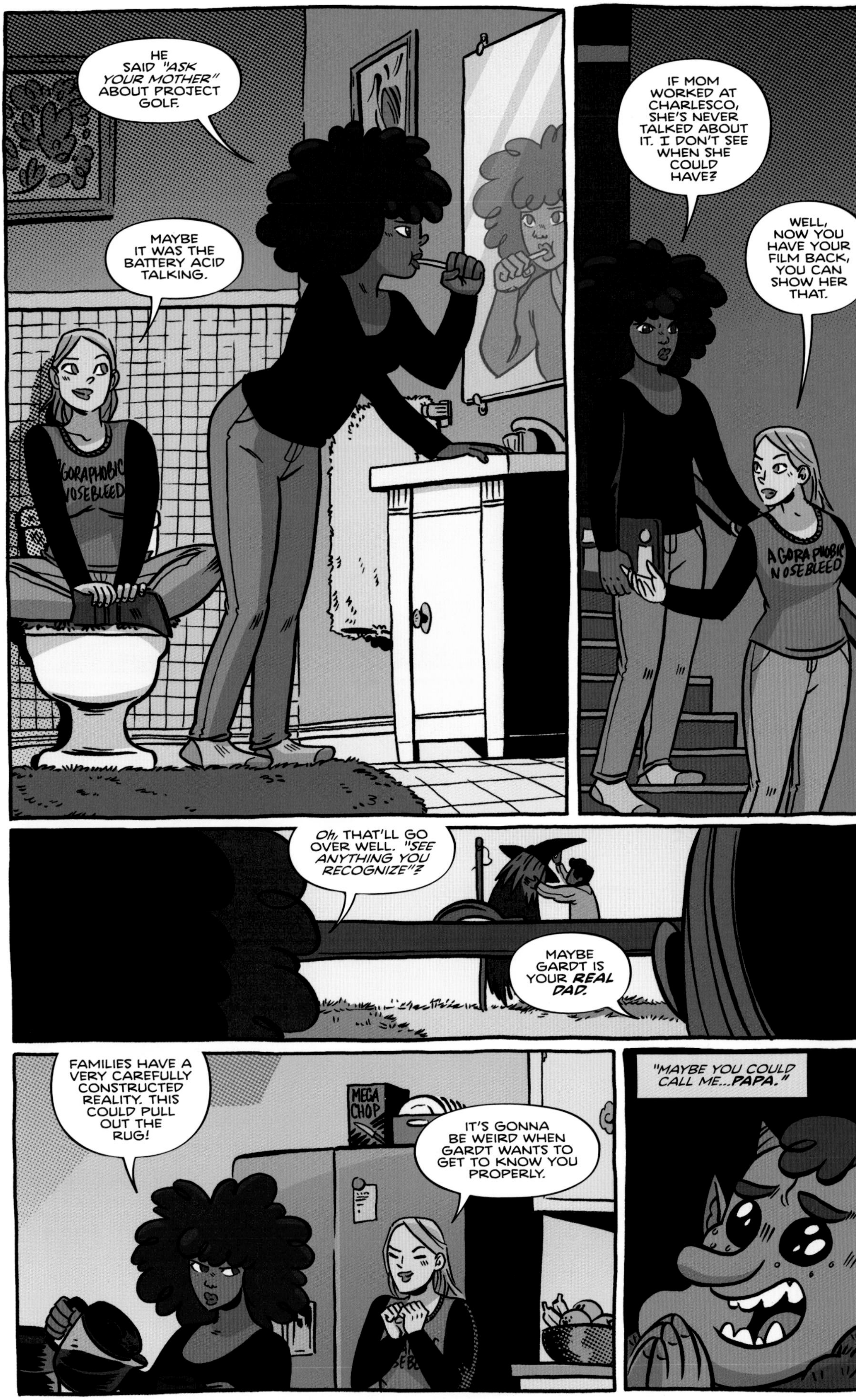
HE SAID "ASK YOUR MOTHER" ABOUT PROJECT GOLF.
MAYBE IT WAS THE BATTERY ACID TALKING.
AGORAPHOBIC NOSEBLEED
IF MOM WORKED AT CHARLESCO, SHE'S NEVER TALKED ABOUT IT. I DON'T SEE WHEN SHE COULD HAVE?
WELL, NOW YOU HAVE YOUR FILM BACK, YOU CAN SHOW HER THAT.
AGORAPHOBIC NOSEBLEED
Oh, THAT'LL GO OVER WELL. "SEE ANYTHING YOU RECOGNIZE"?
MAYBE GARDT IS YOUR ***REAL DAD.***
FAMILIES HAVE A VERY CAREFULLY CONSTRUCTED REALITY. THIS COULD PULL OUT THE RUG!
MEGA CHOP
IT'S GONNA BE WEIRD WHEN GARDT WANTS TO GET TO KNOW YOU PROPERLY.
"MAYBE YOU COULD CALL ME...***PAPA.***"

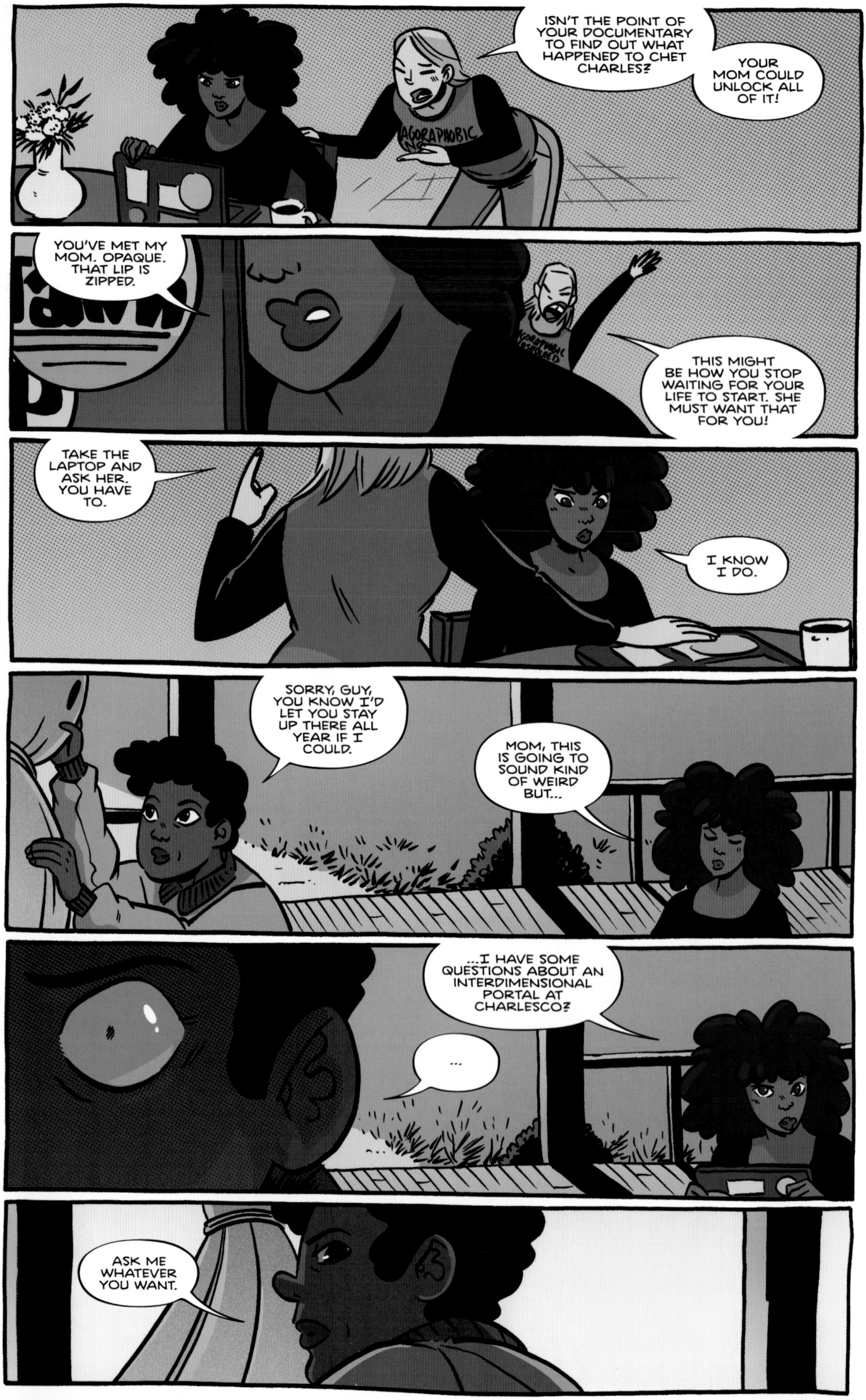
ISN'T THE POINT OF YOUR DOCUMENTARY TO FIND OUT WHAT HAPPENED TO CHET CHARLES?
YOUR MOM COULD UNLOCK ALL OF IT!
AGORAPHOBIC
YOU'VE MET MY MOM. OPAQUE. THAT LIP IS ZIPPED.
THIS MIGHT BE HOW YOU STOP WAITING FOR YOUR LIFE TO START. SHE MUST WANT THAT FOR YOU!
TAKE THE LAPTOP AND ASK HER. YOU HAVE TO.
I KNOW I DO.
SORRY, GUY, YOU KNOW I'D LET YOU STAY UP THERE ALL YEAR IF I COULD.
MOM, THIS IS GOING TO SOUND KIND OF WEIRD BUT...
...I HAVE SOME QUESTIONS ABOUT AN INTERDIMENSIONAL PORTAL AT CHARLESCO?
...
ASK ME WHATEVER YOU WANT.

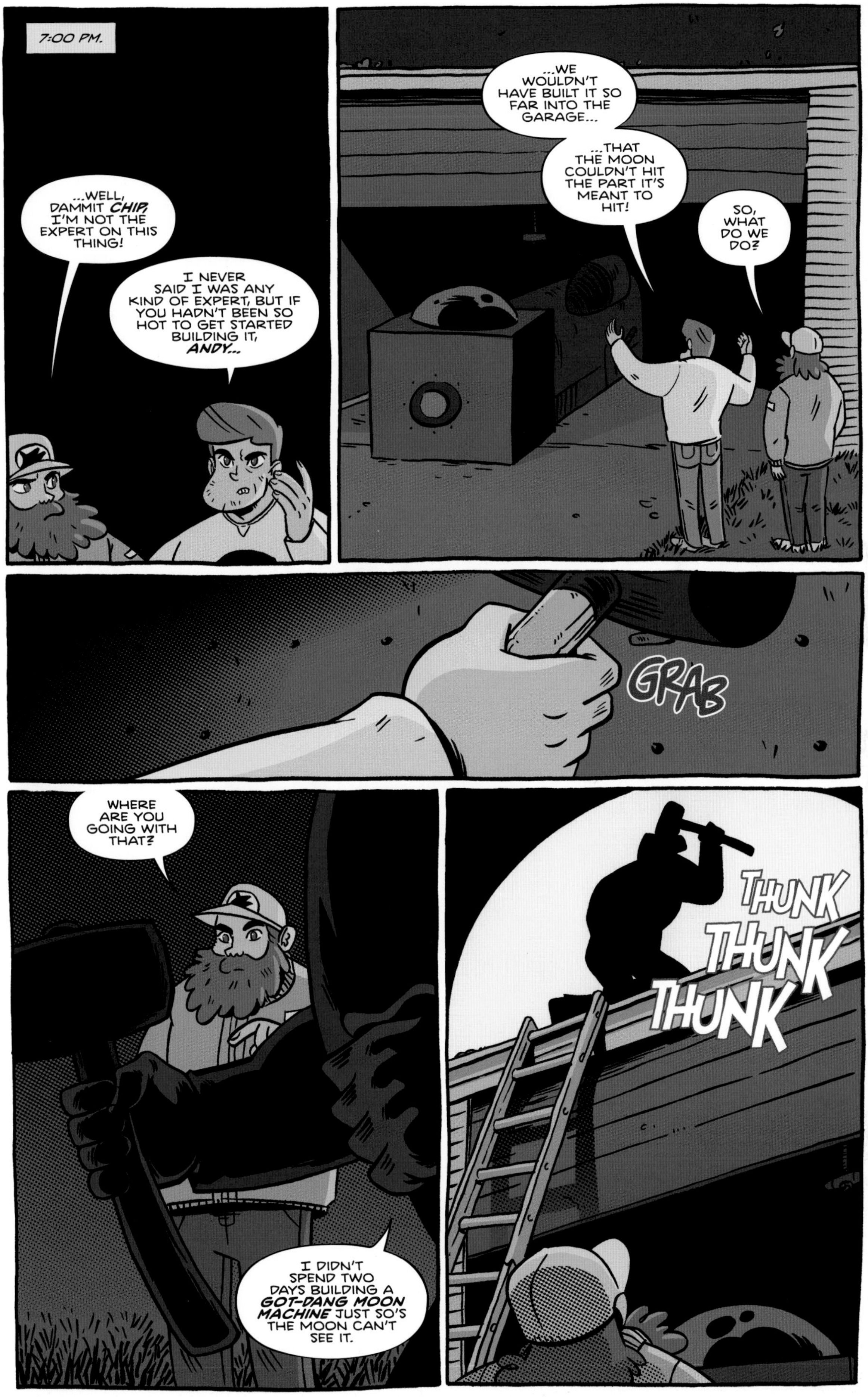
7:00 PM.
...WELL, DAMMIT CHIP, I'M NOT THE EXPERT ON THIS THING!
I NEVER SAID I WAS ANY KIND OF EXPERT, BUT IF YOU HADN'T BEEN SO HOT TO GET STARTED BUILDING IT, ANDY...
...WE WOULDN'T HAVE BUILT IT SO FAR INTO THE GARAGE...
...THAT THE MOON COULDN'T HIT THE PART IT'S MEANT TO HIT!
SO, WHAT DO WE DO?
GRAB
WHERE ARE YOU GOING WITH THAT?
I DIDN'T SPEND TWO DAYS BUILDING A GOT-DANG MOON MACHINE JUST SO'S THE MOON CAN'T SEE IT.
THUNK
THUNK
THUNK

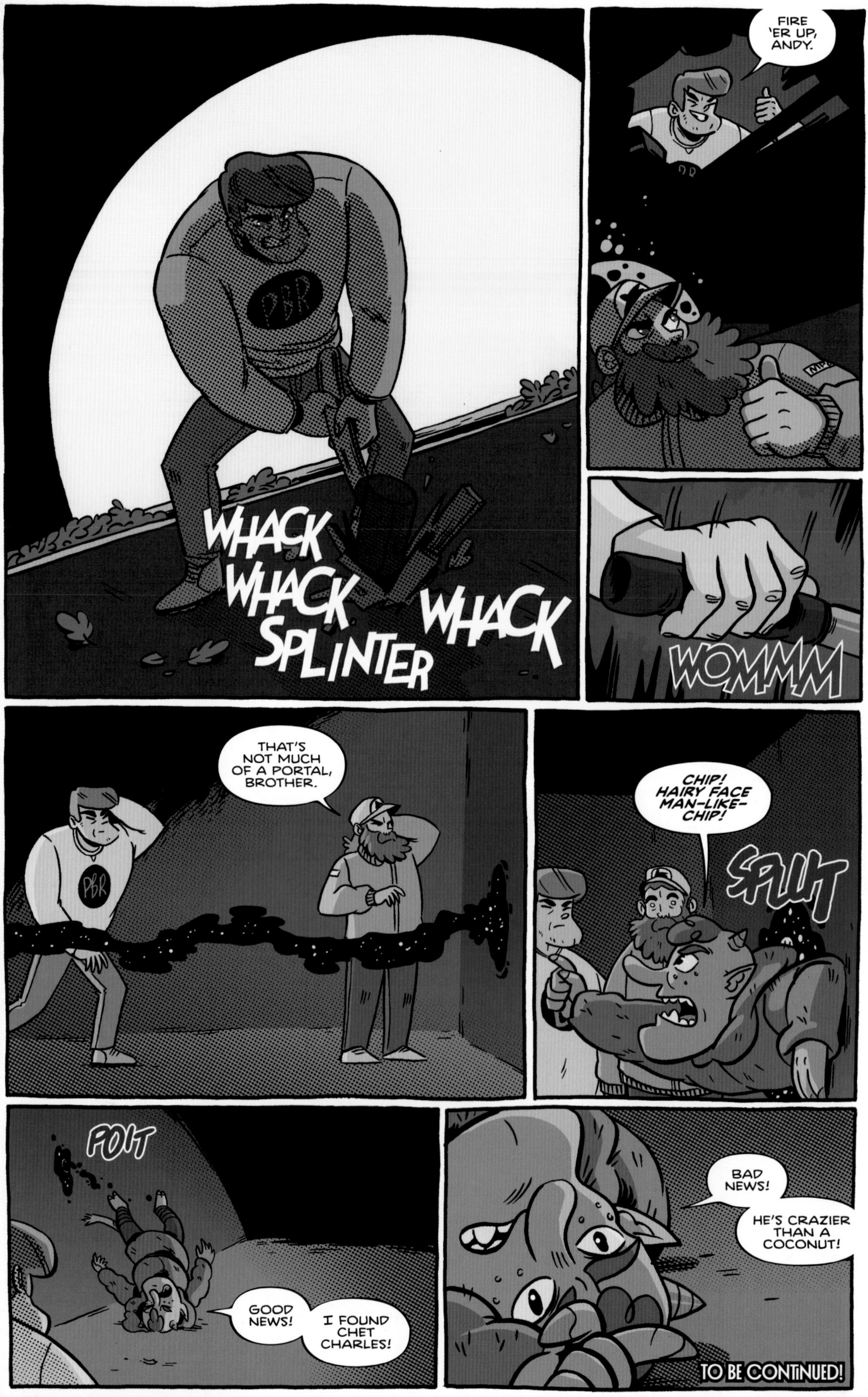
WHACK
WHACK
SPLINTER
WHACK
FIRE 'ER UP, ANDY.
WOMMM
THAT'S NOT MUCH OF A PORTAL, BROTHER.
CHIP! HAIRY FACE MAN-LIKE-CHIP!
SPLUT
POIT
GOOD NEWS!
I FOUND CHET CHARLES!
BAD NEWS!
HE'S CRAZIER THAN A COCONUT!
TO BE CONTINUED!

Cover Gallery

Issue 5 Main Cover by
Christine Larsen

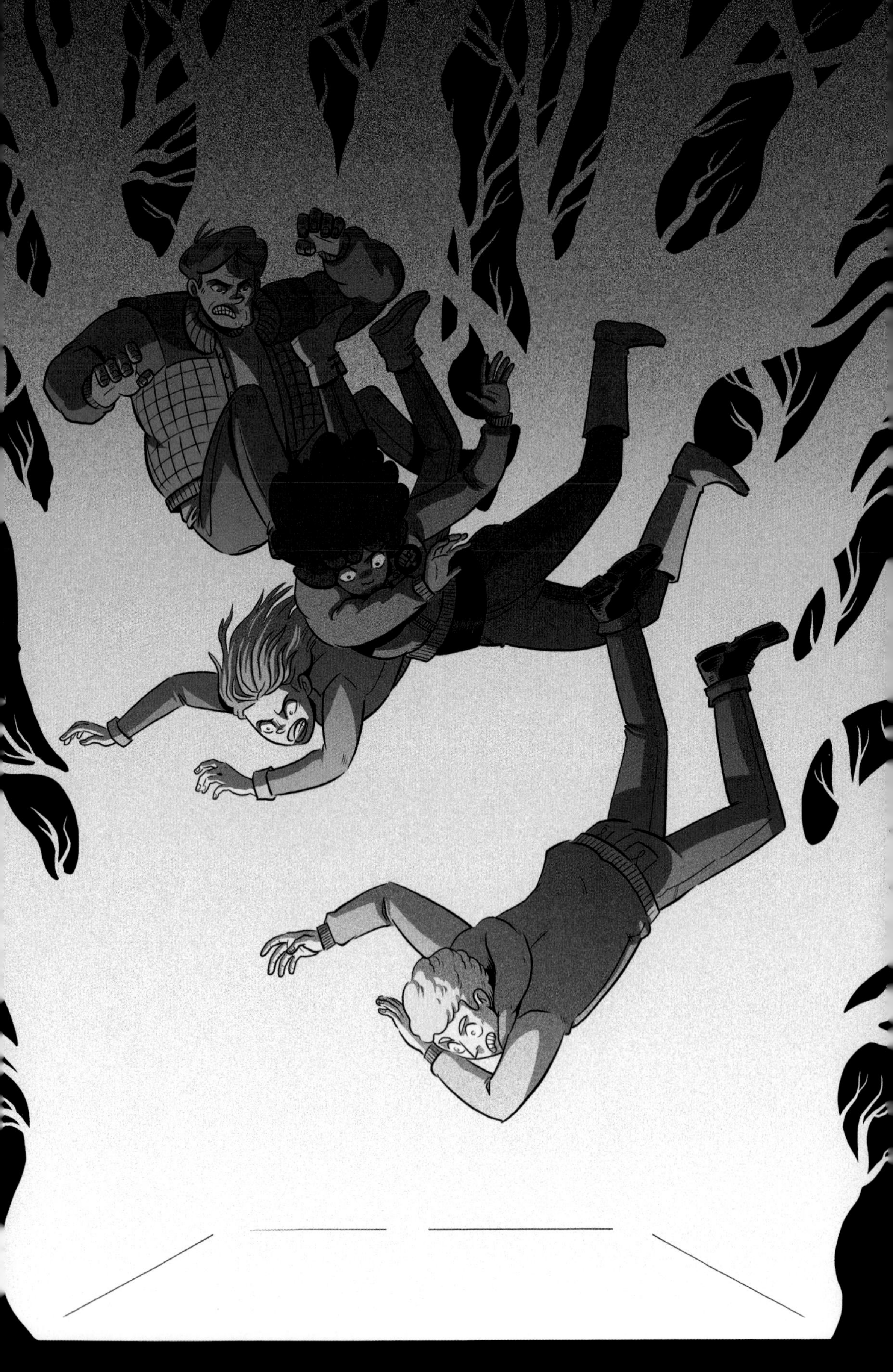

Issue 5 Preorder Cover by
Sarah Stern

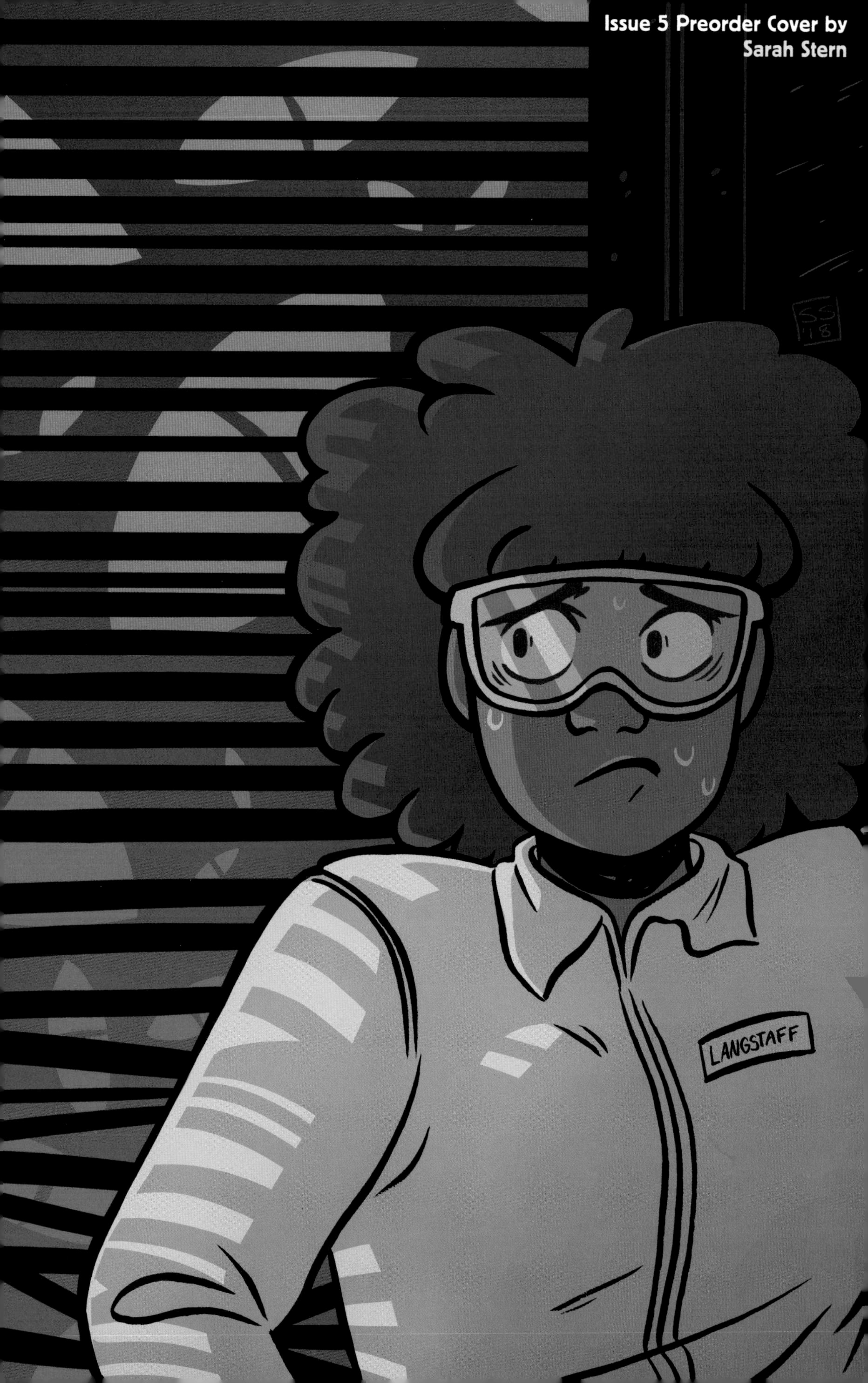
SS '18
LANGSTAFF

Issue 6 Main Cover by
Christine Larsen

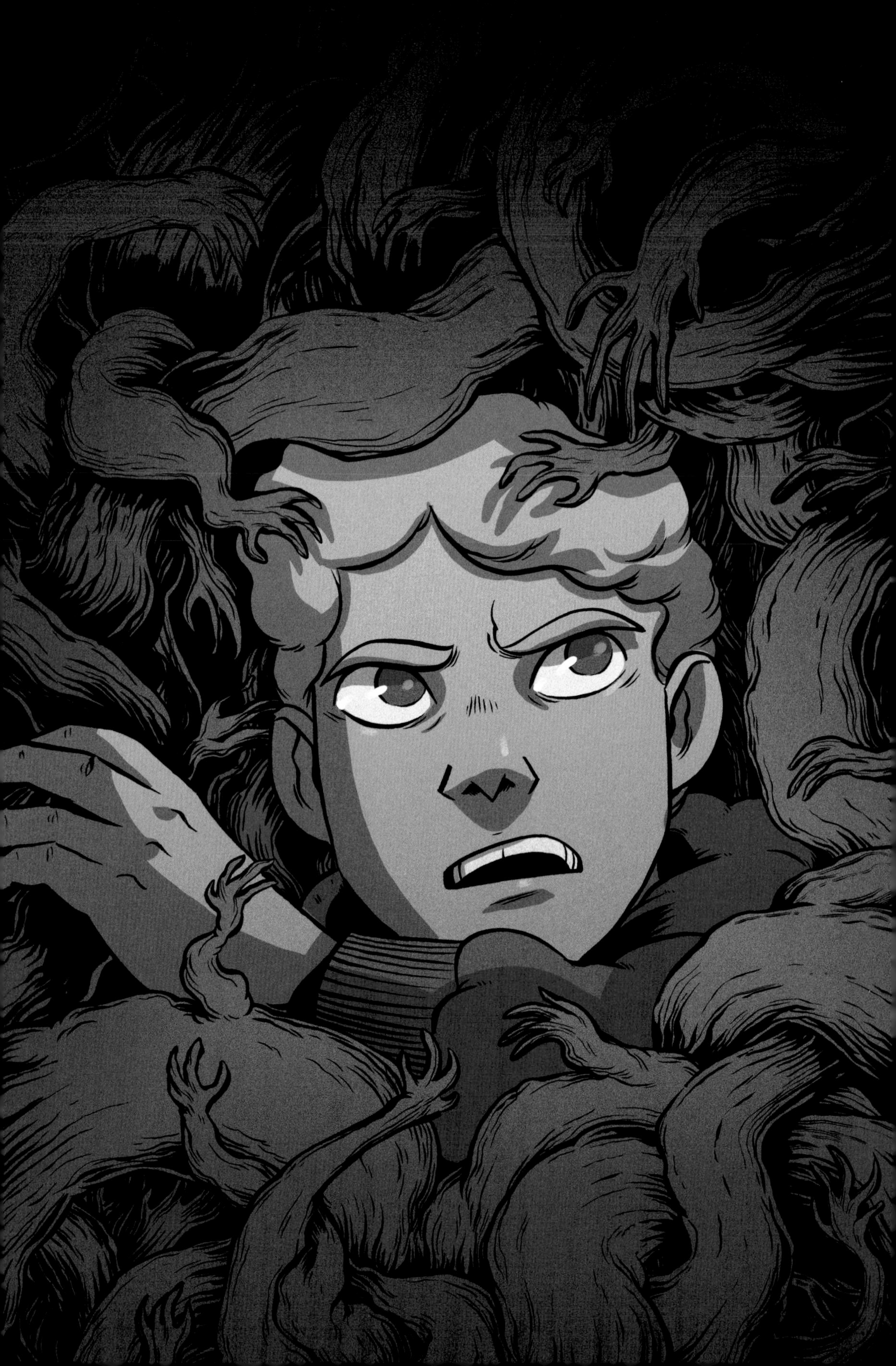

Issue 6 Preorder Cover by
Sarah Stern

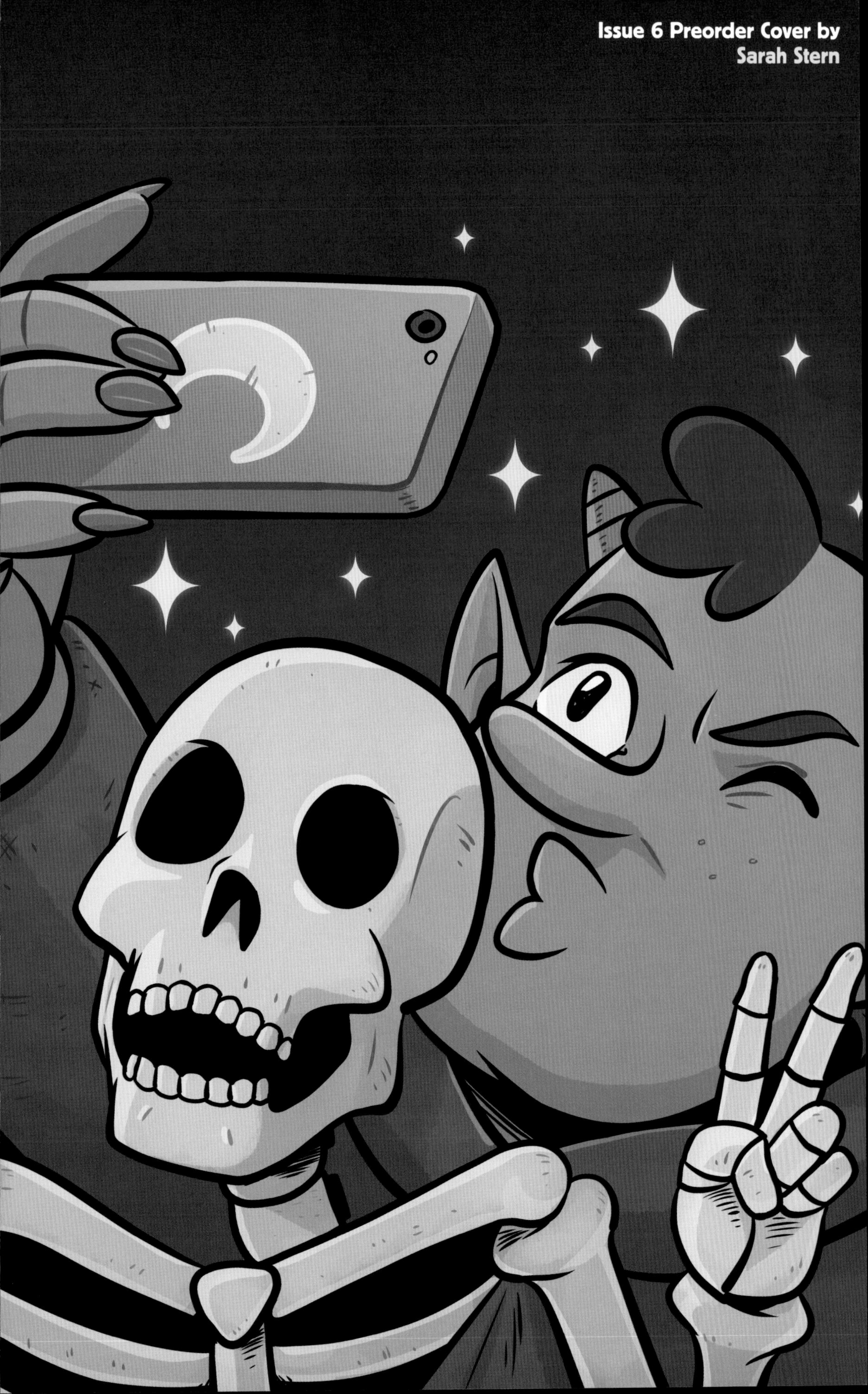

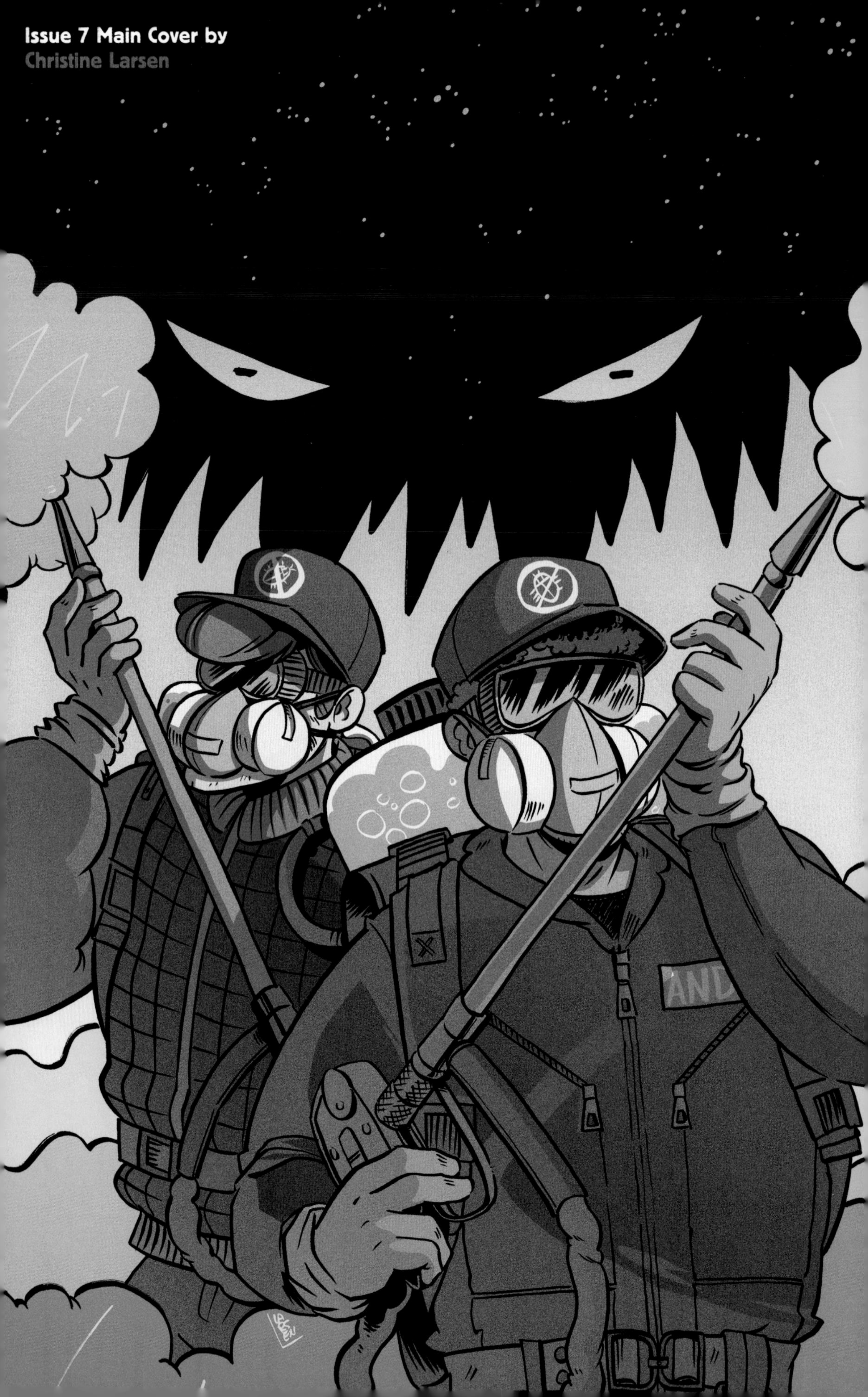
AND

Issue 7 Main Cover by
Christine Larsen

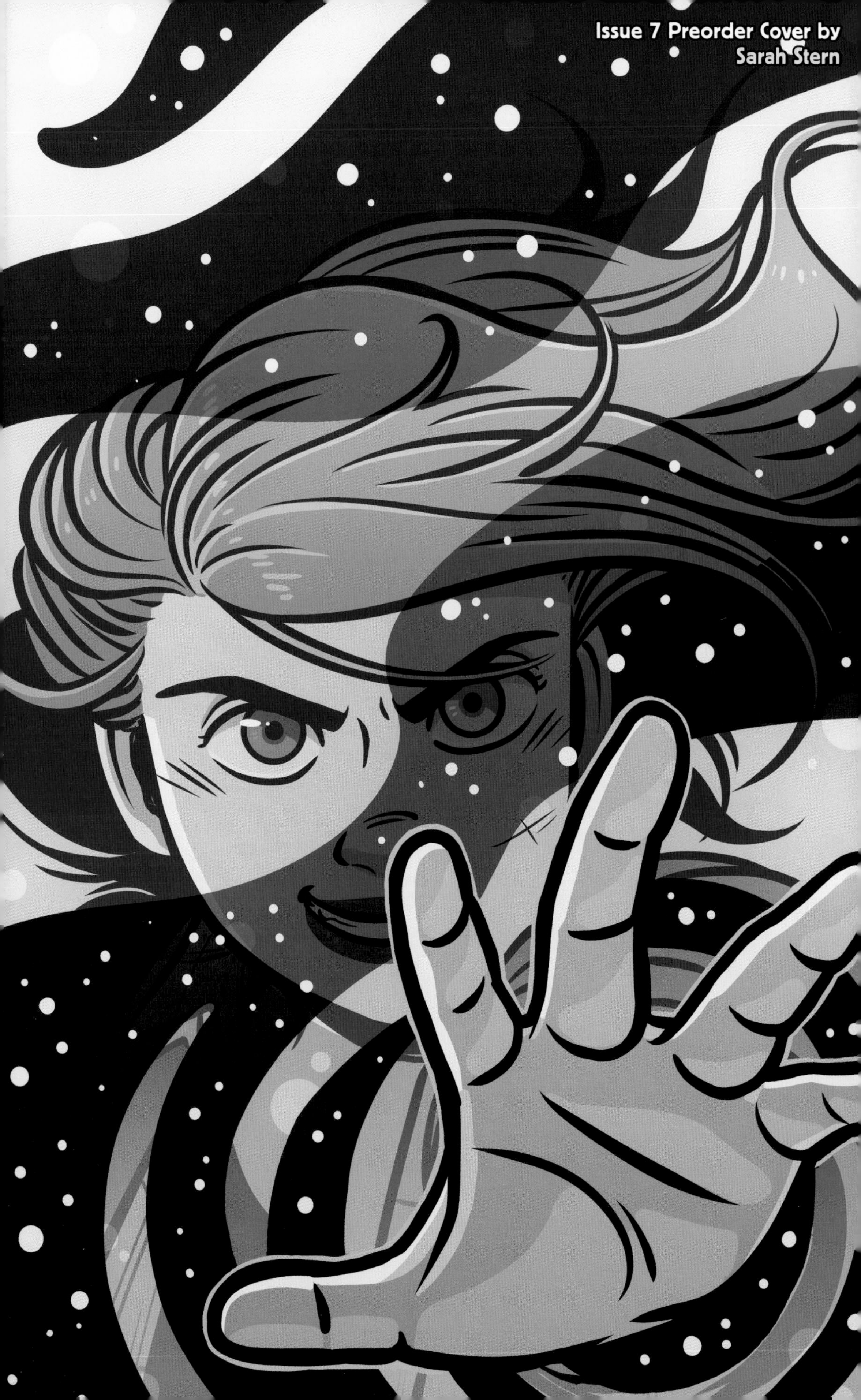

Issue 7 Preorder Cover by Sarah Stern

Issue 8 Main Cover by
Christine Larsen

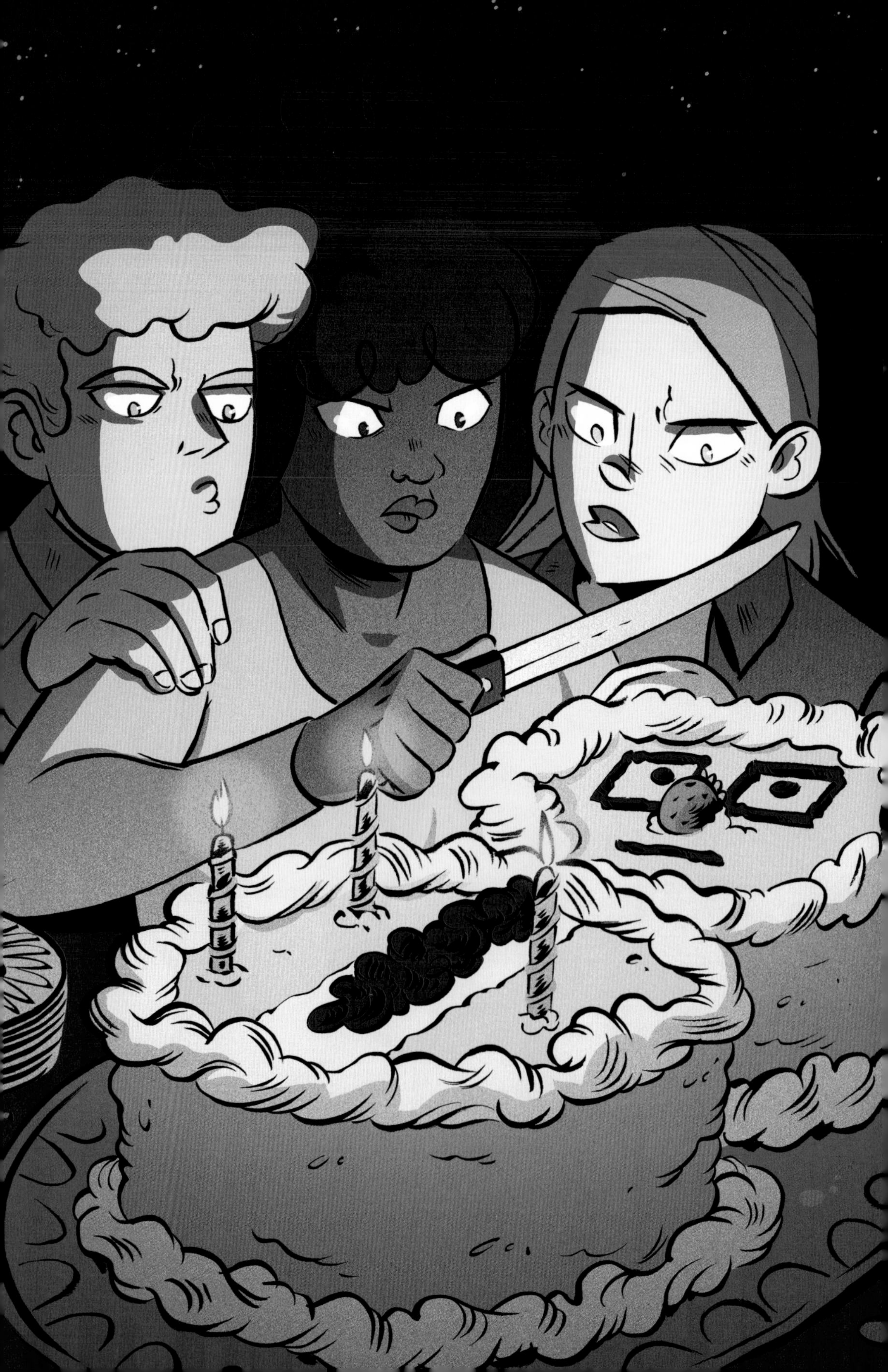

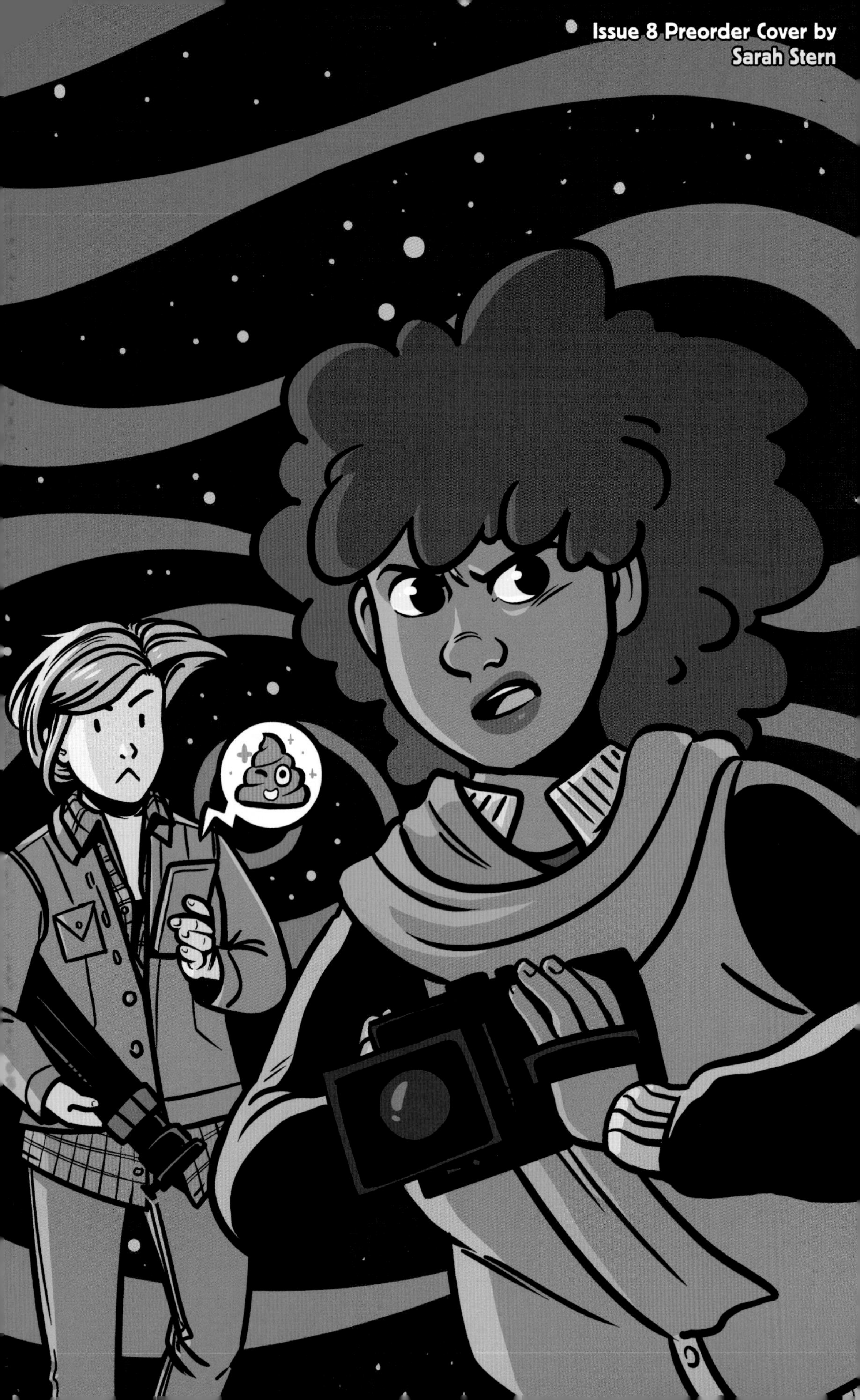

Issue 8 Preorder Cover by
Sarah Stern

Heather Meadows
by John Allison

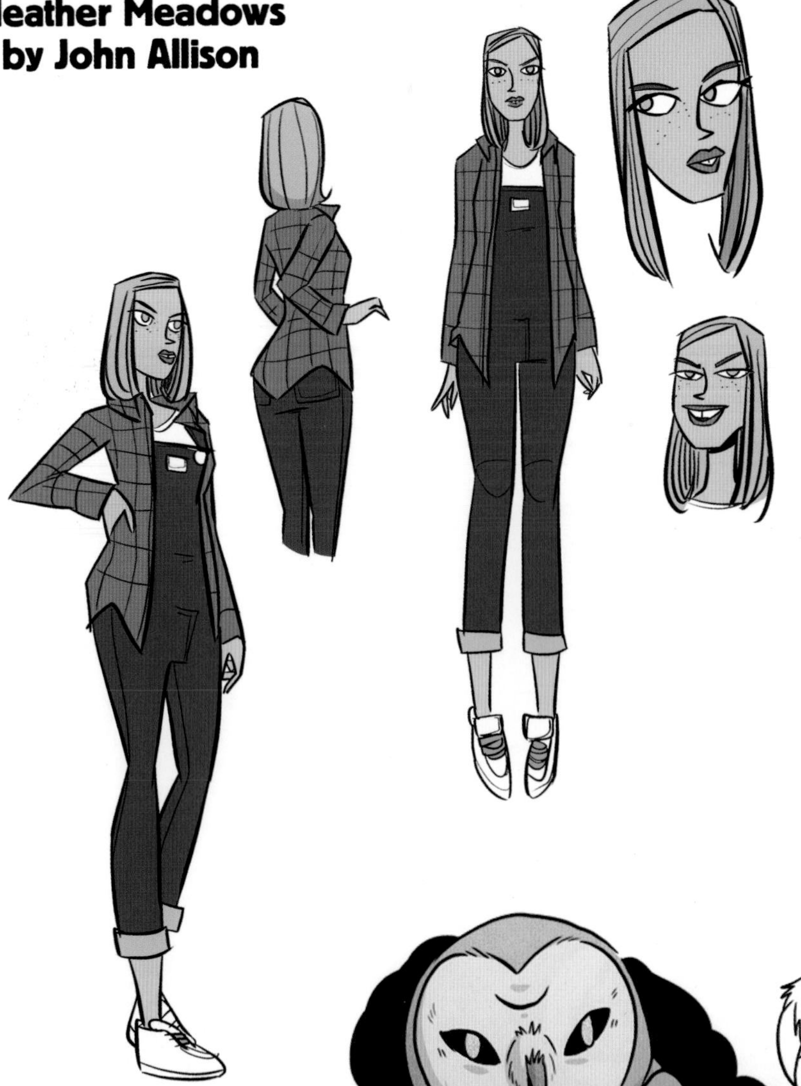

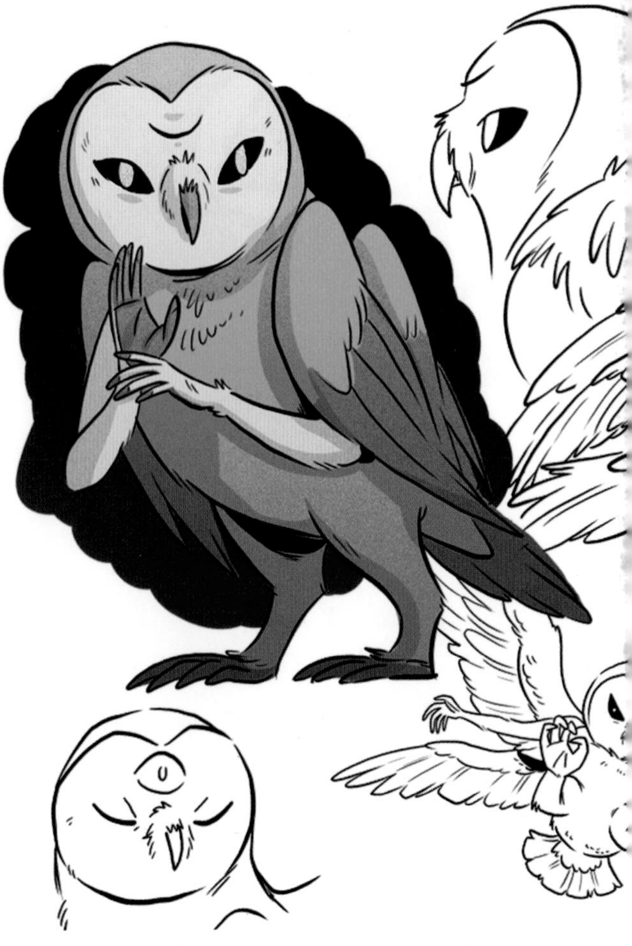

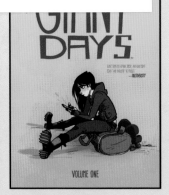

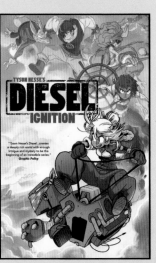

Lumberjanes
Noelle Stevenson, Shannon Watters,
Grace Ellis, Brooklyn Allen, and Others
Volume 1: Beware the Kitten Holy
ISBN: 978-1-60886-687-8 | $14.99 US
Volume 2: Friendship to the Max
ISBN: 978-1-60886-737-0 | $14.99 US
Volume 3: A Terrible Plan
ISBN: 978-1-60886-803-2 | $14.99 US
Volume 4: Out of Time
ISBN: 978-1-60886-860-5 | $14.99 US
Volume 5: Band Together
ISBN: 978-1-60886-919-0 | $14.99 US

Giant Days
John Allison, Lissa Treiman, Max Sarin
Volume 1
ISBN: 978-1-60886-789-9 | $9.99 US
Volume 2
ISBN: 978-1-60886-804-9 | $14.99 US
Volume 3
ISBN: 978-1-60886-851-3 | $14.99 US

Jonesy
Sam Humphries, Caitlin Rose Boyle
Volume 1
ISBN: 978-1-60886-883-4 | $9.99 US
Volume 2
ISBN: 978-1-60886-999-2 | $14.99 US

Slam!
Pamela Ribon, Veronica Fish,
Brittany Peer
Volume 1
ISBN: 978-1-68415-004-5 | $14.99 US

Goldie Vance
Hope Larson, Brittney Williams
Volume 1
ISBN: 978-1-60886-898-8 | $9.99 US
Volume 2
ISBN: 978-1-60886-974-9 | $14.99 US

The Backstagers
James Tynion IV, Rian Sygh
Volume 1
ISBN: 978-1-60886-993-0 | $14.99 US

Tyson Hesse's Diesel:
Ignition
Tyson Hesse
ISBN: 978-1-60886-907-7 | $14.99 US

Coady & The Creepies
Liz Prince, Amanda Kirk,
Hannah Fisher
ISBN: 978-1-68415-029-8 | $14.99 US

Jane Langstaff
by John Allison

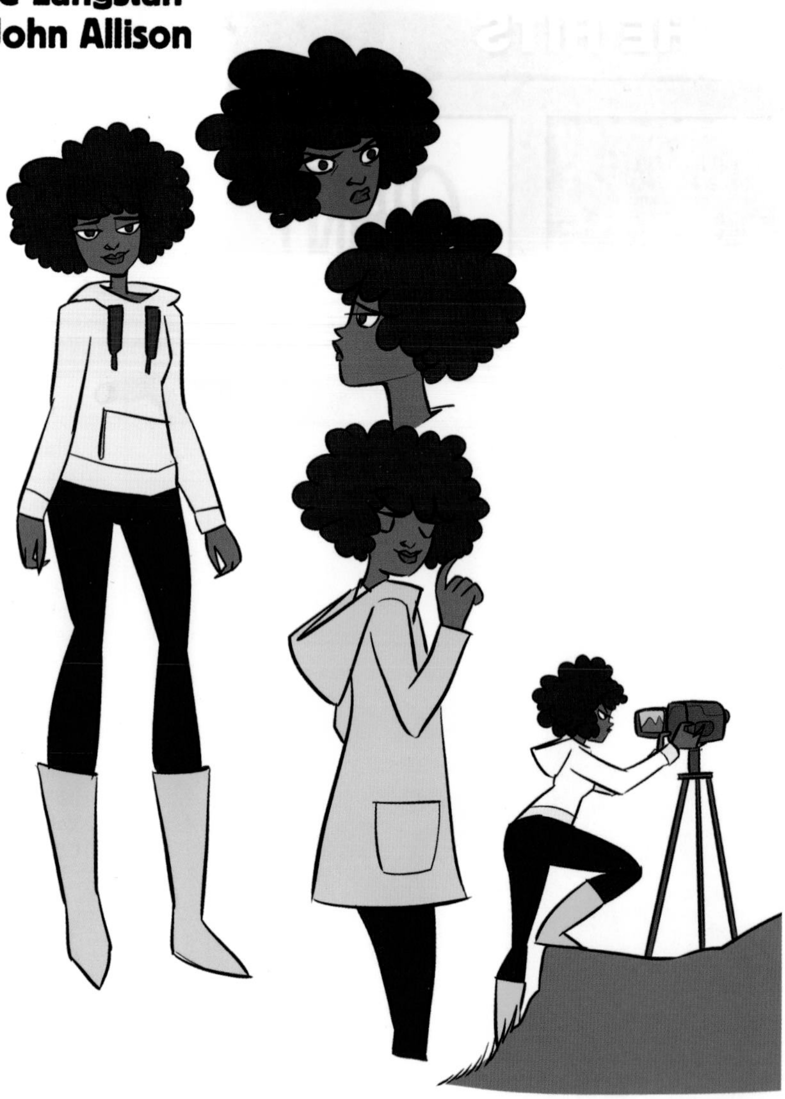

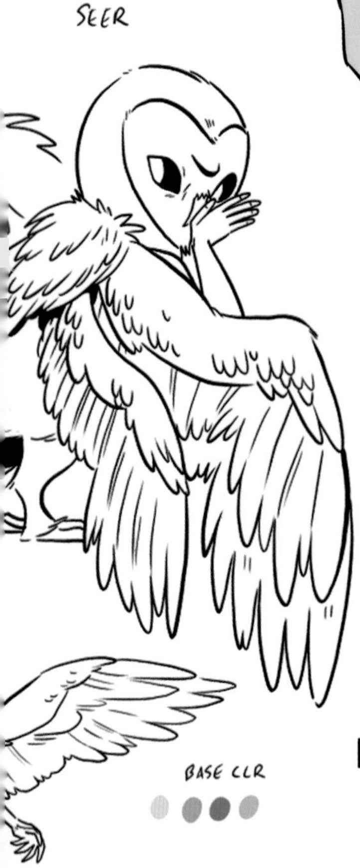
SEER
BASE CLR

The Seer
by Christine Larsen